Finding the Phoenix

Book One of The Celestial Talisman

CAITLIN O'CONNOR

To Gio, for helping me realise the story started sooner, and to my mom, for her unwavering support. Thank you.

iv

Acknowledgements

Thanks to Allex, Colleen, Ellen, Jacques, and Jilly for taking the time to read Phoenix and give me input.
Special thanks to Gio, Shawn Spjut, and Tito Martinez for their input and critique.

TABLE OF CONTENTS

Chapter One..1
Chapter Two...13
Chapter Three...30
Chapter Four..46
Chapter Five..55
Chapter Six...69
Chapter Seven...84
Chapter Eight..108
Chapter Nine...124
Chapter Ten..139
Chapter Eleven.......................................154
Chapter Twelve.......................................168
Chapter Thirteen.....................................176
Chapter Fourteen.....................................185
Chapter Fifteen......................................193
Chapter Sixteen......................................208
Chapter Seventeen....................................220
Chapter Eighteen.....................................242
Chapter Nineteen.....................................257
Chapter Twenty.......................................273
Chapter Twenty One...................................282
Chapter Twenty Two...................................289
Chapter Twenty Three.................................301
Chapter Twenty Four..................................314
Chapter Twenty Five..................................325
About the Author.....................................343
Glossary of South African Vernacular.........345

Bonus Features:

Playlist...................................351
Preview Scar...........................353

1

The dream faded into absolute darkness colder than the Atlantic in winter. Her shoulder blades ached from the unyielding pressure of the surface beneath her. Attempting to roll over placed pressure on her left arm and screaming agony rocketed through her. She cried out, and the sound echoed close around her.

It must be a small space, a new punishment Trey had cooked up? Had he broken her arm and stuffed her in a freezer? It seemed screwed up even for him.

Deep breath and exhale. She concentrated on her right hand and tried to move it. The joints were stiffer than arthritis. Muscles she'd never realised existed, exploded with pins and needles. She pressed her fingertips against the hard surface beneath her and used them to lever her hand closer to her thigh.

"You can do this." Her words came out in a hoarse whisper, but the warmth of her breath blew pleasantly across her face. It brought sensation back to numb skin. She'd get out of here and everything would be—wait, this wasn't right. She exhaled again, felt it on her skin. Air shouldn't do that, unless her face was covered.

Her breaths sped up and her face got warmer. She used her fingers to crawl her hand up her thigh, and realised she was naked.

She mustn't panic. He wouldn't kill her, not like this anyway. Trey had a nuclear temper and could be cruel, but this was too calculated.

She forced her arm upwards. The sheet resisted her movements so she curled her fingers into a fist, but that made her hand spasm. Her arm fell back down to her belly, and she bit her lip.

"Hey!" she yelled, wincing at the loud echoes, "Let me out. Trey!"

So quiet, she shouted again. She sucked in a deep breath, and heard a thump. Next, a sharp vibration moved through her. There was another thump, accompanied by a strong tremor through the surface beneath her. Something clicked just above her head and she flinched.

A rolling sound filled the small space, and whatever she was lying on jerked backwards. The cover pulled back and light smacked her in the face, blinding her.

"I found you."

A male voice, but not Trey, this man had a deeper voice and a typical South African accent. He touched her left arm, and she cried out as the pain shot up to her shoulder.

"Sorry," he muttered. "Don't worry that can be fixed up as soon as we get out of here."

What? Light reflected off metal surfaces in a dazzle of bright sparkles that made her head hurt. She squinted at the fuzzy, dark shape to her left as he lifted something and spread it over her, something soft and warm that smelt of lavender. Gentle fingers tucked the edges around her, as he leaned over, he blocked out the glare and she stared up at him.

An oval face crowned by waves of dark hair hovered over her, blue eyes framed by thick eyebrows that pinched together in a frown as he fiddled with the blanket. He looked like he should've been chubby, but his chest and shoulder muscles bulged against his shirt, and biceps as large as her thigh flexed beneath the material as he bent closer to lift her.

She gulped, and all the times that strong hands had grabbed her by the wrist or thumped into her stomach flashed through her mind. She remembered the stab of broken ribs, and her toes straining to reach the ground as Trey held her by the throat.

Fear and adrenaline gave her the strength to lurch upwards, but she collapsed back onto her right elbow a second later. There was space to her right. She could throw herself in that direction, but he'd get her. She couldn't run.

Her elbow slipped out from under her, but he caught her before she hit the hard surface beneath her.

"Easy, I'm here to help you, I'm your Guardian," he said.

What the hell did that mean? She looked at him, then past him to the bank of square, steel doors set into the wall in front of her, to the square, black hole past her feet. She'd been in a place like this when her parents died; their bodies had been behind square doors. A little while ago, she'd been behind a square door.

Oh God, it was a morgue.

Her scream came out as a strangled groan, which he muffled by covering her mouth with his hand. Being naked didn't matter as much as escape as she wrestled with the blanket and tried to get away. Her heart crashed against her ribs, and her skin went numb again as panic raced through her veins. She caught him in the ribs with her knee, but he tightened his grip on her. He lifted her upright in one smooth movement, and tilted her head forwards, holding it with one arm.

"Sorry."

Sharp, sudden pressure at the back of her head, the edges of her eyesight blurred, and everything went dark again.

**

Blake sighed as the girl's body slumped against him. He wrapped the blanket around her like a cocoon, and lifted her into his arms. It wasn't safe manipulating pressure points on somebody in her condition, but he'd already taken too long here.

He lowered her into the wheelchair he'd left by the door, and backed out through the entrance to the morgue. The corridor was empty. As he strode towards the end, the rubber soles of his boots squeaked on the linoleum, and he winced at how loud it sounded. He left the wheelchair and crept forward, pausing to listen for footsteps before peeking round the corner in both directions. None of the nurses had been down here when he entered, but the security guards would make rounds of the whole hospital. He had no desire to fight his way out of here.

Nothing, he straightened up, and returned to the chair. His nose wrinkled at the disinfectant smell as he pushed her towards the lift down the hall, and pressed the button.

While he waited, he pressed his fingers against the girl's carotid artery to check if she was still all right. All the struggling back there had freaked him out, why had she reacted like that?

The ping and sliding sound of the doors opening startled him. He quickly got her inside and pressed the button for the first floor. Blake tapped his foot as he watched the orange light move from the basement level to the ground floor, and tried not to clench his hands around the handles of the wheelchair. The doors hadn't even opened properly when he pushed her through them, and made a sharp right turn.

The foyer lights were dim, but it was still brighter than he liked. Too bright to hide what he was doing. This subversive stuff wasn't Blake's cup of tea; teamwork and the cover of darkness were far more familiar than sneaking around in the open. A quick scan of reception reassured the Guardian that the area was deserted. He sighed softly, and pushed the chair toward the passage that led towards Emergency.

As he turned the corner, the edge of the wheelchair bumped against the feet of a security guard sprawled in a chair. The man blinked up at him, shit!

Blake scowled at the guard and lowered his voice to an angry rumble. "Is this what I'm paying for at this place, security guards sleeping in the passage?" He made a show of checking the girl then shook his finger at the man. "If you'd woken her, there would've been hell to pay."

"Excuse me, sir, but…" The man straightened up and frowned, apparently unaffected by his intimidation efforts.

"I don't want to hear it, and I will report you to your supervisor as soon as I get her back to her room." He walked away with his heart thumping, please let the guy just go back to sleep and forget about this.

Footsteps squeaked on the tiles behind him, but he didn't look back. It was tempting to speed up, but he kept his pace normal and carried on walking as though nothing was wrong.

"Sir, that's the wrong way."

Blake glanced over his shoulder, turned the corner, and pulled the Taser from his pocket. As the guard rounded the corner, he shoved the device against his belly and shocked him.

One of the guard's arms shot out, and Blake ducked. He fell, jerked a few times, and went limp. Blake dragged him back to his chair, and propped him up in it, then returned to the girl. He wheeled her to the fire door near the admin offices.

Earlier on, he'd wedged it open with a brick, and fortunately, it was still there. He turned and shoved the door open with his shoulder, kicked the brick out of the way, and manoeuvred the wheelchair through the gap. It shut itself with a thud behind them.

Wind tore at the blanket, and he tucked it tighter around the girl. Squinting through his hair as it whipped across his face, he pushed the wheelchair to the car, and opened the passenger side door. As soon as he lifted her from the chair, it went careening across the parking lot. He strapped her in with the seatbelt, closed the door, and ran around the back of the car.

Heavy clouds hung low in the sky, black smudges with glimpses of pale grey in the distance. Blake peered up at them as he climbed in and started the engine. He wasn't familiar with Cape Town's streets, it would be better if he were out of the city before the rain started. All it would take was one idiot who couldn't handle a car on a wet road to mess up his nerves entirely.

He drove through the empty parking space in front of him, turned the car around, and sped out through the ambulance exit. It took a few minutes to reach the highway. Soon the city was nothing but lights twinkling in the distance, and the dark outline of Table Mountain against the clouds.

It was time to revive her, but he waited until he could pull over. He parked on the gravel verge, switched the engine off, and the interior light on.

The orange light cast a weird glow on her pale skin, and etched deep shadows in her eye sockets and beneath her cheekbones. He leaned across and tilted her head forward. With great care, he brushed her long, blonde hair aside to massage the pressure points at the nape of her neck.

A few gentle slaps would help restore the flow of energy, but waking somebody up was more complicated than knocking them out. There were several other pressure points on her head to manipulate. He worked on them from the front, back to 'the gates of consciousness' at the top of her neck.

Eventually she groaned. Eyes that were more grey than blue fluttered open, and he watched her look around. Her body went rigid as she noticed him.

There could be no mistake about it—she was scared of him. It didn't make sense. The odds of having two different women alive in the morgue simultaneously were too small to consider. This woman had to be the Child of Heaven.

"You don't remember anything, do you?" he asked.

***

Anxiety clenched in her stomach and tightened her throat. Who was this guy, and where the fuck was she now? There was nothing but darkness beyond the windows. It was impossible to tell which road this was or how far they'd travelled.

He cleared his throat, and she stared at him, watching his hand as he lifted it to rub the back of his neck.

"No, you don't." He shook his head. "Shit, no wonder you're so freaked out."

What was he on about? Nobody had forewarned her about waking up in a morgue, or a strange dude kidnapping her. That wasn't the type of message you forgot.

"Firstly, I'm Blake. What's your name?"

She arched her eyebrows. Appearing friendly didn't count for much in her book. When in doubt, stay silent.

He sighed, leaned sideways against the seat, and rested one arm across the steering wheel. His body looked awkward in the cramped space; she could use that to her advantage. Could she undo her seatbelt, get out of the blanket, and open the door before he grabbed her?

Not likely.

"I'll start at the beginning and maybe it will come back to you." He nodded as he spoke, the corners of his mouth turned down, and a frown etched on his forehead. "I'm part of a group known as the Circle, and we're a little different from the rest of humanity. We're made up of male Guardians and female Wielders, with a Keeper to guide us. Most of us are born into the Circle, but in every generation, there's one Wielder who isn't. She's a normal person with a spiritual link to us, a link that becomes active once she's died."

10

He's crazy, or into a dodgy variety of witchcraft. She could almost see this bullshit on one of those pamphlets promising to bring back lost lovers, solve financial problems, and enlarge penises. Next, he'd pull out a mirror to reveal everyone who wished her harm.

"What about the Between?" he continued. "It's a place with bright colours and no sense of time or direction. There would've been people there, or maybe just voices, the Phoenix?"

There had been a bird feathered in flames, its song sweeter than anything she'd heard before. She'd dreamed about it for the past two weeks, a vague creature that had become more definite every night. They'd flown together the last time, up into the sky, through clouds, and past the edge of Earth's atmosphere. She'd looked back and seen Africa curve away from her, the night chasing the sun across the ocean.

Then light and colours that drifted like visible wind had enveloped her, filled with the intense emotions she normally deadened with alcohol and drugs. There'd been an overwhelming lack of hurt and tension, and she'd felt so alive, like a song given flesh. There were voices, faces that blurred in her memory. They'd offered her a choice…but what was it? She tried to recall the rest, but it was like water falling through her fingers.

Her head felt heavy and the weakness in her body returned. It felt as if she was shrinking. All she could manage was a nod, but she looked him in the eye to show him she wasn't afraid anymore.

Blake's lips curled into a faint smile. "Glad to see it's coming back to you. We should get going again; I want to reach Hex before dawn."

He had to mean the Hex River Valley, why would he take her there? It was all orchards and vineyards, wasn't it?

"But first…" He twisted in his seat and reached into the back of the car. A second later, he sat up with a bundle of fabric clutched in one hand. "This should help you warm up, and cover you."

He turned his head away as she took the bundle from him. A jacket, she draped it over her front rather than spend strength she didn't have to put it on. The car engine purred and he turned back onto the highway. Once they hit the asphalt, the car sped up fast. She leaned back and sighed. Despite the freakiness of everything that had happened tonight, she couldn't help being relieved. She was free of Trey, at last.

2

The journey had become monotonous a long time ago, but now the road twisted and the car was climbing. They must be heading into the mountains. Lights blinked in and out of sight past shadowy obstacles, but no matter how hard she peered out the windows, she couldn't tell if they came from houses, or what was obscuring them.

Blake turned the car, and she had a brief view of a wire fence and gateposts. Had they reached their destination?

The road was uneven now, not enough to rattle her teeth loose, but every bump rippled through her. Eventually a light appeared straight ahead and growing closer.

A bare bulb shone from the veranda of a building in front of them. Its exact size was hidden by the night, but she made out red bricks faded to pink, and white paint on the veranda, window sills, and door.

It looked like it belonged in a horror movie.

Blake parked on the paving in front of the building and climbed out, reappearing at her door.

"Do you think you can walk, or should I carry you?"

She frowned at him and shrugged free of the jacket. He plucked it from her lap as she fumbled to unbuckle her seat belt, holding the door as she gripped the blanket and climbed out.

The paving bricks were rough and cold beneath her feet. It seeped through her soles. Before she took take another step, he draped the jacket over her shoulders, and she tensed. Instinct told her to defend herself, but it was just a jacket. He was being nice.

He'd wrapped her left arm in a fold of the blanket, but the right was free and she wriggled it through the sleeve.

"I should've brought a warmer blanket, you're shivering like a leaf." Blake looked at her as he shut the door.

She shrugged. She'd been shivering for a while now, feeling nauseous too. Her heart was racing in her chest and her head still ached, but she put it all down to anxiety.

She leaned against the car and took a step, legs wobbling under her. When she reached the edge of the bonnet, she paused and measured the distance to the door of the building with her eyes.

It wasn't far, but she didn't know if she'd make it, not with her body so weak.

"Here."

Blake's blue eyes regarded her as he offered her his arm. They reminded her of tranquil pools of water. She eyed his muscles again, and swallowed hard before resting her hand on him as lightly as possible.

Her left arm throbbed from the small effort of keeping the blanket pressed against her. So far, she'd tried not to think of her nudity, or how much he'd seen of her body, but now she worried that the blanket would slip off. The jacket, though helpful, wasn't much cover. When they reached the door, she let go of him, adjusted the blanket, and pulled the jacket closed. He watched her like a concerned parent until he realised she was watching him.

Blake glanced away and opened the door, staying close as she shuffled through the entrance.

The scent of citrus was so strong it made her eyes tear. Directly ahead of them a teenage boy was whistling as he mopped the floor of the tiled passage.

"Hey, trainee, where's Jake?" Blake asked.

The boy looked up at them, his eyes growing wide when he saw her.

"The Child of Heaven," he mumbled, almost dropping his mop.

She edged behind Blake, using him to shield her body from the boy's stare.

"Dude, snap out of it." Blake snapped his fingers at the kid. "Where's Jake?"

"I'm here."

A man with a narrow face appeared from a room further down the hallway. The bright overhead lights cast deep shadows under his cheekbones, and the glasses perched on top of his head made his short, dark hair spike up at weird angles. Blake started towards him, walking slowly over the wet floor. When she glanced in the boy's direction, he was still staring.

Jake also stared at her, but without the boy's intensity. As they approached, he turned to look at Blake.

"What do you need?" he asked.

"You'll have to summon Adnes."

Jake shot a furtive glance in her direction, and nodded. "No problem, follow me."

The men moved down the corridor so she shuffled after them, her joints complaining with every step. They rounded a corner into another passage. This one was much shorter though, and benches lined the wall directly opposite the only door. Jake was waiting for them. He held the door open as Blake helped her into the room.

It was a large space, tiled in white with walls painted a rosy pink colour that matched the passage outside. A plain hospital bed stood in the centre of the room, but otherwise it was empty. There weren't even any windows.

"Can you hop onto the bed please?" Jake watched her carefully, but the hint of a smile lurked at the edges of his mouth.

She walked towards the bed and leaned on it. The mattress was higher than her hip.

Fingertips touched her shoulder and she looked back to find Blake behind her, his other arm held ready to scoop her up.

"May I?"

She nodded, closed her eyes, and gripped the blanket. He didn't grab her hard or roughly jerk her against him though, and set her down as if he thought she'd break.

Jake had moved to the other side, near the middle of the bed.

He looked towards the back wall as he called out. "Sage Adnes, Blake has brought the Child of Heaven."

She glanced at him. The room had been empty so who was he talking to? Then she noticed the branches of a sapling behind him, growing longer and taller before her eyes. She sat bolt upright, watching leaves appear; pale green that darkened as they unfurled and grew larger. Grass grew through the floor in fast forward and more trees rose all around them. Walls disappeared behind the vibrant flora and even the ceiling vanished. Clouds drifted high above the branches that waved overhead.

There was a rustle behind her, and she turned to see a person walking towards them. A hood shadowed his face, but not the bushy, grey streaked beard that brushed his chest. An old-fashioned robe of heavy looking material in a dark shade of purple framed his body about as well as a large sack. He could've hidden an extra pair of arms under there if he had any. It was also far too long, trailing over the grass and making a soft rustling sound as he walked.

Although most of his identifying features were obscured, he seemed familiar—a bit like one of the people from her dream.

"You've done well, Guardian of Heaven, how is she wounded?" The robed man stood beside Jake and swept the hood back from his head. His face was lined with age but it was his eyes that captured her attention. The irises were violet and the whites around them so bright they looked silver.

"Her arm." Blake glanced at her as he reached across and gently unwrapped the blanket from her left arm.

Blood stained the fabric. The rich odour of metal and raw meat invaded her nose, and her arm...she backpedalled on the bed, as though she could get away from the gaping slash dividing her flesh from wrist to elbow.

"Easy, he's going to heal you."

She glanced at Blake, back at her arm, and dry-retched. Jake reached out to take her wrist, and she pulled back, kicking wildly at him. She missed just as wildly, lost her balance, and fell against Blake's chest.

"Hold her," Adnes commanded.

Blake's arms closed around her and she struggled. Jake caught hold of her left hand. She dug her nails into him, and twisted her head to bite Blake at the same time. He caught her jaw in his hand and she cringed, expecting his fingers to slide down and close around her throat. Instead, he turned her head to face him.

"Nobody's going to hurt you, we want to help. Sit still, please. It will only take a moment."

Too many people touching her with their strong hands and arms, and she was so weak, too weak to fight anymore. She squeezed her eyes shut, trembling violently, and braced herself for whatever Adnes was going to do to her.

"There we go." Blake spoke in a soft, soothing voice, and rubbed her back. "I didn't realise you'd forgotten about your arm too, I'm sorry I didn't think of it."

She snapped her eyes open, he was apologising to her?

Gentle warmth flowed into her left arm, and she craned her head to see what Adnes was doing. The wound was closing. Near her elbow, the skin was already whole again. A breath hitched in her throat. The freaky-eyed man wasn't even touching her, just holding his hands over her arm. It was like magic.

"Most peculiar."

She looked up and found Adnes staring at her.

"It's rare that a Child of Heaven uses such violent means to end her life," he continued, a frown crinkling his forehead.

"She remembers nothing, Sage Adnes, just the Phoenix. Right?"

Blake was also looking at her, and she nodded. End her life? She hadn't done this, it was impossible.

"It must have been painful." Adnes sounded sad. "What have you told her, Guardian?"

"The bare basics about Wielders and Guardians," Blake replied. "None of it clicked until I mentioned the Phoenix."

Adnes withdrew his hands; the wound now healed, and tucked them into his robe as he stared at her. Jake released her hand, and Blake let go of her. She glanced between their faces nervously.

"I've done what I can to help your body recover from death. You'll be replacing blood and damaged tissue at a much higher rate over the next day or so, and you'll probably be rather hungry because of it." Adnes tilted his head. "What's your name, lass?"

"She refuses to talk, not a word since I picked her up," Blake answered for her.

"One of the more extreme cases perhaps, nevertheless, it should clear up in a day or two. In the meanwhile, she can listen. Do you remember the place in the light?" he asked.

She replied with a hesitant nod.

"Good, that is where all souls go when the body dies. Some call it Heaven, but it's really a place between worlds. A plane where the soul must choose what becomes of it. A few develop into spirits and move to the soul plane, others are reborn in the bellies of pregnant women." He sighed and looked down as though he were uncomfortable. "For some, the decision is already made. People who live less than gracious lives in the material world weigh their soul down with their harmful actions." Adnes speech had slowed, his voice rougher than before. "They wander in the darkness forever unless they free themselves of that burden. Those that choose to die—that commit suicide—usually count amongst them. That would have been your path except for one thing: you are the Child of Heaven."

She blinked, was he talking about reincarnation? Last she checked that wasn't immediate, or into the same body you'd vacated. Even if she'd died, she certainly hadn't killed herself. This was all so bizarre.

"You are the gift of light into the darkness that grows in the world," Adnes continued. "For weeks we sensed your coming, and prepared for you, Child of Heaven. We chose Blake to be your Guardian, and the Phoenix sought you out in the physical plane."

He was talking about her dream, like Blake had. How did they know about any of this? It was impossible.

She looked at the trees surrounding them and remembered how she'd watched everything change. Only the door remained, like a prop erected in the middle of a forest as somebody's idea of a joke. The new scar on her arm, where they claimed she'd killed herself, was a wide, pink band, streaked with dried blood. She pressed her finger against it, and crusts of dried blood fell away, but it felt normal underneath. It didn't hurt when she pressed against it.

Another wave of nausea hit her and she covered her mouth. Clouds floated through her head, saturated with fear, and her heart was going to explode in her chest, she knew it. Something wasn't right here, and she couldn't brush it off as the after-effects of a very strange night anymore.

Everything happening here could easily be a symptom of a drug Trey had given her.

Adnes sighed and she shrank back. Would he punish her for not knowing what he was talking about?

"It's been a long night, maybe she just needs rest." Blake's voice was low.

Jake nodded in agreement. "Might be that she needs a little time to adjust," he said to Adnes.

"Fair enough, good luck to you." Adnes nodded then turned and walked away. The grass sank through the floor in his wake, and slowly the room faded back to the way it was before his appearance.

"Let's get you to your room." Blake smiled at her but it didn't reach his eyes. He held out his hand, and she had to lean on him as she slid off the side of the bed.

"He said himself that it could take a day or so." Jake spoke to Blake like she wasn't even there, but flashed her a smile when he realised she was looking at him.

"Yeah."

She kept her hand on Blake's arm, and allowed him to lead her through the building while she lowered her head and tried to think this thing out. They couldn't know about her dreams, and she wouldn't choose to bleed to death.

A cold shiver ran down her spine as she remembered a pig shrieking, her father's farmhand plunging the knife into its throat, and the spray of blood that had landed on her shirt. No ways, if she'd accidentally overdosed then maybe she'd buy it, but not that. This couldn't be real, and the sudden forest in that room proved it.

What happened before the dream?

Trey had been angry because she'd tried to sell his stuff to a man who turned out to be a cop. It had cost him most of the afternoon's profit to convince the man to let them go. When they got home, Trey had thrown her around like a dog with a child's toy. Her skull had cracked against the wall, and then his fingers tangled in her hair as he jerked her head back to look at him.

"I've had enough of your bugger ups, Chantelle."

His cheeks and ears had reddened with fury, and she'd smelled mint and brandy on his breath. He'd hit her until she fell then dragged her. Abrasive beige carpet had changed to the rubbery linoleum of the kitchen. She'd hit her forehead when he released her hair.

***

Fingernails dug into his arm. He glanced at her, but all he saw was blonde hair and the top half of her forehead.

"Are you okay?" He placed his free hand over hers.

She tensed, and shot him a wide-eyed look before nodding.

They'd reached the door to the clinic. The kid who'd been mopping earlier still lingered nearby, and he opened it for them.

"Thanks for your help." He smiled politely at Jake before glaring at the boy, who was staring at her again.

It was raining outside, but so softly that he barely heard it falling on the roof above them. At the edge of the veranda, he paused to eye the path that led uphill toward the dorms. It was a gentle slope, but he doubted she'd manage it, and carrying her was awkward, not least of all because she clearly didn't like being touched.

"That's where we're headed next." He pointed to the shadowy outline of the ivy-covered building where the senior Guardians lived. "Think you can make it? I don't want you to get soaked, but there are clothes waiting for you."

She stared at the building, and then down, seeming to follow the path with her gaze. Her head tilted slightly, and she shrugged.

At least she was honest.

"We'll see how far we get, okay?"

They stepped out into the rain, and it was like walking through a mist of ice. Both his hair and the top part of his shirt clung to his skin by the time they reached the foot the path. She looked even worse, as though the wet weight of his jacket was dragging her down to the ground.

Blake shook his head. "I know you don't like it, but I'm going to lift you."

He picked her up, ignored her flinch, and strode up the path. It was almost double the distance they'd just covered, but took half the time.

The only light here came from a stuttering fluorescent tube under the overhanging roof of the mess hall across the way. All he made out were the edges and corners of the terraced front of the dormitory building. Door handles glinted as he passed them; he counted them, and stopped outside the seventh door.

"This is you." He set her down, opened the door, and stepped inside to switch the light on. "These are Guardians' quarters so it's nothing fancy, but it's comfortable."

She peeked inside, snuck through the doorway on her tiptoes, and eyed her new surrounds warily.

"The clothes are in the cupboard." He sidled round the bed to the built in pine cupboard that covered the opposite wall. Part of it was recessed to form a desk with a stool stored in the leg space. "And you have your own bathroom through here." He opened a door next to the desk to reveal the small bathroom behind it.

She stared around the room, trembling from head to foot. When she caught him watching her, she lowered her head to look at the floor. He kept his sigh silent as he retraced his steps to the door.

"I'll leave you to it then. If you need anything, I'm just next-door." He smiled and pointed at the wall behind her before leaving.

This was a disaster. He pulled his phone from his pocket and strode into his own room. He dialled the number as he closed the door. It was just past five in the morning, but Robert answered his call after two rings.

"Is she secured?" A deep voice inquired.

"Yes, Keeper, I had no major problems getting her out."

"Excellent, well done, Guardian. How is she coping?"

"Not well, I'm afraid. She doesn't remember much."

"Care to elaborate?" He drew out the words and Blake could almost hear him frowning.

"She slit her wrist, but when she saw the wound she freaked out. She had no idea who I was, and when I tried to explain, she looked at me like I was crazy. The only thing that gets through to her is mentioning the Phoenix or the Between."

"I see." He went silent for a while. "It's not an entirely unusual reaction, Blake. Waking from death is bound to be a harrowing experience."

"I know," Blake sighed. "You said I'll need to be patient, Keeper, but I don't think that will be enough. She doesn't speak, practically has a fit when anyone tries to touch her, and seems scared of everything. I think there's something very wrong with her."

"She committed suicide; of course there's something wrong with her. That's why I instructed you to take her to Hex, so she'd have time to adjust and get over whatever it is that made her kill herself. It's isolated and peaceful there, and safe from the Covens."

"Yes, Keeper." He made it sound so simple, but Blake doubted it was. People who venture so deeply into depression that they contemplate suicide don't just get over it.

"Report again at the end of the week with her progress, and inform me if anything untoward occurs in the meanwhile. I doubt her essence will Awaken rapidly, but one must be prepared in any case."

"Yes, Keeper, I'll do that."

"Very good, now try to get some rest."

The line went dead. Blake sighed, put his phone on the bedside table, and stripped his wet shirt off. A shiver rippled through his skin, and goose bumps rose across his scarred chest and stomach. He snatched a dry shirt from his bag and pulled it over his head. While he was at it, he kicked his boots off and changed his jeans for sweat pants before collapsing onto the bed. As he stared up at the ceiling, the events of the night flashed through his mind.

He'd been excited a few hours ago when the Keeper called him with her location, and had driven to Cape Town on an adrenalin high. He'd known she'd be disoriented, nervous, and possibly even violent, according to the Keeper and Elise. He'd prepared himself for that, but this silent girl who wouldn't be touched and seemed to be waiting for something awful to be done to her was a different kettle of fish.

Maybe he'd been overconfident, expecting her to be one way without allowing much leeway for anything else.

"Just have to see how it goes," he whispered to himself.

3

She found a tracksuit in the cupboard that almost fit her, loose enough to be comfortable without swallowing her in folds of fabric, but she couldn't sleep. Her situation was too uncertain, and her nerves were shot.

The light felt too revealing, so she sat in the dark with the duvet from the bed draped around her. Nothing made sense, and she had to face the facts; as pleasant as it was to be around nice people, this couldn't be real. She'd hit her head before, hard enough to cause brain trauma? Or had Trey given her something to send her on a bad trip?

That could account for her shaking fingers, racing heart, and the apprehension boiling in her guts. But her legal guardian had put her through GHB withdrawal before, and the first few hours had been similar to this. Afterwards, the DT's had started, and the hallucinations.

She couldn't remember much after that. So much of her life was lost in drug-induced blackouts that it had become normal. Most of it she didn't want to remember, but sometimes, she hated it.

Eventually he'd given her pills, and that had cleared it up. If this was all an elaborate hallucination then he'd bring her out of it at some point.

She lay down on her side and curled up into a tight ball. She didn't want to be back with Trey—it was much nicer in her delusion. Even if she had to live with this horrible scar, at least she didn't have to suffer his abuse here.

Religion was something she'd lost a long time ago, but now she silently prayed to any God who might listen, and pleaded for reprieve from the hell she'd lived in for so long. It gave her something to focus on.

Words wove into a mantra, and the warmth of her cocoon soothed her. Her stomach tingled. It was a strange sensation, uncomfortable but not unpleasant. It spread through her body, and she felt lighter, as if she was floating in the ocean and drifting toward the horizon.

A faint melody filled the air. The notes vibrated against her skin, no, beneath it. It grew stronger, like a symphony which starts gently and builds to a triumphant wave crashing over you. Phoenix song. The music lifted her, and the world seemed brighter, but now heat prickled her skin and beads of sweat trickled across her forehead. She couldn't see the bird, but its heat was all around her, would burn her if it came any closer.

She wrestled the duvet, kicked and flailed against it until she tumbled free, and rolled off the edge of the bed.

"Ow." Her elbow knocked against the floor, and she sat up.

Pale light shone through the blinds on the window. Had she fallen asleep after all? Her body felt stronger, it wasn't a great effort to lift her arm level with her eyes, and pull the sleeve up.

The scar was still there, a ridge of thick, pink flesh running from her wrist almost to her elbow.

She pulled a face, jerked the sleeve down to her wrist, and rose. The rain had stopped and the sun hadn't fully risen yet. Everything outside her window was painted a pre-dawn grey. Not that she could see much: the edge of the cement patio, a neat stretch of lawn, and the white building opposite her.

Another dig through the closet produced jeans, a t-shirt, and a hoodie with a smoking skull on it. All the clothes were men's sizes, and too big for her. It was the same with the shoes, but at least she didn't have to wear a dress anymore.

She opened the door to her room, eased it closed behind her, and walked to the edge of the patio. The upper storey and roof of a building similar to this one was visible over the low structure across the lawn, but she wasn't interested in meeting people. To her right, the ground sloped down, and she diagonally crossed the lawn in that direction.

From the end of the white building, she saw the dirt road leading to the clinic she'd been in last night. Blake's car was still parked outside the building. A tall, evergreen hedge separated the property from a huge stand of trees planted in long rows, their branches all bare. More trees were visible off to her left, beyond another hedge.

An orchard perhaps, which meant she was on a farm. She certainly wasn't close enough to any town or city to see it. She stepped away from the building and looked back, the grassy slope crested a bit higher up, and further on, the mountains reached to the sky. Wispy clouds in hues of pink and orange hid the peaks from view.

Thudding footsteps snapped her out of her reverie, and she turned to see a gang of teenage boys jogging towards her. The same boy who'd stared at her earlier that morning ran at the head of the pack. She started back towards the white building, but he'd already seen her. His eyes went wide, and he stopped on the metaphorical dime.

Some of the boys behind him ducked sideways, but a few crashed into him, and soon the entire group was in shambles. Most of the group lay sprawled over the short, dry grass. The rest either milled around behind them, or stood a metre away from her looking bewildered and amused.

"What's going on here?" a male voice boomed from somewhere beyond them, and she tensed.

The group parted as a man appeared, older than Blake, but cut from the same muscly, super-fit cloth. A scowl creased his face, pulling at a scar that sliced through his eyebrow, passed millimetres from the outer corner of his eye, and ended on his cheek. The boys scrambled over each other to pick themselves up.

"Carl stopped."

"It was Carl's fault, sir."

He raised one hand and all the talking stopped. Her awestruck admirer, Carl, she assumed, had lifted himself to one knee. He stared at her avidly, the only member of the group unaffected by this man's obvious authority.

"She's the Child of Heaven." Carl pointed at her.

Now they all gawked at her as though a naked supermodel had sprouted from the ground in front of her. She lowered her head so her hair would fall across her face.

"If you lot are going to fall over yourselves every time you see a Wielder then you're more useless than I thought." The scarred man slapped Carl's arm down as he moved to the front. "Get up and get off with you, now!"

The group sprinted off, and every last one of them gave her and the man a wide berth. He waited until they'd left before approaching her, and she gulped.

"Please excuse them, word got out that you'd be staying here a while, and the trainees don't get much excitement," he said.

She nodded, glancing back as the last of the teens disappeared through a gate in the hedging.

"I'm Declan, by the way, one of the trainers here at Hex."

He held out his hand for her to shake, and she stared at it a moment before hesitantly offering her own.

"I heard that Blake returned with you this morning, but I assumed you'd both spend most of the day sleeping."

She shook her head, and inched away from him as she cast her gaze about for an excuse to get away.

"Would you like breakfast? The trainees won't be back for a while, and most of the others only get up in another half an hour, so you should be able to eat in peace." He smiled, and the tail end of his scar pointed at the corner of his mouth. It was even scarier than his frown.

She nodded. With any luck, this would get him to leave her alone.

"This way." He gestured to her to go with him.

She followed him round the corner and through the double door entrance to the white building. Inside was an open, utilitarian space filled with old wooden benches drawn up to steel tables. A long counter at the near end separated this area from a pink tiled kitchen. Four or five people bustled around inside it, but only two of them seemed to be cooking.

"There should be coffee shortly, please help yourself."

She nodded in Declan's direction, and walked to the far end of the counter, where a large tray of muffins sat under a cover. Her stomach had become a growling pit. She put a lemon and poppy seed muffin on a plate before choosing to sit at a bench near the wall.

This place was huge, and if that was anything to go by, there had to be at least a hundred people here, more like two hundred. Would they all stare at her?

She pulled the jacket hood over her head, just in case anyone else appeared.

* * *

Blake felt like he'd only just closed his eyes when an insistent rapping on the door woke him. He groaned, couldn't he ignore it and go back to sleep?

The continued knocking didn't think so. With a sigh, he pulled himself up and shuffled to the door.

"At least one of you got some rest. Your Wielder is in the mess and she seems antsy." Declan frowned and Blake tried not to stare at his scar. "Perhaps you should keep an eye on her, Blake, we wouldn't want her getting it into her head to run off."

"Yes, thank you, sir." He sounded hoarse, and cleared his throat before continuing. "I'll get dressed at once."

Declan nodded then walked away. Blake closed the door, yawning as he flapped open his gym bag. His shirt was rumpled from the few hours he'd slept, but otherwise fine. He left it on, but tugged a clean pair of jeans from the bag and pulled them on. After brushing his teeth, he splashed cold water on his face then shuffled across to the mess hall.

She sat alone on the far side of the room picking at a muffin. Long, blonde hair spilled from the hood of her jacket, and past the edge of the table.

He filled two cups with water from an urn nearby. To hers, he added coffee, milk and sugar, but just coffee to his—eight spoons full of the instant, no-name brand crap. He'd probably regret this toxic concoction after he'd tasted it, but he needed as much caffeine as he could get. Too little sleep was far worse than none at all.

He headed across the room and sat down opposite his charge. Her gaze flicked up at him, steel grey eyes narrowed into a look that could peel skin from bone. She relaxed when she recognised him, so it seemed, at any rate, and watched as he set her coffee down in front of her.

"Aren't you tired?" he asked, stifling a yawn.

She replied with a stiff shake of her head.

Blake groaned and took a sip of coffee. It tasted much like burning tyres smelled.

"You were woken up because of me?"

Her voice was melodic, and just loud enough to carry across the table. He looked up, uncertain he'd really heard her, and found her watching him expectantly. This was good, he'd get to know her if she was talking.

"Yes," he replied, "but it's fine, it's my duty."

"Why?"

"Because I'm your Guardian, I'm here to protect you."

Her face contorted as though he'd presented her with a handful of maggots, and a fearful sort of anger sparked in her eyes. He watched her fingers tense on the muffin, and send a cascade of crumbs falling to the plate. Blake set his mug aside, well out of the line of fire in case she threw her food at him.

"I realise that this is all new to you." He cleared his throat and prepared to dodge. "But I'll explain everything, starting from today. I can start right now if you want."

She broke off a piece of muffin and daintily popped it into her mouth while her features smoothed into a blank expression.

Oh holy crap, this girl was complicated.

She swallowed and seemed to examine her food. "What does it mean, being this Child of Heaven?"

"It's an honorific name we use for Spirit Wielders, because they have to die first. You may be human in a genealogical sense, but your soul is connected to the Geead Lyana, the first children created by the Mother."

She pushed her muffin aside, only a quarter of it eaten, and closed her hands around her mug. She was still shaking, he noted, and looking at him as if he'd spoken a foreign language.

Blake gulped down another mouthful of coffee. "To start with, the Circle has nothing to do with religion or magic, although certain elements of both might seem to apply to it. The simple reason for this is that we have the oldest and most intact records of humanity's origins. Many modern religions and magical concepts are rooted in what we know, but the truth has been twisted over the centuries. The Geead Lyana have been misinterpreted as Gods, the seemingly supernatural abilities of the Awakened, confused with magic, and..." She was pulling a weird face, like she wanted to puke.

"And I'm not explaining very well, am I?" he asked.

"Not really," she mumbled.

He smiled at her. "Sorry about that. If it helps at all, I know how you feel. My uncle told me about all of this when I was twelve, he inherited the Awakened genes but my Dad didn't, so I was oblivious up til that point."

In that moment he'd wondered if Mom was right to say Uncle David had a screw loose. Not that she said it in front of him and his twin, but he'd overheard her on the phone many times. David had taught both him and Maya martial arts from a young age. She hadn't enjoyed it as much as he had, skipping lessons as often as she attended. It was on one of those afternoons, when he'd been training alone, that David had told him he was a Guardian.

How different things might've been if Maya was born a Wielder. She should've been, they were twins, after all.

"Being Awakened means you have genes from those Geead thingies?"

He looked up and brought his focus back to the present. "Yeah, some of them had children with humans, and that's how the Awakened came to be."

"How is that possible?" She frowned at him.

"The two races must've been similar enough to interbreed. Like lions and tigers can, or horses and donkeys. Obviously in our case, the offspring aren't infertile."

Her head tipped forwards, and she pressed the heels of her hands against her eyes.

"Male children have increased strength, agility, and speed," he continued, quirking a brow at her. "We train from a young age to be Guardians of the women, the Wielders. Each Wielder has an affinity for a certain element, Earth, Fire, Air and Water; they can channel the elements and control unique abilities associated with them. For example, Water Wielders tend to be empathic, Fire Wielders can teleport, Earth Wielders use telekinesis, and Air Wielders are telepathic. You are the Wielder of the fifth element, Spirit, but the books are unclear about your specific ability. They just call it 'knowing'."

"Knowing what?" She removed her hands to frown at him.

"I'm not sure. The only well documented aspect is the premonition that Spirit Wielders get when they're about to die, the second time, that is."

She sniffed and shook her head.

This wasn't going as well as he'd hoped. He shouldn't have mentioned the premonitions, or death. Good thing he'd started slowly—she wasn't close to ready to hear about the Skaath.

"It's a lot to take in, especially if you're religious..."

"I'm not."

"Okay," he paused. There must be a way to explain this that'd be easy for her to understand.

"I don't believe in anything," she continued.

"This isn't something I'm trying to convert you to, it's real, but I don't expect you to blindly take my word for it. If you keep an open mind, you'll see for yourself." Seeing was believing, after all.

"Sure."

A non-committal response if ever there was one. "Since you're speaking now," he said. "I still don't know your name..."

She shook her head again.

"I guess I'll just have to call you Heaven."

***

"Fine by me," she replied. Her heart had taken up a high tempo dance beat again. She spread her hands over the table, and breathed slowly to slow her heart rate. It was pointless, but she had to try. This was definitely withdrawal, and the possibilities scared her. DT's killed. She wasn't at that point yet...but that 'yet'.

That weird episode this morning, and all the stuff he was telling her. He spoke so rationally, but it made little sense. Everything seemed off, as if the sun had suddenly risen in the West. This shit was down the rabbit hole.

"Since we're both up, why don't I show you around?" His smile was forced, for her benefit, she supposed. The guy kept trying to put her at ease and she wasn't sure why he'd bother.

"Sure." Despite her hunger, the muffin was making her nauseous, and the coffee wasn't helping. She stood up without bothering to finish either, and watched him in her peripheral vision as he downed the contents of his mug.

"This way," he said, standing up and moving away from the table.

They left through the doors on the opposite side from where she'd entered, and emerged a short distance from where the human pile up had occurred earlier.

"That was the mess hall, as you know. Breakfast is served between five and six thirty on weekdays, and six and eight over the weekend. Lunch is at twelve and supper at six, but there are usually snacks available throughout the day if you're hungry. Those are the trainees and novices' quarters, not much to see there," he said as he pointed at the building in front of her.

It was an exact replica of the building she'd stayed in last night. She frowned at it then turned away to follow him.

A wide path led them across the neat lawn to the crest of the hill. Tall pine trees grew here and there, and narrow flowerbeds bordered the smooth cement. From the top of the rise, she saw a long building squatting in the approximate centre of the tiny valley below.

The path led them towards it.

"This is basically a school." Blake gestured to the building in front of them. "When people realise that their son is going to be a Guardian, they usually send him here to begin training."

"How do they realise that?" she asked.

"It's little things, really. A protective instinct, fast healing, the physical traits I mentioned earlier. Most kids are compassionate by nature, but if your son bends an opening in a fence to stop two dogs from fighting then you're likely to recognise something unusual about it."

Bloody hell. If a child was that strong then how much stronger was an adult? If she wasn't already trembling then she would've been now.

"Where are the Wielders?"

"They don't train with us." He glanced at her as they approached the building. "For some reason, Guardians outnumber Wielders, so there's really no need for them to go to a centre. They usually mentor under an older Wielder of the same element, and only come out for combat training."

Combat training? Her head swam with images of people attacking each other, blood, and the crack of bone. Her chest closed up and the nausea kicked up a gear. She thought she might fall over, so she leaned against the wall instead. Fear wasn't real, just a stupid emotion. She had to pull herself together.

"Are you okay?"

Blake stood in front of her, but colours floated at the edges of her field of vision, and the weird, warm tingles had returned. She was losing her grip, but she lied, nodding at him.

His brow furrowed. "Heaven, if something is wrong then you can tell me."

She was a dancing flame, but instead of shadows, she cast colours around her like a prism. Her time was up. She had to trust him and hope for the best.

"Withdrawal, it stirs up your head," she muttered.

"What did you take?"

She waved her hand to dismiss his question. "I'm not an addict…pills'll fix me."

"I'm taking you back to the clinic, can you walk?"

There was no walking through this stage of it, you crawled or you sank.

"I won't sink."

4

Blake paced the hallway outside the room where Phillip was examining Heaven. He should've insisted that Jake check her out last night. He'd seen the way she was shaking, but assumed it was a combination of the cold, and her revival from death.

He'd been a fool.

The door swung open, and Phillip came out. He rubbed his index finger between his eyebrows as he marched past Blake, and down the hallway.

"Phillip, what's going on?" He fell into step at the man's side.

"I'll tell you as soon as I know," Phillip replied brusquely.

"There must be something you can tell me, is she going to be okay?"

Phillip slowed and turned to look at him. "I'm a field medic, Blake, not a doctor. I'm not equipped to deal with this, none of us are. But I'm going to phone Elise now, so don't worry, she'll be okay."

He ducked through the door to the office and Blake stopped outside. The door closed in his face, and he looked back toward Heaven's room. Elise would know what to do about this, and she'd have access to whatever medication Heaven needed at the hospital.

"...tachycardia, tremors...no, she hasn't..."

He turned his head to listen more closely.

"Blake said she mentioned being treated with tablets on a previous occasion...it isn't that severe...I do, yes."

There was a long pause; he heard the click of a pen and paper rustling.

"Got it, thanks, Elise...I will."

Blake turned and jogged down the hallway, through the door to Heaven's room. She was sitting on the bed staring at her fingers.

"Hey," he said.

She looked up, her eyes wide and scared. "Hi," she muttered back.

"It will be okay." He forced a smile as he stood at the side of the bed, and looked down at her. "Phillip should be back soon and he'll sort you out."

She nodded, "This isn't the worst."

She spoke so softly that he wondered if she was reminding herself of that.

"Here we go." Phillip entered the room with a small cup and a syringe on a steel tray. "This should ease the immediate symptoms, and help you sleep. You said you've been through this before, right?"

"Once, worse than this."

Phillip shook his head. "Madness. Anyway, I'm going to keep you here tonight, and if you're responding well then you can go tomorrow, and just take a short course of medication to help your body adjust to being clean." He leaned towards her and narrowed his eyes. "Just so you know, we don't keep alcohol here at Hex, and all the scheduled medications in the clinic are tightly locked up, so don't get any ideas."

"I'm not an addict." Her lower lip quivered as she spoke.

"Uh huh."

Phillip didn't believe her, obviously, but he didn't have to be so rude about it. Making her feel bad about it was probably the worst thing he could do. Blake knew what it was like to crave something bad for you, and how easily the thing you used to cope could start controlling you. He had the scars to prove it.

Blake lowered his hand, offering it to her, even though he doubted she'd welcome the contact. She stared at it and he felt like an idiot. Just when he'd decide to retreat gracefully, she lightly folded her fingers around his, and squeezed as Phillip gave her the injection.

She drank the pills from the cup while Phillip looked on, and then the medic ordered Blake out with assurances that she'd probably fall asleep soon. Blake nodded, but chewed the inside of his cheek as he left the clinic. He leaned against the hood of his car as he took out his phone and called Elise.

"I knew you'd call."

He smiled in spite of himself at the sound of her voice. "Is she going to be okay?"

"Probably...I can't go into specifics, but it sounds like she's doing better than she should be," Elise said, her voice husky but sweet.

"Okay, thank you."

"Are you okay?"

"Yeah, just worried about her," he sighed.

"She's going to be all right...I'm sorry, but I have to go. I'm fully booked today."

"No problem, thanks, Elise."

"Anytime."

She hung up. He shoved the phone back in his pocket, and sternly reminded himself that Elise was off limits.

Or was she? He'd be moving to Denysrus now that he'd been assigned to Heaven, maybe he'd get a chance to pursue a relationship with her. Provided she felt the same way about him.

Blake sighed and strolled back the way he'd come. He was thinking too much, as usual.

***

Colours wrapped around her, a visible wind that caressed her skin like silk. Everything glowed, and her footsteps caused the hues beneath her feet to ripple and swirl together like wet paint. There was music too, but it was inside of her, warming her as it vibrated through her cells.

She smiled as she pushed through a violet breeze, and giggled when it tickled her skin. Something smelt like ginger biscuits baking. She closed her eyes as she inhaled the scent, so much like home and childhood.

"You have to love again, Child of Heaven, everyone and everything, it will save you. Do not be afraid, for every light casts a shadow."

Those voices, they were the same as before. She looked for the source of the words but they were drowned out by a hiss. It sounded like it was coming from her right, but when she looked in that direction, there was nothing there. She waved her hand to disperse green and butter-yellow drifts of air, and waited.

Another hiss, behind her now, and accompanied by a waft of cold air against her back. Heaven stood perfectly still; too nervous to turn around. What could be large enough to breathe against her like that, and why was it cold?

The warmth of the music faded and the colours on the air turning to brittle wisps of grey. A bitter chill crept up her legs, and when she glanced down, she was standing in a pool of darkness that expanded as she watched.

Hiss…and a foul scent of rotting meat. Damp, almost feverish heat prickled the back of her neck as something entered her peripheral vision, small and black. Crimson eyes without pupils, or irises, that nevertheless seemed fixed on her. A forked tongue darted from the snake's mouth, and it was a pale, cyanotic blue, like some dead thing.

Another snake pressed against the back of her arm then wiggled between her arm and her side. Another skimmed against her thigh, yet another slowly coiled around her wrist like thick rope. She tried to move, and they tightened their hold. More wound around her waist, her elbows, her throat. She opened her mouth to scream, but there was no sound.

The snakes engulfed her. They bound her so strongly that she couldn't move, couldn't breathe. They began moving her, turning her around to face a pitch-black jackal, lithe and lean. The snakes poured from its gaping jaws. Its eyes were yet another set of endlessly deep crimson embers. It was like staring into lava, and she felt like they were burning into her, charring her skin away to bare her bones, and every terrible secret hidden in her soul. She struggled against the snakes: wrenching joints and muscles until they ached, ignoring the strange scrape of scales against her skin. The jackal stepped closer, and the serpents' grip tightened.

The snakes wound around her chest and throat were horribly tight. All she could see was black and the burning eyes of the jackal. It was suffocating her, and she was powerless, she'd die.

But would that really be so bad? To return to the dream place, and be back where she was so deeply loved that she could physically feel it in her heart? She relaxed as she recalled that feeling. Her situation no longer seemed so perilous, in fact, she welcomed it, welcomed the opportunity to die.

The jackal shattered like glass, and she was falling into the blackness at her feet. Thick and cloying, heavy like mud, it resisted her as she struck out for the edge of the pool. It got into her mouth, and it tasted like blood.

When she screamed, it flooded her throat and choked her. Darkness filled her lungs until she could feel the weight of it inside her, dragging her down, drowning her.

She woke with a start. Somebody touched her arm, and she pulled away so hard that she nearly fell off the bed. The room was dark, but enough light came in through the door for her to make out the face of the first medic, Jake.

"You were having a nightmare," he said, giving her an odd, but friendly look before pouring a glass of water, which he held out to her. She moved around until she was sitting in a more comfortable position then sipped at the cool glass.

"I owe you an apology." He tilted his head as he spoke and rubbed the back of his head. "I should've checked you out last night; maybe I would've noticed that something was wrong."

She frowned at him then shook her head. "I thought it would be okay."

"It will be." He smiled. "How do you feel?"

"Awake, pretty clear headed."

"That's good. The drugs Phil gave you seem to have alleviated most of your symptoms. We'll probably be able to release you in the morning."

"And then?"

"A short course of Valium, if necessary. You'll have one tomorrow, and Blake will keep the rest. I'm sure you know that they're addictive, so he'll have strict instructions to only administer them when needed."

"I'm not an addict," Heaven muttered, staring down into the glass.

"I didn't think you were. When Phil told me about your condition, I did some research into GHB and alcohol withdrawal. It seems to me that you wouldn't have been strolling around if you were heavily addicted to either of the two. The fact that you slept for so long also suggests that you don't have as high a tolerance as expected."

All she could do was stare at him.

"That being said," Jake continued, "you were obviously regularly partaking in heavy doses of both to develop symptoms at all. The combined effects of your blood loss and Adnes's healing may well have compounded what should've been a minor withdrawal issue."

She nodded, it sounded plausible enough to her.

"Still, you shouldn't be afraid to ask for help, Heaven." He smiled. "Now, I'd like to check your heart rhythm, and then you should try to go back to sleep."

She thought about her dream while he checked her pulse. It had been so much like death, the place they called the Between. How could something that felt so honest and complete, be nothing but a transient nowhere? The unadulterated sense of love and peace she'd experienced there made the earthly versions seem like cheap plastic knock-offs.

The voices had asked her to love, and it had seemed so simple there. It was a con and she'd fallen for it. The beauty of the Between was impossible to reproduce here.

Don't be afraid? Yeah, right.

5

Jake had left by the time she woke up the next morning, but Phillip released her before midday. She wasn't hungry, but Blake made her eat before giving her another pill. Afterwards, she went to bed again, and took refuge in the familiarity of a drug-induced serenity before falling asleep.

She woke shortly before dawn, but cuddled into bed rather than face the world already. She still didn't feel right in her skin.

There was a gentle rapping at her door. She lifted her head, and hoped that if she stayed quiet then whoever it was would go away. She wasn't that lucky. The knock was louder the second time. She sighed and got up to answer it, but pulled the over sized shirt she wore up to cover her shoulder her shoulder first.

"Morning, Heaven." Blake grinned. "I brought you breakfast."

She looked at the mug of coffee and muffin he held then stepped aside to let him enter.

"Did you sleep okay?" He glanced in her direction as he put the mug and plate on the bedside table.

"I did...and you?"

"Very well, I don't think I even dreamed last night. Come and have your breakfast in bed, your body has been through a lot, and you deserve a little spoiling."

Was he ever not nice? She shrugged, climbed back onto the bed, and settled against the pillows before swallowing some coffee. Blake pushed the door closed, and sat on the edge of the windowsill.

"How are you today?"

"I'm fine," she muttered.

"You look better." He nodded. "How would you like to take a trip into town? The Keeper contacted me last night to let me know that he's put money into my account for clothes and anything else you need."

She blinked a few times; surprised that he was willing to take her shopping, and that something as minor as her comfort could be important.

"Yes...thank you."

"No worries, you can't keep wearing second-hand stuff, and smelling like the trainees' cheap aftershave."

Her eyebrows flashed upwards, and she bowed her head to stare into her coffee. When last had need been so simple? Too long ago.

"We aren't staying here much longer, you should know that. Soon you must start training." Blake stared past her as he spoke.

"What type of training?"

"Your essence will Awaken at some point. You need to learn how to control it, and how to channel the Phoenix."

"Essence?"

"If your soul had a fingerprint, it would be your essence. It's also the source of a Wielder's abilities."

"Where the similarity to magic comes in?"

"Yeah." He shifted his weight on the sill and rubbed the corner of his mouth. "Wielders train from the moment their element Awakens, learning to build up their essence, and to control it. Spirit Wielders aren't able to do that, so things happen in reverse. They're given one of the four Heavenly talismans to give them a boost, so to say, the Phoenix talisman, in your case, and the ability to channel the Fire element. Then it's just a matter of waiting for your Spirit abilities to Awaken."

"Does every element have its own talisman?"

"Yes, but we only have three of them. The Earth talisman was lost when the last Child of Heaven died. You can read about most of this in the lorebook the Keeper has for you, all the general info will be explained in that."

"Law book?" She frowned. "Like rules and stuff?"

"No, L-O-R-E," he chuckled as he spelled the word out. "Every Wielder and Guardian has a family lorebook which is passed down from one person to the next, it explains our history and…well, it's rather like a school text book. The Keeper has a generic version you can use."

There was always one more thing. But if reading some book was the price she had to pay for her freedom, she'd take it. There was still a lot she didn't understand about all of this, and these people, maybe this could clear that up too. The mystical essence stuff she'd believe when she saw it.

She downed the rest of her coffee.

"I'll take that for you." He got up and held out his hand for her mug. "And leave you to get dressed. Just come and let me know when you're ready."

"I will."

After he left, Heaven picked out a pair of jeans that wasn't too baggy and a long sleeved shirt that would cover her scar. Once she'd finished her shower and dressed, she stared into the mirror.

Any other day, she would've put make up on now, and styled her hair to look presentable and feminine. The years spent being acutely aware of how much sun reached her skin had kept her face pale, and the freckles that dotted her cheeks faint. She lifted a hand to her wet hair. Trey had kept it blonde after Anna left, and she'd never been allowed to cut it either. Six years of nothing more than an occasional trim had produced a curtain that fell to her waist. It was heavy and thick, and the roots were growing out in her natural mousy brown.

Blonde hair, pale skin, and grey eyes, she was a monochrome personification of what Trey had wanted her to be. He'd taught her to do her hair and make up just so, and he'd made her wear dresses and stockings to create the perfect aesthetic. He'd turned her into a perfect little doll with correct posture, faultless manners, and a head full of subversive conditioning, a poor replica of Anna, with a twenties' housewife twist.

His blissful smile as he'd said that word, 'perfect', flashed into her mind. She snarled at her reflection, the baring of her teeth turning into a grin of approval at her feral appearance.

She wouldn't be an imitation of the girlfriend who left anymore.

The desk drawer stuck when she pulled on it, a quick tug didn't help, so she peered into it. Empty, and the second drawer as well. Not even a blunt nosed paper scissors you'd give to a kid in Pre School. She groaned, put her hands to her head, whirled around, and strode to the door.

She looked around, walked the short distance to Blake's room, and knocked; shifting her weight from one foot to the other until he opened.

"Hey…are you ready to go?"

"No. I need scissors," she said.

"Scissors? Sure, come in, and I'll see if I have one," he replied as he turned away from the door.

His room was carelessly neat. The bedding pulled up but not properly made, shoes lying together but not perfectly aligned, and a leather jacket hung over one of the doorknobs on the cupboard. It smelt of him; a clean, rain on warm soil sort of smell with a sharp tang of aftershave, and a vague bottom note of feet and sweat, but she liked it. It was an improvement on Trey's obsessive neatness.

"That's the first time I've seen you smile," he remarked.

She swung her head around to find him watching her with the scissors in his hand. She shrugged and held out her hand.

"Hang on a moment." Blake held up his hand with the palm facing her. "Don't take this the wrong way, but I must check what you want this for, just in case…you know. Its my orders. I have to protect you, even from yourself."

She scoffed and lifted a lock of her hair. Blake arched one eyebrow then shook his head as an amused look crept over his face.

"You want to cut your hair?" He smiled, and she nodded in reply.

"It will look a mess if you cut it yourself, can I help you?"

She hated to admit that he had a good point. Did she care if her hair was a mess? Not really, but he might not give her the scissors if she didn't agree. She nodded, and indicated a length slightly longer than her jaw line.

"That's a lot of hair, are you sure?" He arched his left brow at her.

Again, she nodded.

Blake shrugged. "Your wish is my command."

Damn, she could get used to hearing that.

He brushed her hair back over her shoulder with his fingers, apologising when they touched her neck.

"It's okay," she replied, surprising herself as she realised that she didn't mind. Maybe it was because he'd been gentle with her so far, and never seemed to get perverted thrills from touching her. Despite his scary proportions, Blake was remarkably unthreatening.

She stood still as he moved around behind her, her arms crossed, and her hands clenched in her armpits as she listened to the soft snipping of the scissors. The ends of her hair brushed against her neck as he progressed. When he stepped in front of her and held out her hair in his fist, it looked like half a metre. Her whole head felt lighter.

"I feel like I just barbered Rapunzel." He chuckled, and she briefly smiled at him.

When she looked in the mirror, she felt as though she didn't even know herself. Blake had done a good job, but something still bugged her. She stared, and stared, used her hands to lift her hair away from her face, and covered the blonde so she could only see the dark roots.

"Do you like it?" he asked from beyond the door.

She lowered her hands, went to stand in front of him, and pulled her hair back while pointing at the darker colour on her roots.

"Shorter," she said.

"That's drastic." He frowned. "If it's the colour you don't like we can always get you dye in town."

"I want it short, like a boy. And dye."

"Are you sure, Heaven? You might miss your hair."

"I won't!" The words came out in a harsh tone. Blake's thick eyebrows shot up in surprise.

"Please," she pleaded, "I don't want to be somebody else anymore."

His expression softened, and the frown melted from his face. "Okay," he sighed. "But there's a clipper in the bathroom cupboard that will work better than scissors."

She nodded, and stepped aside to let him pass. This time, she watched in the mirror as her hair fell away.

"All done," he declared after a while. It wasn't quite as short as she'd wanted it, but it would do.

"Thank you…now I'm ready to go."

Blake chuckled and she met his gaze in the mirror.

"It's nice to meet you." He grinned.

***

The drive into town was just long enough to be boring. There was nothing to see along the way except fields of bare trees and vineyards. The town wasn't impressive either. At a guess, she'd say that nearly everything of interest lined the main street.

Blake parked the car outside a building of stained and weathered stone with a modern shop front. The sign over the door, and the branding in the window displays, identified it as one of the cheaper clothing chain stores.

"I reckon this'll be a good place to start."

She followed him inside. There weren't many people around, but it was still easier to get through them if she stayed in his wake. Once they reached the women's section, she moved among the clothes hesitantly, occasionally touching fabric, or gently pulling an item so she could get a better look at it.

"Take a few things and try them on."

He was standing a short distance away with his hands in his pockets, and his hair hanging in his face. He seemed relaxed, so maybe she'd imagined the impatience in his tone, but he obviously thought she was dawdling.

Heaven stared at the folded piles of jeans at the end of the aisle. It had been years since she picked out her own clothes, she wasn't even sure what size she wore. She snatched two pairs of jeans and moved on, looked at some long sleeved shirts that were on sale and took two of those as well.

"Get a black shirt and a pair of black pants," Blake said over her shoulder. "T-shirts too, since summer is coming."

"T-shirts won't cover my scar," she muttered as she grabbed a black long sleeved shirt and moved away to look for black pants.

She tried on the clothes then changed one pair of jeans for a size bigger, and grabbed some underwear, socks, and a pair of shoes. Blake had been quiet since she mentioned her scar. He gave the cashier his card without even checking the total.

He carried her shopping bags to the car and locked them in the boot.

"The chemist is nearby, we'll get your toiletries and dye there, but there's a place I want to stop at on the way."

"Okay," she said, it wasn't as if he needed her permission.

The place in question was a boutique shop with designer clothes that were odd to say the least. If they were just brightly coloured it would've been one thing, but nearly everything also had ruffles, or lace, or jewel studs, or a combination of them. Surely even the blind could tell how tasteless these clothes were. What Blake wanted in here was beyond her imagination to guess.

She examined a dress in peacock print with a gathered and ruffled hemline while Blake spoke with the middle-aged woman behind the counter. Maybe he had a girlfriend with bad fashion sense, or he was a cross-dresser.

Nah, even the plus size dresses would never fit his frame. She pretended to look through the rest of the rack while moving closer, hoping to overhear his conversation.

She peered over, and watched as he selected something from a tray the woman had on the counter. He held it in his hand as she rung up his purchase on the till then stuffed whatever it was in his pocket, and came towards her.

"Off we go again," he said with a smile.

She picked out toiletries in the chemist with little care, but spent a long time staring at the hair dye displayed on the shelf. She'd never touch blonde again, and brown seemed too plain, like the drab version of blonde.

"Black?" She held up a box of blue-black dye and looked at Blake.

He shook his head. "Your skin is too pale, you'll look like a movie vampire."

"Probably right," she muttered, even though the colour was beautiful. Next, she lifted the last box of a dye that was more purple than red, and smiled. Maybe the same people who'd bought out nearly all the stock were also walking around in clothes from the little boutique of horrors.

"That's bright," Blake remarked behind her. She shook her head before returning it to the shelf.

"Too bright," she replied and turned her attention to the reds, eventually picking out two boxes of different shades. She held them side by side and finally put the lighter shade back, keeping the colour that was somewhere between crimson and auburn. He nodded, and then they went to pay for everything, and made their way back to the car where he put that bag in the boot with the others.

He didn't start the car immediately once they were both in, but instead reached into his pocket,

"Here," he handed her something black in a cellophane bag.

It had to be what he'd bought at the boutique, and that made her twice as wary as she took it from him and opened it. Two pieces of soft, satin-like material were inside, and she unfolded them on her lap.

They were gloves; long enough to reach her elbows, the sort of gloves that elegant women wore to fancy parties. They repulsed her because they were so ladylike.

"Do you like them?"

Blake gazed at her, and she nodded, automatically reverting to the manners Trey had beaten into her.

His eyebrows pulled low over his eyes. "It's okay if you don't, you know. I just thought it would be the easiest way for you to cover your scar."

Her throat felt tight. She looked down at the gloves again and bit her lip.

"They're perfect, thanks."

"It's really fine if you don't like them," he sighed.

She reached across and hugged him. An awkward gesture that she hoped would convey what her words did not. He tensed, but then gently rubbed her back with one hand.

"So long as you're happy, Heaven."

"I think I am," she answered as she sat up again. She'd almost forgotten that good emotions could be just as intense as the bad ones.

Blake had been nothing but kind to her. Sometimes he was weird and almost shy, but she'd yet to see any signs of him having a hidden agenda. He'd said that Guardians protected Wielders. Maybe she was a fool to believe it was that simple, that he'd keep her safe from the world, but she thought he truly meant it.

6

Heaven dyed her hair as soon as they returned to Hex, and tried on her new clothes again. Her mind felt sharper than it had been in too long, and she delighted in the power of that simple feeling. She felt like she finally felt, and looked like herself.

It was freeing, not having to project somebody else's lie anymore.

She braved the Guardians' stares to eat in the mess, and used the time to observe them. Most were boys aged from around ten to fifteen, she guessed. There were very few older boys, and around ten adult men. The only woman she saw were those who worked in the kitchen.

There was a strict hierarchy in place among the Guardians—it was obvious in the way they treated older members. Blake was quite high in the rankings judging by how they looked at, and addressed him.

Mealtimes weren't quiet though. Guys who sat together at the tables spread through the large room always spoke at high volume and laughter often rippled through the atmosphere. It created quite a cacophony when the hall was at its fullest, but it was nice.

Therefore, the silence startled her when she and Blake went to eat supper four days after she arrived. Nearly all of the kids were gone.

"Where is everybody?" she asked.

"Home for the week end, today is Saturday."

"Oh…"

They dished up rice and beef stew with a spicy aroma then she followed Blake to an empty table. It was eerie to eat in such silence when the place was usually so lively, and it made her feel small.

She pushed her bowl aside when she'd finished eating and sat sideways on the bench, one leg folded under her. Most of the older Guardians weren't here either, just Declan and another two dudes she'd seen at mealtimes.

"Heaven." Blake cleared his throat. "We're leaving for Denysrus in the morning."

She stared across the table at Blake. All the fear and uncertainty that had just begun to sink below the surface bubbled up again.

"I know it's sudden, I'm sorry. I got the message just before supper."

She nodded, and resisted the temptation to ask him for one of her pills, just to take the edge off.

"It'll be okay, Heaven." He was studying her as though she might freak out.

She rolled her eyes at him and faked a smile. "Sure it will."

What did he know? He wasn't an outsider, nor was he in a position where the goodwill of strangers meant life or death. But it wasn't like she had a choice, nor was there anything they could do to her that was worse than what she'd already been through.

***

They left just after breakfast, and Heaven felt a twinge of sadness as they drove away from the valley. Something about the place reminded her of her childhood home and leaving it now, with the unknown looming in front of her, was a lot like when Amanda had taken her after her parents died.

Amanda was supposed to have taken care of her—her parents had appointed her as legal guardian. She wished she knew why the woman had taken her to Trey instead.

"Can you drive?"

The random question snapped her out of her reverie. "So long as it has a manual clutch, yeah…I also had a scooter for a while, why?"

"You'll need a way to get around now."

"You guys are giving me a car?"

He laughed, possibly at the disbelief in her voice, and looked at her with a hint of affection. "And a place to stay...the Keeper will arrange everything. You'll also get a job, a way for the Circle to pay you a legitimate salary, even if it isn't a fortune."

"This sounds more and more like a dodgy business."

"We have to operate in a certain way, but I assure you, we're the good guys."

"There aren't any good guys, just better or worse guys." She turned her head to look out the window again.

"I can't decide if you're a cynic or a philosopher."

"Neither, I'm a realist." From the corner of her eye, she saw him shoot a thoughtful glance her way.

"The Keeper will want to know your name," he said in a low, gruff voice.

She glanced across at him and shook her head.

"If you don't mind me asking, why is it so important to you to be a Jane Doe?"

She didn't know, not really. Hearing her name had come to mean that she'd done something wrong. It was a harbinger of painful bruises, her blood, and hospital if Trey was violently angry. Perhaps it would be different in different voices, but she wasn't ready to find out.

"My name is a swear word, I'd sooner be called bitch." She shrugged.

"Never," he replied.

She saw his fingers tighten on the steering wheel as he frowned deeply. Heaven stifled a chuckle; Blake was softer than a marshmallow.

They drove in silence for a while.

"I could just choose a name for you…something like, Gretchen? Or Anastasia…"

She arched her eyebrows, did he just offer to lie for her? She stared at him while he continued.

"Tallulah…Myrtle…Eunice…just stop me when you hear one you like, okay? Beatrice, Ingrid, Elvira, Bertha, Gertrude, Maude, Agatha."

"None of the above." He was just teasing her.

"Oh come on, don't you have a sense of humour, Tallulah?" He chuckled.

She smiled faintly and rolled her eyes. "Just carry on calling me Heaven, or a nick name if you think of one."

***

She wasn't quite sure what to make of Denysrus at first. Plenty of old buildings lined the streets, mixed with a few newer ones here and there. She vaguely recalled that the city had historical significance, possibly to do with The Great Trek, but not the details.

It looked like a place stuck in the past. Cape Town may still have cobbled streets, but they were a charming feature, like the brightly painted houses that lined them in Bo-Kaap, a quaint reminder of the city's age and origins.

This place? It was trying to get somewhere but the vibe was off. She saw it in the faces of the people they drove past, so many disapproving frowns, and kids trying too hard to be fashionable. It screamed 'small town attitude'.

Blake slowed as they approached a long building filled with shop fronts then turned into an alley. Behind the building was a narrow strip of concrete, and a row of cars parked under a shabby strip of shade netting attached to the wall opposite the building. He stopped his car in the only open spot.

"This is it?" Heaven asked.

"Yeah…you'll see when we get inside."

She unbuckled her seat belt and followed him across the concrete to a plain door. A passage lit by bare bulbs stretched out before them. It was suspiciously normal looking.

Blake moved ahead of her, the plain wooden floorboards creaked beneath their feet. He stopped outside the second door on the left and knocked politely.

A man a little shorter than Blake appeared in the gap as the door jerked open. He had what she was starting to think of as the typical Guardian look, except that he was more lean than bulky. His skin was caramel coloured and stubble lined his jaw. He reminded her of somebody, but she couldn't think who.

"About time you got here," the stranger said. "We've been waiting."

"Its not like it's just down the road, Al," Blake said.

The man smirked and looked at her. His brown eyes widened and she heard his breath hiss.

The teenagers had gawked at her at Hex, but he was staring as though he knew her and this was the last place he'd expected to see her again. Did she know this guy? Had she and Trey ripped him off sometime?

She took a slow step backwards, but he ducked back into the room. Blake entered, and she followed a moment later.

The small room was filled with expectant faces, both male and female. She felt trapped the instant she heard the door close behind her.

"Welcome home," a deep voice rumbled.

Her head snapped forward to where a middle-aged man with a sandy beard and vivid green eyes stood beside a large desk. He had to be the Keeper, not simply because he was the eldest, but for the authority he exuded. She unintentionally found herself wanting to please him, to gain this man's approval.

The little voice that should've been her conscience wanted to stab him.

"Keeper, this is Heaven," Blake said, stepping aside so that the path between her and the Keeper was unobstructed.

She wanted to stab Blake as well now.

"Heaven?" The bearded man looked at Blake then frowned at her. "Surely you have a proper name?"

His words came with a polite smile but it didn't put her at ease. She stared at him, flinched without meaning to when she heard movement close behind her, and then edged towards Blake.

"She's still a bit wary," Blake said.

"I can see that."

The silence didn't last long but it was heavy while it did. The strangers looked baffled now, except the guy at the door. His eyes were shrewd, and she had the feeling he was sizing her up.

"Well, Heaven, the people you see here are the other members of the Circle. I am Robert, the Keeper here. Elise is our Water Wielder." The Keeper gestured towards an attractive blonde woman who looked to be in her thirties. Her face was impassive, perhaps even a little cold, but her eyes felt like mirrors to her deeper self. The nervousness she felt spiked upwards, along with her heart rate. Everything she felt intensified.

"Dylan over there is her Guardian."

She looked away with relief to the man beside Elise. Black hair hung in his face and he had a piercing in his lip. He nodded but did not smile.

"Then we have Janine, the Wielder of Earth, and her Guardian, Michael."

The pair nodded at the same time: a dark skinned woman with high cheekbones who looked almost as buff as the tall guy at her side. He had very short, white blonde hair and the arms crossed over his chest showed off thin, surprising delicate, lines of tattooed script.

"Alistair is the Guardian of Fire."

The man at the door continued to stare at her.

"And I'm Nadia, the Wielder of Fire." A tawny-haired girl interjected with a thousand watt smile.

There was something exotic in her milky complexion and the slant of her eyes but Heaven couldn't decide what it was. She waved at her, and Alistair sniggered behind her. Nadia shot him a pouty look, but that only made him laugh harder.

The Keeper gave them both a stern look as he cleared his throat. "Rochelle is our retired Wielder of Air, Paula is her student, and Darren is Paula's Guardian."

The man was easily the youngest Guardian in the room, not much older than eighteen, she reckoned. Although his curly blonde hair and cherubic features could make him seem younger than he was. Paula stared at the floor with a shoulder length veil of thin, platinum blonde hair obscuring her face. The older woman looked around forty. She was neatly dressed and wore her short, dark hair pulled back from her face. She smiled faintly, but her eyes were the sharpest of all. As Heaven looked into them, she felt memories rising—unbidden and unwanted—into the front of her mind. Terrible things she'd buried for the sake of her sanity.

Heaven ducked behind Blake, using his body as cover. What the hell was it with these women and their omniscient eyes? If this was how it was going to be then she'd have to walk around backwards with a mirror, like that myth about Medusa.

"Heaven?" Blake asked softly over his shoulder, but she ignored him to focus on breathing.

"Did I miss something? Or do..."

"Shh."

Nadia's cheerful voice was cut short.

"Hey, there's no need to hide, sweetheart, come out." A hand appeared in front of her.

She followed the arm up to find Alistair looking at her with his lips curved into an affable smile. Heaven bit her lip, remembering times when Trey had thought she was looking too hard at another man.

She crossed her arms, dropped her gaze, and backed up to press against Blake's broad back.

"She's scared, Al," Blake said.

"I can see that, that's why I'm trying to be friendly."

"I'd say that brings this introduction to an end," Robert sighed. "Alistair and Nadia, stay, the rest of you are dismissed."

She listened to the others leaving, but decided that she was still better off in the shelter of Blake's body.

"She just needs more time, Keeper," Blake said.

"Maybe, but we cannot sit idle while time passes. She needs to become acquainted with using the Phoenix."

"Yes, Keeper."

She lifted her head and turned, intending to peer around Blake, but Alistair was still there, still looking at her with his dark brown eyes. She scowled at him and he smiled,

"You're not cowering back here; it's just a tactical retreat..." His voice was so low that the only other person who could have heard it was Blake. "...not scared then, smart. I wonder what you'd do if I grabbed you out of there."

"I'll scratch your pretty boy face off," she snarled, lowering her hands and flexing her fingers.

"Don't touch her, she doesn't like it." Blake turned his head and spoke at the same moment she did.

She felt his body tense beside her as he moved his arm back to separate her from Alistair. Her jaw dropped and she stared at his profile.

Alistair grinned triumphantly, revealing a narrow gap in his front teeth. "Hear that, sweetheart? Us Guardians are wired to protect our Wielders even without being used as a meat shield." He patted Blake on the shoulder as he turned away. "I was just proving a point, bro."

Blake shook his head and dropped his arm.

Freaking strange dude. She stepped out to follow Alistair with her eyes without even realising she'd done it until Blake's hand gently rested on her shoulder.

"May we continue now?" Impatience laced the Keeper's voice, but when she glanced at him, his face was calm.

"Heaven, you haven't had much time to become accustomed to your new situation, and unfortunately you aren't going to get any. Blake will have informed you about the Geead Lyana by now, how we're descended from children they had with humans, but there's more to the story than that."

She tilted her head, waiting to hear how much crazier it could get, but instead he lifted a book from his desk and held it out to her.

"Most of the Awakened have a lorebook that's passed down to them when they come of age, this will serve as yours. Study it, Blake will elaborate on anything that seems confusing, and make sure you memorise it well because it could save your life."

She took the book and looked at the cover. It was bound in plain, faded leather with a strange design on the top half, like a tiny square with large looped corners joined by a circle.

A thump drew her attention and she looked back towards the Keeper as he raised the lid of a wooden chest on his desk.

"Please come closer, Heaven." He looked at her.

She glanced up at Blake, he nodded, so she cautiously left the safety of his shadow and approached the desk. She felt more confident when she sensed Blake come and stand behind her.

"This is the Phoenix." The Keeper lifted a necklace from the chest and a golden bird the size of her palm swayed from the chain as he moved around the desk towards her. "It's the Heavenly talisman of Fire. It will allow you to control this element, and bolster your essence until it Awakens."

She nodded as she looked at it; the bird looked like it was moving as it swayed on the chain. Light caught the detailed markings on the feathers etched into the metal, and highlighted a ruddy tint she hadn't noticed at first. It seemed impossible that any artisan could have created such a thing.

He opened the chain, moved his arms to lower it over her neck, and she shied backwards against Blake's hard chest. Those large hands and a chain near her throat didn't seem like a good combination.

"It's okay, he won't touch you, Heaven, he just has to put the talisman on you."

The Keeper was scowling, but she didn't care. She shook her head.

"Heaven, I won't let anybody hurt you." Blake's voice was a whisper close to her ear. When she turned her head towards it, his face was calm and confident.

She would give him another chance to earn her trust.

She turned back to Robert and nodded. As his hands passed her face, she tensed, but they soon withdrew and she looked down at the talisman. It wasn't nearly as heavy as she'd thought it would be.

"Keep it under your shirt where nobody can see it," Robert said before lifting his gaze to speak to Blake. "Take her to the main centre and begin her basic training. Alistair and Nadia will join the two of you everyday so she can learn pyrokinesis."

Nadia smiled at her. Alistair was scratching his chin but he looked at her just as she looked away, and there was nothing nonchalant in that brief instant.

She might not be good at being normal or mixing with normal people, but she knew how to spot a shark. That cop she'd tried to sell to might have fooled her with his hungry eyes and watchful self-possession, but anybody could fall for a good actor. No member of the Circle she'd met so far seemed to be acting on that level.

Blake was safe, she felt sure of that now, but these others...some of their faces were open, some guarded, but none quite as analytical as Alistair seemed—or the Keeper, for that matter. Both had the same air about them as a stalking leopard.

"You'll be up for assessment in six weeks," the Keeper said.

She glanced back at him as he turned away; that soon?

7

The new centre appeared to comprise only one building at first glance, a large old farmhouse in the Dutch style that was so common throughout the Cape. A patio with bare wooden beams enclosed half the front of the building, and the bare branches of a creeping plant twined around the structure. It looked completely overgrown except where the creeper was pruned away from the sign mounted on the front edge of the rafters.

"Headrush Adventures?" she asked, reading the sign aloud.

"It's a cover, and a way to fund what we do— same as Hex. You only saw the centre but the rest is a thriving farm." Blake stared ahead as he spoke.

Heaven shook her head as she followed him through the front door. A woman sat at a reception desk to their left. She looked up, her cheeks turned bright pink, and she ducked behind the book she was reading.

Blake went directly to a door marked 'Staff Only' and shoved it open.

Two young women dressed in a uniform were giggling to each other, but fell silent as they entered the passage. Both nodded to Blake as he missioned past them. Heaven looked at them but they were already scurrying out through the door they'd just entered.

"How many people know about the Circle?"

"Those who are a part of it. All the Guardians and Wielders, and a few family members who, technically, aren't involved."

"Technically?" She arched her eyebrows.

"Not every descendant of the Geead Lyana has an activated version of the Awakened genes, those who do become members of the Circle. The technical part is that not every guy is good enough to be a Guardian, and you also get girls born with only certain parts activated. Like, that woman at the front desk?" He jerked his head in the direction they'd come from. "She's a partial Water Wielder. She has limited control over the element but none of the abilities."

He paused outside a door with an electronic lock, typed in a sequence of numbers, and pulled the door open to reveal a staircase leading down. It seemed strange to her that the place had a basement, but she didn't dwell on it as she followed him across to a wall, which opened up when Blake pressed his hand against it.

"Through here," he said.

Down another flight of stairs, moving even deeper underground, then down a long passage that was nothing more than wooden beams supporting earth. It didn't look stable, and the air smelled old and dry.

Eventually the passage sloped upwards, and they came to another flight of stairs, this one longer than the first. Her thighs were starting to burn when they reached another door and beyond it, what seemed to be another basement.

"All of that and not a single mole-man, how disappointing," she mumbled.

"What's that?"

"Nothing."

They emerged into a pantry that opened into a sunny kitchen. Blue-rimmed plates were drying on a rack beside the sink, a package of meat was defrosting next to it, and there was a breadboard littered with crumbs on the counter to her left. She turned to ask Blake who lived here, but he was almost out the door. She trotted after him, past the dining room, across a cosy lounge, and up a staircase to the second floor.

"We'll be staying in more luxury quarters now," he said, pausing outside a door with a paper tacked to the wood.

"I've noticed." The paper had 'Heaven' written on it in neat capital letters. "Who lives here, Blake?"

"Rochelle moved out here after she retired, it's just her, Paula, Darren, and us for the next few weeks." He opened the door and a room decorated in lavender and white came into view.

"The Air Wielders?" she tensed as she asked the question.

"Yeah, Rochelle is like everyone's mother, but Paula is quite shy so I doubt you'll see all that much of her."

"Uh huh." Heaven rather hoped she'd be able to avoid all of them.

Blake walked across to the bed and shrugged the backpack containing her few possessions off his broad shoulder. He'd insisted on carrying it for her even though it weighed next to nothing.

"We'll both have to be up early tomorrow to join the others for physical training, I'll be knocking on your door at five thirty."

She groaned and pulled a face.

Blake chuckled. "It's only tough until you get fit then it's not so bad."

"You're crazy." She sat on the edge of the bed, bounced up and down and poked the pillows. Luxury quarters indeed.

"There's something I want to tell you, Heaven, so you don't get the wrong idea." Blake was frowning at her.

"Yes?" She straightened up.

"I didn't tell you the full story at Hex, I didn't want to scare you, but its time you knew. It's not just us, the Circle. There are people who serve dark creatures created after the Geead Lyana, the Skaath Diurga. Most of their followers are women, they call themselves Handmaidens, and they are very dangerous." His eyes flicked over her face.

"In what way?" she asked.

"There are two types of Handmaiden, the Trueborns who are born into the Covens, and the normal, human recruits. All of them bind themselves to a particular Diurga. In return, the Diurga they serve gives them the ability to summon creatures from the shadows using blood. Either the blood of their victims, or that of a Thrall—what they call their men. Skaath beasts resemble normal animals but they're semi-corporeal and a lot more aggressive."

It reminded her of the nightmare she'd had in the clinic. Goose bumps came out on her skin but she played it cool. "Sounds freaky."

"The danger is very real. I'll protect you, obviously, but it's important that you try your best while we're here for training."

"I always wanted to be a super hero." She smiled at him.

"I'm serious, Heaven…"

"I know, and I'll try to be awesome, okay?"

"You will be." He nodded as though he knew it for certain.

"Don't put all your chips on me." She stood up and walked around the room, glancing at a painting on the wall.

He shook his head and adjusted his own heavy looking bag, lifting it higher on his shoulder as he headed to the door. "You'll be okay."

She turned toward the window as she rolled her eyes. There was something weird about Blake, she'd done nothing to lead him to believe in her, yet he did. It didn't make sense.

A hissing noise startled her and a jet of water arced out from somewhere below the window. Diagonally across the narrow strip of lawn, another sprinkler rose from the ground. She closed her eyes and took a deep breath, opening them again as she exhaled.

Beyond the wall, grew tall, skinny trees, lots of them. Many were bare but others were evergreen, it was like living in a forest. Through the sparse branches, she made out a building similar to the dorms at Hex nestled beneath a small hill. She was fairly certain that the building they'd first entered was in that direction. Was that little hill supposed to hide this section from adrenalin junkies?

Farther along the crest of the hill was a concrete water tower, stained by age. It looked like a huge castle from a chessboard; all it needed were crenellations. She'd wondered what the world looked like from up there.

**

It had been less than a fortnight since Blake left Headrush to take up the responsibilities of being a full Circle Guardian. Not very long, but it somehow seemed strange to be back here when it wasn't his home anymore. Especially here, in Rochelle's house.

He dumped his bag on the bottom part of the bed, turned and walked out the door. As he passed Heaven's door, he knocked and loudly told her he'd be back soon.

The man-made forest that surrounded the house was the largest in the area, tended by the partial Earth and Water Wielders who worked at Headrush. It spread down the hill to the obstacle course and paintball arena near the main building. Usually you could hear the echoes of people shooting at each other on the paintball course, but it was quiet now.

He strolled down the dirt road that led to the main building and entered through the front doors again. This time, Marike skirted around the front desk and scurried towards him,

"Blake, was that her?" Marike asked in hushed tone.

He didn't even have to ask what she meant. "Yeah, that was Heaven. Sorry, Marike, but I'm in a bit of a hurry."

He went through the same door as before, but turned down a side passage. He soon reached a door marked with a small sign announcing it was the Accounts office, and knocked twice.

"Come in."

Rochelle sat behind a pine desk arranging invoices and receipts into neat piles across the surface. It was tidier than the one occasion he'd seen her desk during tax season, but not by much.

She looked up and smiled when she saw him. "You must've left less than fifteen minutes after us, what took you so long?"

"I took Heaven to the house first, she gets uncomfortable around strangers. Maybe people in general," he said with an apologetic smile.

"I noticed, she's very self-contained."

Blake chuckled, talk about an understatement. "It's very polite of you to put it that way," he said.

Rochelle gave him a sharp glance then shook her head. "It isn't funny, Blake. People who have such deep mental and emotional scars, and the sheer volume of such people in the world today, indicate exactly how strong the Skaath have become."

"People don't do bad things because of the Skaath…" he began.

Rochelle's voice cut through his. "They do it because these things have become acceptable, because it's everywhere. I'm not blaming the Skaath for human depravity, but we all know they feed on the corrupt actions of humans, and how the Handmaidens recruit abused girls with promises of power."

Blake stepped closer to the desk, tilting his head as he looked at her. "Is something bothering you, Rochelle?"

She waved her hand dismissively then lowered it to play with a charm bracelet on her right wrist, her brow furrowed. "Being in town tired me…I've become so comfortable being a recluse that I'd forgotten what its like to be around so many people."

"I can imagine, all those thoughts…"

"Yes." She cut him off again then gave him a thin smile. "How is your uncle? I haven't heard from him in weeks."

"He's fine, he's an instructor at a martial arts school now."

"That's good, a much better fit than…what was he doing? Selling real estate?"

"Yeah, I think he was hoping to find Coven houses."

Rochelle rolled her eyes. "Not everybody can retire gracefully. Will steak be fine for supper? Or is Heaven a vegetarian?"

"She never objected to meat dishes at Hex." He shrugged.

"Good, maybe a home cooked meal will help her feel more comfortable."

"It might," he replied.

It was unusual to see Rochelle flustered. Come to think of it, Heaven had only hidden behind him in Robert's office after being introduced to the Air Wielder. Had something happened between them?

"I must get back to work," Rochelle said, picking up a pile of papers. "You'd be amazed how disorganised people can be. I'll see you later, dear."

"Sure." He smiled at her then headed for the door.

Had she overheard his thoughts just now, and avoided his question by dismissing him before he could even ask it?

Blake sighed and headed back the way he'd come. He still had to report to Bryan, the Guardian in charge of basic training. Something he was not looking forward to.

He'd avoided him ever since he became a senior because the guy was a jerk. Requesting his permission for Heaven and himself to join the trainees for morning exercise was just a formality, but he had to follow the chain of command.

It was a few minutes past eleven o'clock so he headed up to the Guardian Complex at a slow walk. Bryan would be holding the Novice Combat classes now, putting a fresh group of teenagers through hell.

The double doors to the gym were roughly in the centre of a long building that also housed the medical centre and School. When he pushed through the entrance, he was greeted with the smell of sweat, and grunts and yells of exertion.

Trainees punched bags and wooden dummies around the far edge of the room, and near the centre, two pairs of teenagers sparred on the mats. Bryan stood between them, upper lip curled into a sneer and arms folded across his chest as he watched the boys fighting.

One of the boys hit the other in the face, hard. The boy wailed and went down clutching his nose.

"Stop crying and get up, Freebie," Bryan said in a droll tone.

Blake narrowed his eyes and sped up.

"Righty-oh," Bryan continued when the boy didn't get up. "Finish it, Ed."

The boy who was still standing advanced on the fallen boy, but Blake reached him first. He gripped Ed's shoulder and pulled him back, then crouched down beside the kid on the mat.

"Hey, you okay, kid?"

The boy moaned intelligibly and covered his nose with his hands. Blood streamed over his cheeks and his eyes had filled with tears. Blake glanced up, and looked over the other trainees who'd gathered around.

"What the hell do you think you're doing, Cake?" Bryan growled close by.

Blake swallowed his anger and pointed to one of the other boys. "You, take this guy to a medic."

The boy glanced at Bryan fearfully.

Blake stood up to loom over him as he spoke again. "Now. That's an order."

A hand gripped his shoulder and tugged, Bryan was behind him.

"You don't give orders in here, laddie," he snarled.

"If you don't take your hands off me, I'll lay you out. And, it's Blake. I earned my name back from you a long time ago."

Bryan's eyes narrowed but his hand retreated. He glanced at the trainees and cleared his throat. "You ladies are dismissed."

The boys headed for the door, many casting curious glances back over their shoulders. Blake paid little attention to them, he was too wary of what Bryan might try once they were alone.

"How dare you undermine my authority?" Bryan leaned closer to him.

95

"That kid's nose is broken, he needs a medic."

"No, what the little dumbass needs is to learn to keep his guard up."

"And encouraging your favourites to bully him is the answer? You're a sadist." Blake spat the words out as though they were poison.

Bryan smiled. "Big talk for somebody who's proof that my training methods work."

Blake's hands curled into fists and he resisted the temptation to deck him. "I am what I am in spite of you." He turned and walked away. "My Wielder and I will join the trainees for morning exercise, starting tomorrow."

"Is that so?"

Blake paused at the door and looked back at him. "I'll take any reason I can to report you, Bryan. Any reason at all."

***

Alistair stared at his feet as he walked into the kitchen of Stillwater house. He could still see that girl's eyes looking at him as clearly as if she was standing in front of him.

Sure, those grey-blue eyes were unusual, but she wasn't a striking beauty, so why couldn't he get her out of his mind?

He didn't notice that the room wasn't empty until he felt the touch of cold metal on the side of his neck, pressed against his pulse.

A familiar, husky voice whispered into his ear. "You just earned the privilege of buying the next pack of beer."

"Get bent, Dylan." He jerked away and twisted around to face his housemate. "Next time, I'll break your arm regardless of whether I recognise your voice or not."

"You walk around with your head in the clouds, that's what you get," Dylan replied, grinning as he spun the butter knife in his hand. "Got the Spirit Wielder on your mind, brother?"

"Why would I?" Alistair snapped.

"You do have to help train the skittish girl. But mainly because couldn't stop staring at her." Dylan waggled his eyebrows at him.

Alistair wanted to thump him but he sniffed instead. "I was observing her, not checking her out."

"Of course." Dylan nodded earnestly and moved towards the fridge. "I also get starry eyed and drool when I observe pretty women."

"Fuck knows why when you might as well be one with this random interrogation."

Dylan snorted, took two beers out of the fridge, and offered one to him. "If you weren't all about the one night stand then I wouldn't get so happy on these rare occasions. I already marked it on the calendar."

Alistair took the beer then punched him on the shoulder. "Stop being such a dumbass, bro."

"Tell me about the staring."

"I think she looks cool." Alistair shrugged. "She has an edge to her, I like that."

"That's it? Come on, man." Dylan pulled a face.

"Seriously, cut it out." He twisted the cap off the bottle and swallowed a mouthful.

He hadn't realised how obvious his staring had been but damn, something in that girl's eyes had been like a fist in his guts. Something about her seemed so...

"You're daydreaming again." Dylan's voice cut through his thoughts before he could decide what it was that struck him about her.

"You're being annoying again." He scowled at Dylan.

"Can you blame me? You're a man-whore and Blake is like a celibate old priest. Both of you desperately need a good girlfriend."

"And you're out buying a ring, I suppose?"

Dylan shrugged one shoulder and smiled. "I have my woman; she's all I'll ever need."

Alistair stared at him. Dylan had never mentioned a girlfriend, nor had he noticed anything to suggest his friend wasn't single.

"When the hell did that happen?" he asked.

"While ago."

If it weren't for the stupid look on his face, Alistair might've thought this was more bullshit, but Dylan clearly had it bad. Either he'd grown so relaxed around the Water Guardian that he'd stopped noticing the small things, or Dylan had put a lot of effort into keeping this secret.

"Why didn't you say anything?" he asked, leaning back against the wall behind him.

"We've been taking it slow," Dylan shrugged.

"Does she know about you?"

"Being awesome? Anyone who's spent five minutes with me knows that."

"Being a Guardian, bro."

Dylan smirked and took a slow drink of beer, "Now who's playing the interrogator? I'll tell you all about it when you 'fess up about this Heaven girl."

"There's nothing to say." He frowned. This conversation was going in circles.

"But you will be participating in her training so that could change." Dylan winked at him. "Man, its going to be so awesome after Blake moves in, I was thinking we can toss a bucket of ice on him on his first morning."

"What, no tarantula?" Alistair rolled his eyes.

"Hell no, you about scared Spot to death when I introduced her to you."

"She was right in front of my face," he replied through gritted teeth.

Handmaidens, Thralls and Skaath were one thing, but waking up with curved fangs and eight beady eyes in front of you was an altogether different type of frightening.

"I wish I could've put that video up on YouTube," Dylan sighed. "But we wouldn't want the wrong people to find it."

"I'm not willing to die so you can get views." Alistair grumbled as he had another drink of beer. Even Dylan's idiotic rambling couldn't ruin the taste of a cold one.

"I wouldn't want you to." Dylan stepped closer and slapped him on the arm. "I just want you to be happy, you know that, right?"

Alistair smiled. "You've been watching too many romantic chick flicks with your mystery girl, that's why you're suddenly so interested in my love life, isn't it?"

"It beats watching too much porn alone," he laughed. "But I'm serious; happiness is what life's all about."

"I'm serious too, quit being so weird. I'm fine." He raised his beer in Dylan's direction as he moved towards the door. "Before you get too cuddly, I have things to do."

"Does that mean I don't get a hug?" Dylan called down the passage after him.

Alistair shook his head. "Maybe next time, handsome," he yelled over his shoulder.

Dylan was a good guy, but he was annoying when he was in one of his weird moods, more so when he had a point.

Not that it mattered. This was just another assignment, and he'd handle it as professionally as any other, no matter how easy it was.

**

Heaven clenched her hands into fists in her lap and stared down at the plate in front of her. It wasn't just the company making her uncomfortable but her memories as well. She hadn't sat down to eat at a properly set table since before she died.

She could almost hear his voice; feel the string chafing her skin to prevent her from accidentally putting her elbows on the table.

"How long did you live in Cape Town, Heaven?" Rochelle's voice was calm but curious as she looked down the table at her.

The older Air Wielder sat at the head of the table with Paula at her right, and Darren at her left. When they'd all sat down to eat she'd indicated that Heaven take the seat next to Paula and positioned Blake across from her.

It had been a silent meal until now.

"Most my life," Heaven mumbled in reply, taking a bite of garlic bread and hoping Rochelle wouldn't ask any more questions while she was chewing.

"Did you grow up there?"

So much for that. She chewed the bread and swallowed. "No."

"I lived in Pinelands for much of my childhood, even after my abilities came out. I inherited the Air Wielder abilities from my mother and she did my early training."

Heaven didn't answer, but nodded as she took another bite of her food.

"I thought you'd trained with Euphemia, Rochelle," Blake chipped in.

"I did, but only after I'd turned sixteen and come of age. My abilities came out a few years before that."

"So you were an early starter, like Nadia."

"Not quite," Rochelle laughed. "That little imp was starting fires when she was eight or nine. Her father was quite concerned, but Stephen always was a worry wart."

"Still is from what I've heard," Blake said. "Nadia is itching to move out so she doesn't have to sneak out to party anymore."

"And Stephen won't hear of it?"

"Not at all. He wants to protect her when Al isn't around."

"I'm surprised he hasn't booby trapped the perimeter of the house."

"Maybe he has, although it would be pointless considering she can teleport to wherever she wants to be."

Heaven had only been half listening until she heard the word 'teleport'. She'd almost forgotten what Blake told her about the Wielders having extra abilities. Hadn't he said that Air Wielders were telepathic?

"He does her a great disservice by being so overprotective," Rochelle sighed.

Heaven snuck a glance in her direction as she and Blake continued their conversation. Was that why Rochelle had such a weird effect on her earlier, had she been trying to read her mind? How much of what flashed through her thoughts had the woman been able to see, to understand? A chill crept up her spine, maybe she could hear what she was thinking right now.

Heaven rushed through the last few bites of food and placed her knife and fork together, aligning the cutlery at the bottom before ensuring that they were dead centre. The habit was so ingrained that she only realised what she was doing when she'd finished.

"May I be excused?" she asked, still staring at her plate.

"Of course you may," Rochelle replied.

"Thank you." If she could have run from the room then she would've.

Blake watched her go, should he follow to make sure she was all right? She'd been incredibly tense throughout supper and with no good reason, as far as he could tell.

"Let her be, Blake."

He looked up at Rochelle, "Are you sure?"

She nodded and took a small sip of water. "Our abilities make her nervous, but its fear of the past that troubles her most, not the present. That's something she must come to terms with on her own."

He frowned at the older woman but she smiled back at him.

"Don't worry about it, time is a great healer and…" She abruptly turned to look at Paula. The two of them stared at each other as though nobody else existed.

Blake assumed they were speaking telepathically, and Rochelle's next words confirmed that.

"Tell him then," she said.

Paula gulped, her brown eyes widened as she looked at Blake then glanced away even faster.

"Is it something about Heaven?" he asked softly.

"The man…" Her voice was barely a whisper. "He had to have everything perfect, no leeway. If you fetched a tape measure it would be almost exact."

She pointed at Heaven's plate and he half rose from his seat to look at it. The fork balanced lengthways on top of the knife, and it was a little weird, sure, but her words still made little sense.

"'The fork must balance on the knife, Treasure, aligned at the bottom, equal distances from the top and bottom of the plate, a perfect diameter from either side. A lady never forgets her manners'," Paula sighed. "It was running through her head afterwards, but she did it automatically."

"What man?" Blake asked as he examined the plate more closely.

"The one who kept her, he was bad."

"Abusive," Rochelle clarified. "That's why she's nervous."

"Scared…" Paula said, looking more than a little scared herself. "People like that, they change who you are. The worst wounds in life leave our skin untouched but our heart in shreds."

Darren reached his hand across the table to his Wielder, and Paula lowered her head as she took it gently.

Blake was silent as he considered her words, but there could be no privacy with two Air Wielders in the room.

"It's not for me to tell, or you to ask…let time do its work, and your intuition will do the rest." Rochelle gave him a sharp look.

"It seems to be coping so far." He smiled thinly.

"You have some of your sister's instincts, you'll do just fine." Rochelle nodded, and gave him a soft, gentle sort of smile.

It did nothing to lessen the impact of her unexpected mention of Maya.

"Please excuse me, I'm getting a headache," Paula said, running her fingers across her forehead.

"Of course, dear." Rochelle smiled as she stroked a lock of the teenager's hair behind her ear. The girl smiled slightly then rose from the table.

"We can be glad it was me Heaven looked at in the Sanctuary and not Paula," Rochelle said once the girl was out of the room. "Otherwise she may have clawed a hole through the wall."

"Is that what happened? Your telepathy affected her?" Darren asked.

Blake looked at her, waiting to hear her reply.

"Yes…I wasn't looking into her at all, but she triggered something."

"Aren't you always looking into everybody a little?" Blake teased, hoping it would lighten the mood.

"Of course not. I hear background noise, like sitting in a restaurant and overhearing the conversations around you. This was different."

"Maybe it's because she's a Spirit Wielder. Until Robert put the Phoenix on her, she could've taken on any element, as far as I know," Blake suggested.

"Perhaps it was Paula," Darren said in a low voice.

Rochelle's eyes narrowed as she glanced at Darren. "Maybe...maybe not, I can't tell."

"Is Paula really that powerful?" Blake asked.

Wielder and Guardian exchanged a look that almost seemed guilty, much like the way his parents had looked when he confronted them about the divorce.

Rochelle nodded gravely. "She'll surpass my skill before her training is finished."

8

Heaven felt like she was dying in the dew damp grass. Her fingers were numb, her stomach cramped from doing sit-ups, and her arms burned as she tried to do one more push up. A string of swearwords rattled through her thoughts, but as she collapsed on her elbows all she managed to gasp out was, "Fuck."

"C'mon, Wielder, five more to finish your set."

She sneered at the pair of boots in front of her then glanced up at the man towering over her—Bryan, the fitness trainer who imagined himself to be a Sergeant Major.

"I'm already buggered," she said.

"Five more, Red, or you go swimming. The dam is lovely in the winter," he said with a smile that was probably as cold as the water in the dam.

Heaven groaned and glanced to her right. Blake could just as well have been watching TV, and on his other side, Paula didn't seem to be struggling either.

"Your mother," she mumbled. She lifted herself on her arms and struggled through the last five push ups then collapsed again.

She might not be half as fit as a slug, but there was no way she'd be outdone by a schoolgirl.

"On your feet now slackers and get running," Bryan yelled. "First five back here get a head start on the Demon."

The men took off across the wide lawn that separated the gravel parking lot in front of the dorms from the woods that surrounded Rochelle's house. Heaven allowed herself to be swept along with them, but she was jogging at the back by the time they reached the trees.

This wasn't too bad; she'd done athletics for a while at school and her body slipped into a rhythm as she picked her way over fallen leaves and acorns that crunched under her feet. There didn't seem to be a clear path to follow, but nobody seemed lost either.

Except for her, maybe.

"How're you holding up?" Blake dropped back to jog beside her, and the sod was still making it seem like a morning stroll.

"Okay," she puffed.

"I told you it wasn't so bad."

She probably could've tripped him, but it would've taken an effort she didn't feel up to.

"What's...the Demon?" she huffed at him as she jumped over a tree root.

"The obstacle course, but we won't be doing it."

"Thank God."

"It's not that bad."

"Blake, you keep...saying stuff isn't so bad...I'm beginning to think...I can't trust your judgement."

Blake laughed, and she envied him for having the breath for it.

"We'll do it together, later or tomorrow, then you'll see," he said with a grin.

"Like hell."

"It's fun, Heaven."

"I'd rather have a bikini wax." She was far behind now, but still fast enough to keep the others in sight until they reached a large stone and disappeared behind it.

She glanced at Blake; he probably knew this route. He certainly didn't look worried by the others' disappearance. Sure enough, when they reached the stone he ran around it and she saw figures in front of her again. They followed them down the gentle slope until they hit a dirt road. Heaven slowed to a walk, clutching her sides as she tried to catch her breath.

"Come on, can't fall too far behind." Blake took her hand before she could protest and carried on running. She stumbled along until her feet found a rhythm once more.

"I'm not fit enough," she groaned.

"You'll be punished if you take too long to do this, Heaven."

It couldn't be as bad as anything Trey had done to her, but hearing the word pulled her trigger. She surged forward and soon the hill behind the dorms appeared in front of her. The road they were jogging on curved around it then led downwards again on the other side.

She saw roofs and bits of buildings through the trees, a dam of greenish water, and open veld all the way to the road. Then the trail turned away and a tall hedge hid the lower lying area from view.

More importantly, the others were in sight again. Another hill was in front of them, and the front-runners were charging up it as though they planned to invade the water tower perched right at the top.

"You've got to be kidding me," she wailed.

"This is the last bit, almost finished."

She had to walk up the top half of the hill and still arrived at the top wheezing so hard that Blake asked if she had asthma. By the time they reached the lawn where they'd started, all the others had vanished, presumably to play on their obstacle course. Somehow, Blake looked more relieved than she was.

Blake made her stretch, but was nice enough to let her shower before him when they returned to the house. After she came out and dressed, she went down to the kitchen to find something to eat but Rochelle was already on top of it.

An apron covered her navy blue pantsuit and her mahogany brown hair was styled back on her head. Heaven paused in the doorway and watched as she stirred a pot, the dimly remembered scent of mielie meal in the air.

"Good morning, Heaven, how was the first morning of training?"

"Hard," she replied.

The woman hadn't even turned around, but she flashed a smile at her now. "It always is in the beginning...please, help yourself to coffee or tea, everything is right by the kettle."

"Thanks," she muttered, keeping her eyes down as she reluctantly approached the woman to get to the kettle.

She took a mug from the wooden mug tree, switched the kettle on as she measured out coffee and sugar, and focused on the task rather than the telepath less than a metre to her side.

"I think we got off to something of a bad start, Heaven, I'm sorry about that. It wasn't my intention to see your memories." Rochelle said in a low voice.

Heaven stiffened, "But you did."

"Yes, dear, although you should know that it doesn't mean half as much to me as you may think it does."

The kettle boiled and she poured the water into her mug as she weighed the woman's words. She fetched the milk from the fridge and added it to the dark liquid before she spoke. "What do you mean?"

Rochelle switched the stove plate off and removed the pot from the heat before turning to face her.

"In general, thoughts only make sense in context," she said. "More so when it comes to emotional experiences. I saw flashes; fighting, hiding, scraping sounds in a dark place. It's enough to know that you had a few frightening experiences, but it's far from your life story, dear. There's nothing for you to be embarrassed about, and nobody will ever hear of these things from me."

Everything about the woman's attitude as she spoke was neutral, a relaying of facts with neither derision nor any great sense of compassion. No questions either, which was a relief.

"Thanks," she forced a smile and took a sip of her coffee.

"Go on and sit down." Rochelle smiled. "I'm sure you want to rest. I'll bring the breakfast through in another minute or so."

Heaven nodded awkwardly, taking her coffee with her to the dining room, where the table was already set with bowls and spoons. She was tempted to try that trick where you tugged the tablecloth out from under the crockery because she knew it would never work. It would be so awesome to ruin the picture perfect table before her. She could almost see the bowls smashing to pieces.

"You okay, Heaven?"

She spun around so fast she almost sloshed coffee all over her shirt. Either Blake showered really fast, or she'd been standing there for longer than she thought.

"Perfectly fine." A cheerful, automated response, and she wanted to slap herself for it.

"Are you sure? That was just a little Stepford Wives." He quirked a brow at her.

"It's all good dawg." She sarcastically flipped him something like a gang sign with her fingers.

Blake chuckled, "Okay then...how's your coffee? I'm going to make myself a cup now so I could make you more if you want."

"Thanks, but I'm good." She walked into the dining room and sat at the table, sipping her tepid coffee.

She almost made a complete idiot of herself when he surprised her like that. Everything about her situation was so different from what she was used to. It hadn't been so noticeable at Hex but here...she could still remember what it was like to be part of family, and it reminded her of that.

Blake walked in carrying the porridge pot. Rochelle was just behind him, carrying what looked almost like a tall teapot, a jug, two mugs, and the sugar bowl, on a wooden tray.

"I can't even remember the last time I had mielie meal for breakfast," Blake said as he lifted the lid off the pot. "Not to mention percolated coffee."

"You'll have to come out here to visit me more often then," Rochelle smiled warmly at him even as she shooed him out of the way and dished up.

He thanked her as she placed a full bowl in front of him then reached for the sugar and milk jug.

Heaven watched silently as Rochelle spooned porridge into her bowl. She couldn't recall ever having mielie meal, maybe when she was little. Her mother had cooked it a few times, but that was all she could remember. Trey had been particular about what he ate, preferring traditional English food. She'd supposed that it reminded him of home.

She muttered her thanks when Rochelle set the bowl down then copied Blake by adding sugar and milk. It didn't taste marvellous, but it wasn't bad either. She ate another spoonful then poured another cup of coffee. As she took her first sip, Nadia arrived.

"Morning everyone." Nadia beamed at them as she bounced through the door. Her hair was in a long braid that swung as she moved, and she was fashionably dressed. Her make up was applied in a way that looked striking without making you wonder if it had been layered on with a trowel.

"Good morning, dear," Rochelle smiled warmly as the younger girl circled the table to give her a hug, "how are you?"

While Nadia answered, Alistair walked through the door. If the Fire Wielder could be a magazine cover girl, then her Guardian would be her rugged metrosexual counterpart—except for the sullen set of his mouth.

Alistair nodded to Rochelle before draping himself in the seat next to Heaven. He glanced at Blake then turned to her.

"Having fun yet?" he asked, the corner of his lips lifting in a subtle smile.

She looked down at the table. "Am I supposed to be?"

"Not really, but playing with fire is better than running."

"Until you get burnt," she mumbled.

"You won't, Wielders have a level of immunity to their own element, but you should stay away from flammable hair products all the same." He glanced at her hair.

After showering, she'd used hair gel to give it a messy style. She hadn't checked if the goop was flammable, but he was in no position to lecture her since his hair was also gelled.

"Like you do?" She turned her head and arched an eyebrow at him.

"I'm not a noob." He smirked. "I can wear my hair the way I like."

"You're seriously comparing hairstyles?" Blake chuckled from across the table as he spooned up the last of his porridge.

"No, I was advising her against using anything that could catch fire," Alistair retorted.

"At least she can draw her eyebrows back on if they get singed off, how long did it take for them to grow back, Al?" Blake barely contained his smile.

Heaven's snort of amusement earned her a dirty look from the Fire Guardian before he answered. "Long enough...and we'll see who's laughing when this one does the same to you, bro."

"You have one teensy accident and it gets held against you forever." Nadia let out a dramatic sigh as she moved behind Heaven.

"Because I was metres away from the target." Alistair's arm brushed against Heaven as he reached out to poke Nadia, the girl squealed like a teenager and stepped out of reach.

"I still say it wasn't bad for a first try." Nadia grinned as she slid into a chair. "At least I hit something."

"We should get to work," Blake said, pushing his bowl away before looking across at her. "Is that all you're going to eat?"

Heaven nodded, the mielie meal felt like cement in her stomach. Alistair leaned towards her to glance at her bowl. His eyes were too close when he looked at her.

"There's no rush if you want to finish up, no offence, but you are on the scrawny side," he said.

She didn't know what to say to that, but Rochelle didn't give her any time to reply anyway.

"Never tease a woman about her looks, Alistair," the older woman said sternly.

His eyes narrowed and his lip curled, but then he smiled, shrugging one shoulder as he sat back and looked at Rochelle,

"I didn't mean anything by it."

"It's still not nice…women are sensitive."

"Weak people are sensitive," Heaven muttered, louder than she'd intended.

Alistair tilted his head to look at her and Blake frowned. She sipped her coffee and ignored them both, instead watching Nadia grin at her phone as she typed furiously with her thumbs.

Rochelle sighed heavily and stood up, pausing at Heaven's chair as she headed for the door.

"You're not fighting in that sense anymore, dear," she said.

She turned to stare at the woman's back. Telepath or not, what could she know about her struggle? How she'd died inside, the mask of apathy she'd made from the broken pieces of everything she'd lost. All the tiny measures of how much was too much; how much drugs would numb her, how much caring would kill her, how much sanity she could afford to lose.

Heaven sat back in her chair and crossed her arms, keeping her expression blank. She wasn't looking at Blake, or anybody, but she caught him watching her in her peripheral vision.

Blake gulped his coffee. "Let's get to it then."

He stood up, so she did too. She could feel Alistair's gaze on her, but when she looked at him, he stood up and walked around to mess up Nadia's hair.

"Bugger off, Alistair!" Nadia swatted at him.

"Time to get to work, princess, broadcast a 'bbl' to all your boyfriends."

"They are not my boyfriends!"

"Sure…come on, we still have to get the Olympic flame from your boot."

"Hahaha." Nadia dripped sarcasm as she got up and shoved her phone in her pocket. "Aren't you all jokey and cheerful today? Did you get laid last night or something?"

Alistair paused, half turning to look at Nadia. "Manners, princess, what is our new Wielder going to think of you if go around asking people if they got laid?"

Nadia gaped at him and Blake made a weird, choking sound. Heaven couldn't help but smile and walked after Alistair. It didn't take long before Blake joined her and soon they were all gathered around Nadia's car.

When she opened the boot, Heaven saw what looked like a huge candlestick, a shallow bowl half a metre across with three legs extending from the base.

"I trained with this brazier and I thought it might bring you luck." Nadia grinned at her.

Heaven smiled a little and stuffed her hands in her pockets. It looked heavy but Alistair lifted it with ease and slung it over his shoulder.

"Where's the wood?" he asked.

"Back seat," Nadia replied. "Won't you grab it for me, Blakey?"

"Uh, sure." Blake looked at Nadia strangely.

Heaven frowned and Alistair rolled his eyes.

Once Blake had removed the bag of firewood, the Guardians led the way to a dilapidated tennis court half hidden in the trees. Alistair put the brazier down near the centre of one side of the court, well away from the rotting net, then he and Blake packed the logs on top of it.

"Just watch here, Heaven," Nadia said as she pulled a lighter from her pocket. "It's not difficult but it might take a while to get the hang of it."

Nadia flipped the lighter open and struck it in one swift movement then held it up. As she watched, the flame roared higher, then shot at the brazier in a narrow stream, igniting the contents.

Heaven stared at the wood, parts of it blazing merrily now. She'd never seen anything like that. It was like a special effect in a movie.

"Why don't you try?" Nadia smiled at her. "See if you can get the flames to really catch."

Heaven looked from Nadia to the thin flames on the logs then back again.

"How?" she asked.

"Picture it in your head, close your eyes at first…that might help, then just think of the flames roaring higher."

She closed her eyes then imagined the brazier, and the flames tangling around the logs, the wood catching fire and burning.

When she opened her eyes, it all looked exactly the same.

"Just keep trying," Nadia said cheerfully. "The more you practice, the easier it gets."

Nadia's advice wasn't as helpful as she seemed to think it was. Heaven looked across at Blake, hoping he could pull out one of his perfect summaries of how she was supposed to do this, but he and Alistair were talking.

He seemed so relaxed; he and Alistair were obviously friends. It made her realise how careful he always was around her. Alistair said something, she watched his lips moving, and heard Blake laugh.

How could she ever fit in with them? Everywhere she turned with these people, she found a sense of camaraderie, of trust. She wanted it, even though she didn't understand it in the context of reality. How did you let go of the past? How did people trust again? Was it even in her power, something as simple as just deciding to do it?

"You two, go look hot and handsome somewhere else." Nadia pointed at the Guardians as she strode towards them. "You're distracting Heaven."

Both men looked at her and Heaven stared into the flickering little fire, thoroughly embarrassed.

"Is Heaven getting distracted, or you?" Alistair laughed.

"Oh please." Nadia shoved her Guardian "Just get out of here so we can get to work."

Heaven watched them. She knew better than to think that life with her legal guardian had been normal, but it had been normal to her for a long time. The bossy way Nadia addressed the two men seemed so risky to her. Alistair might not be as muscular as Blake, but he was still strong and Nadia was trying to bully both of them into leaving. They didn't hurt her for it, but that didn't mean they couldn't.

"Is that okay with you, Heaven?" Blake looked at her calmly.

His cautious tone, and the fact that Alistair genuinely was a bit distracting, convinced her that she might be better off with just Nadia.

"It's fine." She looked at him and nodded.

"Okay, but I'll be back soon." Blake smiled, gently squeezed her upper arm, and then he and Alistair walked away towards the gate.

9

"What do you think of her so far?" Alistair asked in a low voice.

"Heaven? Tricky question." Blake paused at the edge of the woods to gather his thoughts. "I think there's a nice person in there somewhere, but...I don't know. She killed herself, and it boggles my mind."

"How's that? People kill themselves everyday" Alistair shrugged and stuffed his hands in his jacket pockets.

"They do, but..." Blake frowned. "She slit her wrist, Al. She took a knife and sliced through her flesh, the hell knows how many times to get it that deep. You should've seen what her arm looked like when I got her out of the hospital."

"That bad?" Alistair's eyebrows arched.

"Worse. It reminded me of an anatomical diagram, all veins and arteries, tendons and muscle. I'm pretty sure she'd never have been able to use that hand again if Adnes hadn't healed her." He shivered involuntarily.

"She clearly isn't one to mess around."

"Something like that takes determination," Blake said. "What drives a person to do that? If she seemed depressed, sure, but I don't think she is. Obviously she has issues, but what could've happened to her that was so bad that she chose to kill herself?"

"Lots of things, that girl's more nervous than a virgin bride." Alistair grinned.

Blake briefly wondered if his friend's train of thought had stopped at the wrong station. Al did have a weakness for girls with pretty eyes.

"I'm serious, dude," Blake said.

"So am I." Al glanced at him. "You said she doesn't like being touched, right? Maybe her parents went overboard with discipline, the type that beat their kids black and blue for mundane crap."

"I don't think so." Blake looked down at the grass at their feet, green at the base of each blade but drying at the tip. He remembered what Paula and Rochelle had said about the man who'd 'kept her'.

"Asshole boyfriend then," Alistair shrugged. "Some guys play BDSM without the rules."

"I'm not sure I want to know actually," Blake replied. Al's words were just a bit too close to what he'd been thinking. "She's more of herself now the withdrawal is over. I thought she might never start talking, or allow me to touch her."

Alistair leaned up against a tree, his eyes turned in the direction of the tennis court. "Maybe Nadia will help her relax, she's easy company and the two of them can do that girl talk thing that's so important to women."

"I hope so," Blake sighed.

They were silent for a while, until Blake realised that Alistair was staring at him.

"What?" he asked.

"You're a sucker for damsels in distress," Al said.

He snorted. "A little kindness can go a long way, you know."

"So long as it doesn't lead to complications."

"Like what?"

"She could get all hearts and butterflies over you." Alistair crossed his arms over his chest. "I call it Princess Syndrome, chicks who melt for any dude who saves them, or just expect to be rescued. Works both ways."

Blake stared at him, unsure if he was being sexist or if this was just another one of his slanted views of the world.

"I just don't see her going from being terrified of me to hearts and butterflies," Blake replied. "Stuff like that only happens in movies."

"Maybe...women can be very fickle creatures."

Blake sighed and decided to change the subject. "What's new in the trenches?"

Al's lip curled into a sneer. "There's a lot of tension among the Covens. The Black Rose is gathering and the Ice Flame are closing ranks as well—probably expecting the Rose to hit them. The smaller Covens seem to be lying low for now, like hyenas watching the lions. If those two start a war now...we haven't got enough Wielders here in the Cape."

"We have Heaven now, Spirit Wielders are supposed to be formidable in battle."

"I hope so." Al turned to look at him. "We're bloody lucky we were able to find her without the prophecy."

"Yeah...you can thank the Phoenix for that, apparently. It really makes me wonder what Enid foresaw about her before the Ravens killed her." He frowned. "Do you think any of the Handmaidens heard her prescience?"

Alistair shrugged. "We don't even know for certain that they killed Enid, but if they did, and it mattered to them, then I'm pretty sure that there would've been a couple of Ravens here in S.A."

"The Ravens must have killed her; it's the only thing that makes sense. The Black Rose was founded around that time, wasn't it?" Blake had never noticed how strange that was before.

"Coincidence, what better time to start a new Coven than right after the Ravens broke the Circle in London? I'm sure they aren't the only Coven that sprouted up after that."

"Probably right." He shrugged. "It's weird though...have you noticed that Heaven almost sounds British? Not totally, but there's a certain lilt to her voice sometimes."

"Hard to hear accents in a mumble." Alistair plucked a twig off the tree and twirled it between his fingers. "What drugs was she on?"

"She never told me and I had to leave while she spoke to Phillip."

"That guy's at Hex now?" Alistair snorted. "He's okay for patching you up in the field but I can't see him playing nurse."

"He sucks," Blake replied. "Dude has absolutely no bedside manner. Instead of reassuring her, all he did was upset her. I so wanted to just smack him."

"Protective instincts getting the better of you, bro?" Alistair asked, a knowing smile on his face.

"Maybe." He sighed. "Man, this Guardian of Heaven stuff is trickier than I thought it would be."

"You'll get used to it...once you're used to her. It's that easy, and that difficult."

***

Hours later, Heaven still wasn't having any success. She'd given herself a headache, and every

128

new attempt to make the flames grow only increased her frustration. Nadia seemed oblivious, a little while ago she'd taken out her cell phone and had been engrossed in it ever since. Occasionally she looked up to enthuse over something she'd found on Facebook, or mutter a few words of encouragement, neither of which was particularly motivating. Heaven was past ready to give up when the guys returned.

"Less status updating and more work, Nadia," Alistair yelled as they approached.

"She's had enough for one day, and besides, I'm starving," Nadia replied, pouting miserably.

"No, she needs to get this." Alistair looked at her and she nervously glanced down at her feet.

"A break might help," Blake said.

"Nothing to take a break from, man." Alistair's voice drew closer as he spoke. She glanced up and saw him coming towards her.

"Relax, sweetheart." He smiled at her. "I just want to help. Think you can trust me for a little while?"

She narrowed her eyes suspiciously.

"Look, Blake is right over there" He jerked his head in Blake's direction. "All I'm asking you to do is close your eyes and listen, okay? I won't do anything to hurt you."

Less than half a metre of space separated them, she could make out a faint scar under his left eye and some green in his brown irises. Closing her eyes was a relief.

"Can you hear the fire, Heaven, can you smell it?" he asked softly.

"Yes," she muttered.

"Think about what fire is," he continued, "think of the way farmers burn their fields. Remember what that looks like. Imagine the wind fanning those flames all around you, and the clouds of black smoke billowing in the air overhead. It's hotter than being shoved in an oven, sweat pours off you, and your skin flushes red. The fire roars as it devours everything it touches; you can hear it before you even see the dancing flames." His voice circled behind her and she tilted her head to follow it. Despite the images he was conjuring with his words, his voice was soothing.

"Nothing can stand against such an inferno, it's too powerful. Nothing remains but dust and ash. Fire destroys with unparalleled greed, but it cleanses too. Life starts anew after the flames die down, and the earth is rejuvenated. Some plants need fire to scatter their seeds, without it, they'd die out."

She'd never heard that before, she wasn't entirely sure she believed it either.

"Fire is light, it's the beacon that guides you through the dark and the lighthouse warning ships of danger." His voice was a rough whisper close to her ear that sent a shiver down her spine. He was so close she could sense his body behind hers.

"For our ancestors it meant warmth during winter, safety from predators that stalked the night, and cooked food. It was one of the first revolutionary discoveries of the human species, and it calls to something primal within all of us. Fire is action, it's passion, it's all or nothing. Remember the legend of the Phoenix, dying to be reborn in flames. You are no different, Heaven. You are fire and fervour, heat and chaos, now burn."

He gripped her upper arms and her eyes shot open.

"Don't touch me!" she yelled in fright, throwing her arms up to free herself.

The fire in the brazier made a whooshing sound, blazing up over their heads in a tower of orange and yellow before dying out quite suddenly.

"Nicely done," Alistair muttered behind her.

"I spend half the morning teaching her and you come in here, whisper in her ear, and suddenly she gets it. What the chocolate fudge dude?" Nadia demanded with a hint of outrage, pouting and glaring at him.

"You're forgetting something, princess." He chuckled as he walked towards Nadia. "She's not a natural Fire Wielder. She can't channel an element she's never connected with before."

"Jerk." Nadia punched him on the arm.

Alistair didn't seem to feel it. He slung an arm around Nadia's shoulders and heavily patting her on the cheek.

"I'm just that good," he retorted with a self-satisfied grin.

Heaven couldn't help but stare at them, their easy amity. She wished she could be like that.

"Are you okay?"

She turned to Blake and nodded, smiling as she remembered her accomplishment.

"I did it," she said.

"Yeah, you certainly did." He smiled as he patted her on the shoulder.

"Now it's time for lunch." Nadia put her phone away and headed for the gate. "I'm seriously dying of hunger."

"Always such a drama queen," Alistair said, watching Nadia with a smile as he moved towards them.

"She is a bit..." Blake shrugged.

The men strolled after Nadia so Heaven followed.

"You'll revise that if you ever see her break a heel because of a Handmaiden, entertainment doesn't get better than that."

"She wears heels on raids? I hadn't noticed."

"Nadia always wears heels, always." Alistair turned his head to look at her. "Why do you

132

women do that anyway? There's no way its comfortable, or easy, to run around in stilettos."

"I hate heels so I wouldn't know," she replied.

"That's a first." Alistair made a thoughtful sound as he turned away from her.

When they got back to the house, Nadia was already making a sandwich. The counter beside her was packed with cold meat, mayonnaise, lettuce, and tomatoes.

"If anybody else wants one, speak now." She glanced over her shoulder at them.

"I could go for that." Alistair looked at Blake.

"Same here," Blake said. "Thanks, Nadia."

Heaven ignored the question and went over to the stove to check how much coffee was left in the large pot they drank from at breakfast.

"This is the life, getting to relax while lunch and coffee are made for you," Alistair said.

Heaven froze, clenched her hand into a fist and dug her nails into her palms to restrain the urge to hurl the coffee pot at Alistair. She wasn't anyone's skivvy anymore, and he had a hell of a cheek to assume anything from her.

Something went 'pop' very loudly and Nadia yelled. When Heaven turned around her pants were on fire and Nadia was drawing the flames into her hand.

"Nadia?" Blake sounded concerned but Alistair looked more amused than anything else.

"One of my lighters exploded!"

"How? Are you okay?"

"Yeah, yeah," Nadia replied absentmindedly as she examined the damage to her pants. "That hasn't happened to me since I was twelve."

Heaven turned away and put the stove plate on to warm the coffee. She placed four mugs on the counter, but only added sugar and milk to her own.

"That's not very nice, only making for yourself." Alistair had crossed the kitchen to stand beside her, one hand leaning on the counter.

"I'm not a waitress and your limbs seem to work just fine," she sneered at him.

"Temperamental, aren't we?"

"Yes." She slowly stirred the milk and sugar mixture in the bottom of her mug. Had she really just snapped at him like that?

He nodded slightly then turned to face the counter, standing too close while he added sugar and milk to the other three mugs. Despite her outburst, he was calm, not angry.

"Were you always like that, or are you picking up Fire Wielder personality traits already?" he asked softly.

She glowered at him, unsure if he was teasing her or testing her. "I've always been highly strung; I just used to kill it."

"How'd you do that?" He made it sound like a casual question but the look in his eyes was anything but.

"Literally, I pulled my emotions out and stabbed them to death." She certainly wasn't going to tell him that she took drugs, especially not when he was just pumping her for information.

He chuckled. "How psychopathic of you, I like that. Makes conversation a whole lot more interesting if there's a chance of it ending with somebody getting knifed."

"Even when that somebody is you?"

"Can't afford to lose my edge." He gave her a sneaky smile.

Heaven stared at him. This guy just didn't make sense. She'd threatened him, and he seemed to like it.

The coffee pot shook as it boiled, and she realised that she was still looking at him. She quickly turned away and filled her mug, leaving the pot on the counter for Alistair as she prepared to make her getaway.

"Heaven."

She looked at him over her shoulder.

"Why don't you use your real name?" Alistair asked.

Talk about awkward, the kitchen suddenly seemed very quiet and she felt like they were all watching her, waiting for her answer.

"Why does it matter?" she asked softly.

"Heaven just doesn't suit you, you're too badass…or you act too badass at any rate."

"I'm beginning to understand why Nadia spends so much time hitting you." She laced her words with anger but he just smirked. Her hands clenched around the mug and she considered bolting from the room.

"While I'm semi part of this weird conversation, am I the only one who thought Heaven was your real name and it was just a really weird coincidence that you're also the Child of Heaven?"

She turned to look at Nadia, unsure whether she was truly that vague or was just trying to lighten the mood. The Fire Wielder gave her a half smile and a shrug, but seemed genuinely curious.

"You should've been born blonde, princess." The hand covering his face muffled Alistair's voice, but humour was still evident in his tone.

"Whatever." Nadia rolled her eyes and hooked her arm through Heaven's. "You boys can have your chuckles but we're going to watch TV."

Heaven didn't have any choice but to be dragged along by Nadia while she muttered about how lame men were. The moment they were sitting on the couch she put on a TV show about mobsters because they were all so hot.

Nadia chatted on and on about everything that happened in the show while Heaven just stared at her. Maybe she was only fearless because she was short a few brain cells.

By the time the episode was nearing its end, Heaven felt like she'd been watching the series from day one.

"Vinny…that's what I'm going to call you."

Heaven whipped her head around to find Alistair standing nearby, looking at the TV.

"You clearly haven't noticed that 'Vinny' is a dude," she replied.

"A badass dude…" He smiled down at her "…who just had his finger chopped off rather than betray his family."

"Which makes him a dumbass."

"It makes him a person with honour, looking out for the people who look out for him. He's a fighter." Alistair nodded, as though that was all the approval his words needed.

"That actually works," Blake mused as he dropped into the armchair. "It sounds like a nick name for 'Heaven'."

Heaven frowned and looked back at the TV as Vinny's family blew in to rescue him. It was just a TV show, a fantasy. Honour was dead in the modern world, and nobody looked out for anybody but themselves, or did they?

Guardians protected Wielders. Did that go so far as to include risking their lives for them against those shadow creatures? Or was it just a case of

137

protecting one's assets until they became liabilities?

10

Nadia and Alistair left after lunch and Blake told her they ought to start her combat training. She didn't say anything, just nodded, but he must've sensed her trepidation. All the way through the woods, he emphasised the importance of self-defence, so much so, that it got boring. Luckily, it only took ten minutes to reach the dorms, from there he led her to a low building adjacent to them. The water tower perched atop the low hill on the far end, looming over them from above.

They walked through a set of double doors into a large room. Some wooden dummies and punching bags were arranged near the walls and two Guardians were fighting on a thick mat in the centre of the room. She supposed they were training, but the way they attacked each other looked real.

Her steps slowed to a stop as she watched a blonde guy rapidly throwing punches at his long haired opponent. Long hair dodged and weaved while backing away then suddenly lunged forwards, blocking a punch as he brought his knee up to Blondie's gut. As Blondie folded forward, Long hair struck the back of his head with the side of his hand then twisted one of his arms up behind him. It all happened in one smooth motion and ended with Blondie lying on the mat.

She wished she could fight like that, but both of them were big, and male. What chance could a woman have of being stronger than either of them?

"Heaven!"

Her head whipped around. Blake was standing next to one of the punching bags and she quickly went to join him.

"Have you ever been in a fight before?" he asked when she was closer, his eyes fixed on her face.

Had he noticed the kink in her nose where it had broken? Or was it the scar across her cheekbone? Trey had left very few scars on her body, but most of those came from times when she'd tried to fight back.

"Not exactly," she shrugged.

"We'll start with the basics then," Blake said. "Stand with your feet apart, knees slightly bent, and arms up in front of your body. Keep your abdominal muscles tense, your strength comes from there."

She followed his instructions, but he didn't seem satisfied. He moved around her, correcting her stance with light touches, and then demonstrated how he wanted her to stand.

"First rule when you're using your hands in a fight." He held up his index finger. "It's always hard to soft, and soft to hard. Your fist is hard so you use it to punch soft areas of the body, like the stomach. Don't use your fist on somebody's face or you could break a finger."

"Seriously?" She'd never heard that before.

Blake nodded. "It takes conditioning to get your knuckles hard enough to endure contact with bones, but even then, a palm strike is often better."

He tilted his hand up at what was almost a right angle to his arm and struck the bag, then showed her how to curl her hand up the same way, as well as how to hold her fist to punch. It looked easy enough but when she had to try it, she realised that the bag was heavier than it looked.

"Put your weight behind your blows but don't compromise your balance. If you miss then you need to be able to bounce back and throw the next one."

She nodded and kept practising.

**

Alistair knocked on the door to the Keeper's office once, and entered. Robert was expecting him, and the message had sounded urgent, but he hesitated in the doorway when he realised that Robert wasn't alone. A stocky, dour looking man with dirty blonde hair and weather-tanned skin stood just to one side of the Keeper's desk.

"Come in, Alistair, and shut the door," his mentor said in the very calm tone which usually meant he was highly annoyed.

"Yes, Keeper." He eyed up the second man as he pushed the door closed.

Only members of the Circle ever entered Robert's office. Anything to do with the management of the bookshop was taken care of in the stock room. This guy bore a close enough likeness to a tank to be a Guardian, and was glowering at him with the intense hatred he was accustomed to, but Alistair didn't recognise him.

"I apologise if I'm interrupting..." Alistair began.

"Not at all," Robert interjected. "I called you in because Herman here wishes to speak to you."

Everyone had heard of Herman the Hunter, an Awakened-born cop with the Occult Crimes Division. He was one of the Circle's most important, albeit Inactive, members.

"Certainly." Alistair smiled politely. "How can I help you?"

"You can tell me where you were yesterday evening," Herman said in a low grumble.

"At Stillwater."

"The whole evening?" Herman narrowed his eyes to slits.

"Yes. Why do you ask?"

"Just answer the questions. Can anybody confirm your whereabouts?"

"Dylan was home too." This was like being in training all over again. Bryan had found new things to accuse him of every few weeks, from stealing his car to vandalising the gym.

To be fair, he had stolen Bryan's car, but he was certain Gary was the artist behind that crude picture of Bryan involved in dubious deeds with a Skaath. He'd just laughed at it.

"I suppose you'll want to confirm that with Dylan?" Robert stared at Herman.

"Of course, when I'm done here." Herman's gaze hadn't left him for a second. "Your mother was a Handmaiden, correct?"

"Yes," he sighed.

"Did she teach you the Skaarav?"

"No." Alistair frowned. "I never even heard about it until I started training to be a Guardian."

"You do know about it then?"

Alistair turned to Robert. "What, exactly, am I being accused of, Keeper?"

"All in due time." Robert nodded at him.

He sighed and stared past Herman. "Yes, it's a ritual used to separate a Handmaiden's identity from her soul by severing the connection to the

Diurga. It was widely used in Europe for a while, but has since been forbidden by the Circle as it removes any chance of the soul being reborn."

"Do you agree with that law?"

"Seems fair enough." Alistair shrugged.

Herman humphed and crossed his arms. Before he could ask anything else, Robert cleared his throat.

"I believe Alistair has given us enough information to satisfy your speculation on his involvement."

Herman's upper lip curled into a sneer. "For now. I still need to speak to Dylan."

"Of course. I'll send for him immediately, but until he arrives, you should fill Alistair in on the situation. I'm sure you'll find his insight invaluable."

Alistair bit the tip of his tongue to prevent himself from laughing at the dismay on the cop's face.

"Yes, Keeper," Herman replied. "I hope you're right."

"Alistair is just as valuable as you are in this regard, and I trust him implicitly."

Herman sniffed loudly, and stared at him again. "There's a serial killer targeting Handmaidens. It's been going on for months now, but the ritual aspects of the murders have only recently displayed occult symbology."

"In what way?"

"For one, the latest victim had 'Skaarav' carved into her forehead in the old tongue; I was called in to translate it. Roughly half the skin on her left forearm was removed too, just like the others. That's where many Handmaidens wear their Mark."

"Skaath Marks fade after death. If they were cut off then it must've been done while they were alive." Alistair couldn't help feeling horrified.

"I believe that's part of the Skaarav ritual," Robert said.

"It is, according to my source. The Covens know about it too, they call him the Giyarav Shpyorad."

"Severer of Souls...I've never heard of this, but it might explain why both the Ice Flame and the Black Rose are on the defensive lately," Alistair said.

Herman gave him a sharp look and his lips puckered up like he'd just bitten a lemon.

"I do wonder why only the last Handmaiden was marked on her forehead," Robert said softly.

"If you'll give me access to the Circle's books, I'll find out soon enough," Herman remarked.

Robert smiled. "But of course, Herman. Many refer to the ritual in one way or another, and I'm certain that at least one contains the method of performing it in its entirety. If only I could remember which one."

Robert never forgot anything, or brought up details that may prove irrelevant. He knew exactly where he'd read about the Skaarav, Alistair was certain of it. By far less certain, was the nature of the game he was playing, was he baiting Herman or dropping a clue?

***

That evening, Heaven curled up in bed and looked through the book the Keeper had given her. Right near the beginning was the story Blake had told her about the first children.

In the oldest of times the Mother brought forth the first children of the world, the Geead Lyana. These she moulded from the world itself, gathering the elements into four beings that pleased her in shape, but lacked in their character. It was a matter that perplexed the Mother, and gave her cause for much thought. Her children lived in the sense that they moved and desired to survive, but they were not aware as she was. After observing them, she decided to try another experiment and gathered the dust of the stars to form another child. This time she built the being around a breath of her own life, and so discovered the secret of all life. For when the child of starlight gazed upon the world, she was conscious, not only of the bestial drive to survive, but of her own complexity. Even though she had no perception of the Mother, she seemed aware of her as well, and when she encountered

146

her elder siblings, she knew them, although she knew not how. She recognised the Mother in these creatures and with her own breath managed to bring them fully to life in the way that the Mother had intended. The four Awakened, and looked on the world with new eyes. After a while, they decided to create children of their own, and the first aided them by breathing life into the beings they moulded. So did the clans of stone, sea, wind, and flame come into the world.

The Geead Lyana lived in peace with each other and later, when the Mother brought humans into the world, they lived alongside them and guided mankind in its youth. The first children looked on humans as their younger siblings and gladly shared with them their knowledge, teaching them those arts that the human spirit had strength to master. In the times to come, some of the children of the Geead Lyana even found love with the humans, joining with them, and bringing forth a new race in their offspring.

But there were those among the humans who grew envious of the Geead Lyana and the power that the Mother had embodied in them. The Father, the Void—who balanced out the Mother with shadows and destruction—shared their envy. Ever since he first learned of the Geead Lyana, he had tried in vain to form his shadows into beings just as marvellous, but his efforts always failed.

He approached the humans and whispered to them of sacred knowledge while they lay sleeping in the shade of their caves. Promises were made and the price of their divinity bargained and agreed upon. Within each treacherous heart, the Void placed a shadow, and on the eve of the next day, these humans took the child of starlight and cast her into the Void.

The Pact was now sealed, and with the breath of life held captive within the Father, the shadows in the humans awoke. They possessed the human bodies, moulding themselves around the mortal flesh to create new entities. This was how the Skaath Diurga came into being.

When the Geead Lyana discovered the betrayal, they fought the Diurga, and eventually banished them to the Between. They hunted down their servants from among the humans and cast them out into the wilderness. The first children then withdrew from humankind, their trust in mortals forever broken. Even those among the Geead who had taken human spouses departed, leaving behind their children, the Awakened mortals. To them they gave the task of watching over humans, and a gift of four talismans in the images of the first children.

Over time, humanity's knowledge of this was forgotten, buried in the ruins of civilizations that were themselves forgotten as empires rose and fell.

Victorious marauders burnt libraries and outlawed the knowledge of those they conquered. Elders of all communities died with their wisdom untold. Only the Awakened remember as they continue the battle against the Handmaidens and Thralls who serve the Skaath.'

Child of starlight…was that another name for Child of Heaven? And where could the Geead Lyana possibly have gone?

She checked the time on the alarm clock beside the bed. It wasn't that late so she swept the covers off and tucked the book under one arm. She padded silently down the passage to Blake's room. The door was open and the room was dark. When she peered inside it seemed empty, and there was no discernible lump in the bed.

Muted sounds of voices filtered upstairs from the lounge so she headed down. Blake was sitting on the couch with Paula leaning against him. The TV threw light across them in weird patterns. Heaven paused for a moment then cleared her throat.

"Hey, Heaven." Blake looked across at her. "I thought you were sleeping."

"Reading actually." She lifted the book. "Can I ask you something?"

"Sure, just hang on." He slowly moved away from Paula, lowering her so she eventually lay on the couch. "She fell asleep and I don't want to wake her," he said in a hushed tone. "Let's talk in the kitchen."

She nodded and followed him, asking her first question as soon as the kitchen door closed. "Where did the Geead Lyana go?"

"We were taught that they left their bodies to return to their elemental state while their spirits became part of the Between," he said.

"I still don't get that Between business."

"It's a spiritual plane linking this plane and the soul plane. That's where the Sages exist, the Skaath as well."

"So it's like alternate universes?" She pulled a face at him.

"Not at all." Blake chuckled. "Think of it like pizza."

"Come again?"

"Pizza." He smiled at her and smoothed his hand over the kitchen counter in a circle. "You have a base made of dough, then you put tomato sauce over it, then your toppings, and after that you cover it all in cheese. We are the sauce, the Between is the toppings and the soul plane is the cheese."

"Okay...makes sense, I guess."

"It's all layers that make a whole."

"What about the dough?"

"That's a bit more complicated." He frowned. "The dough is the beginning; primordial soup, hot universe plasma, stardust and dogma. It's the energy that connects us all together, and everything we don't understand about The Mother and The Void."

Heaven rolled that around in her head. "Right…so the dough is the origin of life?"

"Exactly. There is no pizza without the crust."

"And the Sages, Skaath, and Geead all just run around the Between together, or what?"

"No." Blake chuckled and shook his head. "The Skaath Diurga, and all the lesser Skaath beasts, are confined to a part of the Between called the Never. It's believed that part of the reason the Geead left was to keep them from spreading darkness throughout the Between."

"The Geead Lyana became the Diurga's prison guards then?"

"Something like that. They keep them contained in their plane and we fight their influence in ours."

Heaven leaned against the kitchen table and hugged the book to her chest. Could all of this truly be real? It sounded so outlandish.

"You said the Between is a spiritual plane, does that mean its part of my element?" she asked.

"In a way, Spirit is a part of everything. It connects us all together and links us to the Between, but you will always be more closely tied to that plane than anybody else ever could be."

151

"Does that include the Never too?"

Blake straightened up, frowning slightly. "I don't know but I'd imagine so. Spirit is an element with a dual nature. Very much like the concept of Ying and Yang, except that one aspect comprises all the negative experiences that can happen and the other is all the positive."

She sighed softly and ran her fingers through her hair. "This is way more convoluted than I thought it would be."

"Sorry about that." Blake gave her a lopsided smile. "I'm trying to explain simply."

"The pizza dough big bang theory was simple; you could teach science to five year olds."

Blake laughed and she couldn't help but smile. Maybe she could get the hang of being normal after all.

"I doubt it, I like physics because it explains how all of this works." He gestured to include the room, the world, she supposed.

"I don't know anything about that stuff," she said, scuffing one foot on the floor.

"Not many people do." He shrugged. "And I'm certainly not an expert on anything, I just like to know the why's and how's of everything, so I find out."

"Simple as that, huh?"

He grinned as he nodded. "Don't stress about any of this too much, for right now the most important thing is that you learn the spells in the book, theory can come later."

"Spells, seriously?"

"Yes, we'll start tomorrow afternoon, okay?"

"Sure," she sighed.

Just when she thought she was getting a grip on this situation, something new came up to throw her off balance.

"It's not hard, the basic spells are just one word."

"If you say so." She headed towards the door. "Good night, Blake."

"Night, Heaven, sleep well."

"One last thing." She paused as she was leaving. "You and Paula looked a bit cosy in there…"

Blake frowned at her, then his eyes widened and he almost choked on his laughter. "She's seventeen, Vinny, too young for me. Besides, the Keeper has rules about dating."

"Oh." She felt a blush rise in her cheeks. "I was just curious."

11

Alistair sat with his back to the chain link fence of the tennis court and watched as Vinny and Nadia tossed balls of fire at each other.

The more he thought about yesterday's interrogation, the more he worried. Not for himself, he trusted Robert to watch his back, but he had a feeling that Robert knew a lot more than he was letting on.

"…makes them more attractive to other people, think that's right, Al?"

"What?" he turned to look at Blake, sitting beside him with a book on his lap.

"This says that people feel drawn to Spirit Wielders because of their connection to everything." He tilted the book so that the pages were shaded from the sun. "Says that even normal humans can sense a reaction with their deeper self."

"You're saying she's like a magnet for people?" Alistair asked, it felt like he'd been slapped.

"I don't know." Blake frowned. "In a way it makes sense, but I don't think I want to help her just because of a side effect of her element."

"When I came to see you after your sister's accident you were nursing a bird you found in the woods, remember that?"

"It died," Blake replied stiffly.

"That's not the point." Alistair plucked a dry stalk of grass from a crack in the clay. "I never met Maya, but from what you said about her, she was the type to help every broken thing she met. You got like that after she died."

Blake humphed and hunched his shoulders.

"I don't mean it in a bad way, bro." He dropped his hand on Blake's shoulder. "Kindness is a rare quality, but still a good thing."

"I know, but just drop it now." Blake turned his attention back to the book.

He chewed the inside of his lip and carried on watching the Wielders. Maybe there was something to what that book said, it would explain the instant attraction he'd felt towards her.

Vinny fumbled a catch and the ball of flames landed on her shoes. A vulgar exclamation that many men would've been ashamed to utter, echoed around the court, and Blake's head snapped up.

Somehow, it made her more appealing, not less. Alistair bit his tongue to keep from grinning. He

155

was willing to bet that Vinny was all sorts of fun once you cracked that shell of hers.

But she wasn't just some girl, and he'd have to be damn sure about this before he started anything—if he started anything. Spirit magnetism…he'd probably just make a fool out of himself.

"I'm going to duck, Nadia's got this covered," he said, getting to his feet and brushing his jeans off.

"Sure man, see you tomorrow," Blake replied.

"You ladies play nicely," he yelled to the Wielders. "I'm out of here."

"See you, Alistair," Nadia yelled back.

Heaven met his gaze for a moment then glanced away. She didn't say anything, but he thought he could feel her watching him as he walked away.

He snuck up Rochelle's driveway and escaped on his bike without seeing the older Air Wielder at all. She was probably still working, but he'd rather not run into her if he could avoid it.

He ramped a few of the larger bumps in the road on his way down, and paused between the gates to Headrush. If he turned left, he'd be headed home, to Denysrus, Dylan's lingering weird mood, and nothing to do except be bored. If he turned right, he'd be in Cape Town in around half an hour.

He needed a distraction. Alistair turned and drove slowly until the dirt road became tar then he opened the throttle and bent forward over the bike.

There was a little bar in Cape Town that he liked to go to, partly because it was a good place to pick up information, and partly because one of the waitresses was incredibly friendly.

It also had a lot of free parking. He found a space right near the door, walked inside, and scanned the room.

Heavy wooden tables crowded the floor, which was covered in blue-coloured cement, by the looks of it. Plain, but ugly chandeliers hung from the ceiling, ineffectively lighting the badly painted faces of various movie stars on the walls.

Gina was leaning over at an angle that gave him a good view down the front of her shirt. He smiled, and went to sit at the bar, ignoring her completely. It didn't take long before he felt a delicate hand on his shoulder.

"Hi there, handsome." Gina's smile was all brilliant white teeth and dimples, her voice a cigarettes and alcohol sort of husky.

"Hi, Genie, looking lovely tonight." He casually returned her smile.

"Lovely is what makes good tips." She leaned closer, pressing her breasts against his back and arm as she hung on him. "What wish can I grant you today?"

"Just the usual, maybe a burger." He slid his arm around her waist. "I'm not sure if I'm hungry yet."

Her lips pressed together in a pout. "Hmm…I'm taking a break in ten minutes, meet me out back? Maybe we can work up your appetite."

"With pleasure." He lowered his hand to squeeze her hip, and she playfully swatted him away.

"Get my friend here a beer, Andi," she called to the woman behind the bar before she turned and sashayed through the door that led to the kitchen.

Fifteen minutes later, he had Gina pressed up against the back wall of the bar, his hands beneath her shirt as they made out like horny teenagers.

She might've been easy, but he'd figured out a long time ago that she coupled these sessions with a fine sense of timing. There was an always an order waiting for her, or a table to check. Always a reason to leave. It was frustrating sometimes, but ultimately, it suited him.

"I have to get back to work," she sighed with her usual half-feigned regret as she pulled away and looked up at him with big blue eyes. "Maybe you could give me a lift home later?"

This was new. A night with Genie might be just what he needed, but what then? She was too slutty to keep, and too useful to offend.

Alistair tucked her hair behind her ear and smiled. "This is part of an evil plan that ends with you keeping me as a sex slave, isn't it?"

"What gave it away?" Gina chuckled and flashed him that million-dollar grin again.

"I know your type, Genie…and I'd love to take you home, but you'll get the wrong idea if I leave before you wake up, and my boss will give me hell if I'm late to work."

"That sounds a lot like an excuse…" Her eyes narrowed slightly.

Alistair sighed. "I don't live here, and it's a long drive back to Paarl. You can take me home and do terrible things to me next time I stop by."

"That better be a promise." She pulled her shirt down and stepped past him, leaving him in the little alcove formed by two dumpsters.

That was almost too close.

He turned and something gave under his shoe, a partially flattened two-litre juice bottle. For the first time in a long time, it occurred to him that there might be something wrong with feeling a girl up while surrounded by rubbish.

"So much for a distraction," he muttered.

***

Small tongues of flame flickered on Vinny's fingertips. She slowly brought her fingers together, and the flames grew higher. With a little focus, she was able to spin them out on the air, feeding them power until the fire danced and flickered all around her.

"You're getting pretty good at this."

She glanced at Blake and smiled. "I never realised that fire could be so beautiful."

"Most things are beautiful, if you look closely enough," he replied.

She smiled and turned her attention back to the fire, stretched out her right hand, and called the flames back. Orange and yellow tongues settled in her palm and writhed through the air mere millimetres from her fingers. They also twirled around her outstretched arm and the sleeve of her shirt caught fire.

"Bugger." She slapped at her arm to put out the smoking material, but now the dead leaves at her feet were smouldering too. "Blake!" she called out as she stomped on the fires starting up around her.

"Kill it." He was beside her now, also stomping on the flames. "Pull the power out of the fire"

She held out her hands and focused on the energy she felt in the flames, vibrant and passionate as tango dancers. The flames shot up higher and she jumped.

"Shit." Blake leapt backwards as the fire leapt up all around her.

This was bad, very bad. The woods could burn down and it would be all her fault. What the hell kind of idiot was she to play around with fire in the middle of so much potential tinder?

"Don't panic, its not that bad." Blake was looking at her from the other side of the fire, "Call it to your hands."

She took a deep breath, rolled up her sleeves, pulled the glove on her left hand off, and stuffed it in her pants pocket. She focused, and the fire crept closer, burning up the dry leaves and branches closest to her. Her legs were hot now, but when she lowered her arms, the fire jumped on to them quite willingly. Now the ground was clear, but both her arms were clothed in fire.

"Focus it in your hands," Blake said. "Like you're making fireballs."

She just nodded, scared that if she did anything else she'd lose control. Sweat trickled down her temple, but she ignored it and thought of fireballs.

"Just a bit longer, Vinny," he said in a low voice.

"What?"

"Concentrate on holding it, you'll see."

The fire had crept lower and focused mainly around her hands now. Somehow, it seemed less eager than it was before, content to flicker and curl around her hands like a lazy cat. The flames slowly died down, and soon enough she was able to snuff them out in her fists.

"Son of a bitch," she gasped, feeling very tired now that relief was settling in.

"Are you okay?" Blake's hand settled on her shoulder and she looked up at him.

"Yeah, but that was close."

"I knew you could hold it." There was an odd twinkle in his eyes, a bit like pride.

"I call bullshit." Heaven scowled at him. "No way did you believe that."

"I did, and I was right." He smiled. "But if it hadn't worked then we could've just waited until you'd drained both your essence, and the Phoenix."

"That's what the 'bit longer' was about?" she pulled her glove back on and rolled down her sleeves.

"Yeah. Since it's only been an hour or so since Nadia left, I reckoned it wouldn't take that long. Do what you were doing before, with the fire on your fingers."

"Are you insane? I nearly set the woods on fire, and you want me carry on?"

"If a horse throws you, you get straight back on. If you take too long to think about things then you start getting nervous, or scared of doing it again. I don't want that to happen to you," he said.

She groaned, but pulled out the lighter anyway and lit a flame, drawing it into her right hand before she could think about it.

"Good." Blake smiled. "See if you can keep it going til we get to the gym."

"Is this really necessary?"

He nodded and carried on walking. Vinny followed with slow, careful steps.

**

Alistair had been drinking for hours by the time Dylan pried the glass from his hand and downed the contents.

"I was drinking that," he growled.

"Now I am. Why are you drinking whiskey without me? Now I have to play catch up." Dylan looked down at him with a slight frown, and the piercing in his lip moved around as he tongued it.

"Go right ahead," he waved his hand towards the bottle on the coffee table, leaned back into the couch, and covered his eyes with one hand.

He felt the couch shift as Dylan sat then heard him pour a drink, but he didn't look at him.

"What's eating you, brother?" Dylan asked.

"Nothing, I'm just a moody bastard, given to occasional bouts of moping."

"No, you're not—that's Blake," he replied.

Alistair snorted. "He has exclusive rights on it now, does he?"

"No." Dylan poked his knee. "Is this about that cop, Herman?"

Alistair sniffed. "He checked my alibi with you?"

"Yeah…are you in trouble bro?"

He could lie, or at least tell a version of the truth that worked for him, but it wouldn't get him answers.

"No," Alistair sighed. "Did you know that Spirit Wielders are supposed to have this magnetic aura or something that draws people to them?"

"Yeah, its pretty basic stuff."

He opened his eyes and sat up to glare at him. "And you still gave me crap about her?"

"The Spirit element has a dual nature; both darkness and light are drawn to each other. Get it?" Dylan smiled as he looked at him expectantly.

"No," he replied.

Dylan sighed. "When Blake heard that he was going to be the Child of Heaven's Guardian, I helped him do research. You know Blake, never met a book he didn't like. Anyway, a couple of them say the same thing—that every light casts a shadow."

"Obviously," he sneered.

"Not just literal lights and shadows, man. It's about balance. Spirit Wielders go through so much shit that they kill themselves, and that takes serious balls. They're drawn towards the most messed up members of society, and vice versa until they literally can't handle it anymore."

"Yeah, this sounds like its going to be a seriously motivating conversation."

Dylan lunged toward him and lightly slapped his cheek. "You dumbass, you're thinking about this all the wrong way. She is light and you have a Skaath Mark, I'm willing to bet she feels drawn to you too."

"You really know how to make a man feel good about himself." He sat up and reached for the bottle on the table.

"Cut the bullshit." Dylan snatched the bottle from his reach, splashed some of the liquid into the glass, and gave him that instead. "You're a good guy, Alistair, and you know it. That Mark isn't who you are; it's just where you came from."

Alistair thought about that for all of five minutes. "It doesn't matter anyway. She's going to think I'm tainted when she finds out about me, she won't be far wrong either."

Dylan laughed and shook his head. "Man, oh man…where do I even start with this?"

"By dropping it." He drained the contents of the glass in one gulp.

"First thing." Dylan took the glass and poured himself a drink this time. "Just because one dumb girl couldn't handle you, doesn't mean that all of them will react the same way. Second, stop letting what the afore-mentioned dumb girl did and said define your estimation of yourself."

"You've been spending too much time with your Wielder. All this amateur psychoanalysis doesn't change the facts, bro. I'm a womanising, Skaath-born fuck up."

"That's how you act, but I know you better than that. Your real problem is that you care too much. If you didn't then you would've brushed Erika's crap off by now. She was wrong about you, Al." He stared at him as he spoke.

Once Dylan was in his 'big brother' mode, there was no easy way to shut him up.

Alistair sneered, "And you're such an expert, Dylan? You have no idea what its like."

"Everybody's an outsider in some way; you just choose to hold a grudge over it." Dylan stood, holding the bottle in one hand and the glass in the other. "You think people don't look at me funny because of my long hair and piercings? I get attitude all the time, but I prove them wrong. I love you, brother, but you seriously have to let go of this shit. All the work you've done just to be allowed to be a Guardian doesn't mean a damn thing if you still think the worst of yourself."

He got up too fast, and the room spun. He squeezed his eyes shut and waited for everything to stop shifting.

"You know, Elise would say that you're only getting so pissed off because you know I'm right," Dylan added.

"Don't make me regret being honest with you," he growled.

"You know what, Al? You want to sit here and sulk, go for it. Knock yourself out. Shit, why not just spend the rest of your life feeling sorry for yourself for never taking a chance."

"Drama queen."

Dylan snorted and left the room, his footsteps echoing back down the passage. Alistair flopped back down onto the couch and stared up at the roof. The bastard knew him far too well.

12

"This is not writing." Vinny pulled a face at the paper in front of her. "It's just a line with a bunch of other lines drawn through it."

"It is confusing at first, but just focus on the alphabet and you'll be able to figure it out," Blake told her.

"Or not." Alistair lay sprawled across the couch, staring at the TV. "Still have to learn the language to read it."

Blake shook his hair out of his face and glared at him. "Not helping, Al."

"I wasn't trying to help."

"If you're not helping then why are you hanging around here?" Blake frowned at him.

"Because Dylan said he'll put Spot's leftovers on my pillow if he sees me before midnight."

"Gross." Blake pulled a face.

"Spot?" Vinny looked at Blake but it was Alistair who replied.

"Dylan's pet tarantula," he said.

"How delightful."

"She's actually quite pretty," Blake said.

"From the other side of the glass," Alistair muttered. He shifted on the couch and pulled his phone from his pocket. After a while, he leaned forward with the screen turned towards her, showing a photo of a large looking spider with golden markings on its legs.

"It is striking," she replied.

"I believe that's code for 'holy crap, its huge'." Alistair smirked as he leaned back.

Vinny balled up the paper in front of her and threw it at him. His hand flashed out and caught it, crunching the paper in his fist before throwing it back at her. She ducked and it sailed over her.

"Might as well call it a day," Blake sighed.

"Does that mean we can do something interesting now?" Alistair sat up as he looked at Blake.

"What do you have in mind, Al?"

"The Demon." Alistair grinned. "Without the usual wager since Vinny will be joining us."

"Says who?" She gave him a dirty look.

"Me, obviously. Come on, its fun."

"You dudes have a weird definition of fun." She emphatically rolled her eyes.

"Well, yours seems to be non-existent," Alistair replied.

He got up, took her by the hand, and pulled her to her feet so casually that it took a moment for her brain to register it. One moment she was sitting on the floor, and the next, she was standing in front of him, looking into his eyes.

"Get off me," she snapped, jerking her hand away and taking a step back.

"My touch isn't toxic and I'm not trying to hurt you," he replied. "But I will carry you outside if I have to."

She thought of the way she'd seen him and Nadia behave over the past few days. Just yesterday, Nadia had tackled him for teasing her and Alistair had let her win. Normal people touched each other all the time and it didn't mean anything.

She couldn't handle that yet, but she could try.

"Fine then," she sighed and walked towards the door.

"You don't have to do it," Blake said when he caught up to her.

Vinny shrugged. "It's no big deal."

Rochelle came through the door just as they were leaving. She smiled at Heaven and Blake then paused. "Alistair, I thought you would've left by now," she said."

"Not yet." his voice came from close behind Vinny, it sounded stiff and tense.

"Stay for supper while you're here." Rochelle's smile widened, and she walked past them. "I won't take 'no' for an answer."

"Okay." He drew out the syllables, making the word sound uncertain.

Vinny passed Blake and halted on the lawn to wait for them. The sun was low in the sky but it wasn't dark yet. Shadows from the trees threw bars of darkness across the garden, and birds were singing loudly in the woods.

The men led the way down through the woods to the obstacle course. She could now see why they called it the Demon. Wooden structures stretched out before her, things for crawling under and climbing over. Tall balance beams and a mud patch with logs sticking out of it like stepping-stones. They could use this place in a game show.

"I would explain the layout to you, but I'm sure you can't keep up so you can just follow Blake." Alistair was looking at her with a cocky grin.

She took a page from Nadia's book and shoved him.

Alistair laughed, but it turned into a yell when he noticed that Blake was already half way across a balance beam bridging a patch of thorns scattered on the ground.

"That's low, man," he yelled as he leapt up onto the beam and took off after him.

"Not my fault you weren't paying attention," Blake replied, jumping down at the far end and running towards a set of logs positioned at various heights.

Blake seemed to slide over the first one then dropped to the ground and rolled under the next before rising to go over the third. He was astonishingly graceful for a guy built like a tank.

Alistair was catching up to him now, so she stepped onto the balance beam to follow them. Both men had run across it but she took her time, holding her arms out at her side so she wouldn't fall. She cheated her way through the next obstacle by ducking under the high logs and stepping over the low ones.

Next there was a rope dangling between two supports, at the top was what looked like a ladder that stretched horizontally across to another set of supports.

Alistair and Blake were already an obstacle ahead of her. She looked up at the ladder and considered her options. Maybe she ought to try doing it for training's sake, but…she tucked her hands into her pockets and walked away.

A strip of dry grass separated the two sides of the obstacle course and she sat down there with her legs crossed. Alistair and Blake were little more than flashes of movement, but she could hear them teasing each other. It was nice.

A group of boys had hung around the athletics field after school, teasing the girls, and smoking in the bushes. She'd considered them her friends for a while, had casually dated Nick until she found out he had a whole string of girls he met up with in the oak trees.

She'd been such a fool, and maybe she still was. She picked a blade of grass and twirled it between her fingers, what did she know about guys or healthy relationships? She'd read a few books and watched some movies, all of it fiction. Most of her knowledge of normal life was drawn from fantasy, and if that wasn't so depressing it would've been funny.

The men were getting closer. Vinny looked up, not paying much attention as they raced through the last few obstacles then drew up a few metres away. They laughed and teased each other for a few minutes until Blake noticed her.

"Damn, Vinny, I never even saw you pass us." He grinned.

"I'm that fast." She forced a smile.

"Lazy." Alistair shook his head. "Typical girl, never want to do anything fun in case it ruins their manicure."

"Screw you; I'm not a typical anything."

"You're not in a position to be objective about that." He smiled at her, but it wasn't friendly.

"My apologies, I didn't know you were such an expert on me. Please, carry on, I'll just sit here and take mental notes with the hope of being enlightened."

Blake covered his mouth as he made a sound somewhere between a snort and a laugh. Alistair arched his eyebrows.

"Aren't you sharp under that veneer of silence?" he said.

Blake cuffed him on the shoulder before she could reply. "Let it go, Al, none of us needs you two getting into an argument."

"I was just making an observation, and I'm right, aren't I, Vinny?"

"I guess," she replied, narrowing her eyes at him.

"See, bro? All friends here." As if to prove his point, Alistair lowered himself to sit near her.

"You're flirting with stiff muscles there," Blake said as he stretched his legs.

"I don't care." Alistair lay back on the grass. "You know, I'll miss this when you move in," he said.

"Yeah, me too."

"You Guardians all live together?" Vinny looked from one to the other.

"Yeah, except Mike," Alistair replied. "He moved in with Janine after they got married."

"Married?" She frowned at Blake. "I thought there was a rule about dating?"

"There is," he replied. "It's not allowed unless you're serious. Break ups and jealousy and all that can be detrimental to team morale."

"How the hell are you supposed to know you want to get serious if you aren't allowed to be casual?" She pulled a face.

"Why are you so interested, Vinny?" Alistair turned his head to look at her.

"I'm figuring out what I've gotten myself into." She met his gaze and shrugged. "You have a problem with that?"

"Not at all." He smiled faintly.

13

Every evening, the Air Wielders watched soapies on TV. Vinny had watched enough of Sleepless Summer to last her a lifetime, so she, Darren, and Blake got into the habit of playing a version of dodge ball to kill time. Heaven used fire, and the Guardians were armed with tennis balls.

Heaven was the fittest she'd ever been in her life, and she'd always been nimble, but it wasn't fair by a long shot...the guys made her look like a one legged drunkard. On the rare occasions that her aim was accurate, they evaded her fireballs easily, but she had to take cover every time to avoid being hit.

She'd just ducked behind a tree when the thrumming of engines in the distance echoed off the panelled concrete walls surrounding Rochelle's house. Shortly afterward, she heard the rough sound of tyres spinning on dirt. Vinny peeked around the side of the tree and saw both Guardians standing in the middle of the lawn with their heads turned towards the dorms.

"What is it?" She left her cover and walked closer.

"A raid," Blake muttered.

"There wasn't anything planned for tonight that I know of," Darren said.

"What sort of raid?"

"A raid is what we call an attack on one of the Coven houses." Blake and Darren shared a grave look before he continued. "You two go in, I'll find out what's going on."

Darren nodded, and Blake left without another word. She wanted to go with him, not stay here with the mind readers, but he didn't even give her a chance to follow him.

***

As soon as he was clear of the house, Blake broke into a run and sprinted through the trees as fast as he could. He didn't want to alarm Vinny, but for the Guardians to rush off without prior planning was abnormal. It meant that something was wrong.

When he reached the long building that housed the gym, medical centre, and classrooms, he wasn't surprised to find the senior Guardians hurrying about. Figures faded in and out of the twilight as they packed supplies into a large, black SUV, or hurried through the doors to the medical centre.

Blake strode towards the car and glanced in the back to gauge how soon the back-up team would head out. A Guardian placing a metal case in the back of the car turned quickly and bumped into him.

"Shit, sorry man," he muttered.

Blake recognised him but couldn't recall his name. "What's happened?"

"Water team called in for back-up, that's all I know."

Blake's stomach turned to stone, and he swallowed hard. "Thanks."

The other Guardian nodded and took off towards the door that led to the gym and classrooms.

Dylan and Elise. This was bad—worse than he'd expected. He looked into the back of the car again, they'd leave soon but he was stuck here…maybe he didn't have to be, he could offer to go along.

But he couldn't. He wasn't a Beta Red anymore, and his place was with his Wielder.

Dark figures jogged through the doors nearby and Blake stepped back, away from the car. The engine started, and it pulled away before the last man in had shut his door.

Blake watched as it disappeared from view, slowly clenching and relaxing his fingers. Being promoted to Guardian of a Wielder was supposed to consolidate your loyalty; he'd never imagined that it could make him feel so torn.

He pulled his phone from his pocket as he headed towards the entrance to the gym and typed a message to Alistair, telling him what he'd just heard. Darren might not know of anything scheduled for tonight, but Al would. He broke into a jog and went straight to the supply cupboard outside the entrance to the locker room.

He reached past a large bottle of bleach and pressed his hand against the biometric scanner concealed on the wall behind it. The wall in front of him slid open to reveal a narrow landing and stairs leading down to the right.

There were several hidden entrances leading to the water tower, but this was the main one. The stairs and tunnel below were lit well enough for him to run down them. Just outside the door to the underground section of the tower, his phone vibrated.

A voice message from Alistair.

"No activity was scheduled for tonight, tried to call you but it doesn't go through so I assume you're at the fort, you should get this through their connection, meet you there."

Blake typed a quick answer then tapped in the codes to enter the tower.

***

Alistair drove to Headrush as though all the Diurga and Skaath of the Never were behind him. He nearly crashed his bike into the gates as he skidded through them, but was able to pull up in time.

He parked right outside the doors to the gym and raced through the tunnel to the fort. Hardly anybody was around. He went straight to the rooms near the centre of the underground section, where the intelligence offices were.

Blake was pacing the corridor, but he looked up when he heard his footsteps and paused.

"Pride won't tell me a bloody thing," Blake snarled at him.

"I'll take care of it." He didn't even stop, just walked straight past him and shouldered his way through the door at the end of the hall.

It was all computers in here, and maps marked with different coloured symbols papered the walls. Five Guardians and partial Wielders were all talking at once into their headsets and tapping at the keyboards in front of them. He couldn't make any sense of what he overheard, but he knew how it worked. At least one of them would be communicating with the leaders of the teams that were sent out, another would be in touch with one of the Awakened-born cops, organising how to control the police response to what had happened. The others were probably talking to Robert and any members of Pride that had gone out to investigate.

A man with long, brown hair sat at a computer to his right. He wasn't wearing his headset and the light from the computer screen washed most of the colour out of his face. Alistair walked over and sat down in the empty chair at the station next to him.

"Here to help or looking for info?" the man asked without even looking at him.

"Info. What happened, Arthur?"

"You know I can't tell you, brother." Arthur glanced at him briefly. "But I can't do much about you looking over my shoulder."

"Thanks, bro." Alistair smiled a little.

"I didn't do anything." Arthur shrugged and pressed a key. A window appeared over the images that Arthur was working on and a dark, black and white video started playing. Alistair watched as three fuzzy figures attacked another. Light glistened off liquid rising from the ground, and the three people on the left of the screen scattered as it streamed toward them. One of the figures drew a blade and rushed towards the other, but a larger shape dodged in front. Darkness rose like a wave and blacked out everything. After that was just static.

"Fuck," Alistair whispered.

Arthur tapped the keyboard again, and the video disappeared. "Cheap-assed DIY security cameras from a shop nearby," he muttered. "Hardly worth the effort to steal the files and upload the video, but I got some facial shots we might be able to use. While you're here you can take a look at them."

Before Alistair could answer, the door opened and a Guardian entered. He looked around then spoke to Arthur. "They're back. Water Guardian took a lun skaath to the abdomen," the man said.

"Fuck me," Arthur cursed.

Alistair just felt cold.

"I'll look at those photos later," he said as he got up and walked towards the door.

Blake was already gone, he must've realised what that messenger meant. Alistair broke into a run, headed for the passage that came out in the medical centre.

He found Dylan's room quickly; it was where the blood trail stopped. A medic came out and he grabbed the man by his arm,

"You know who I am, right? You know what I am. My blood can help him."

"I…" the medic mouthed like a fish as he tried to put a response together.

"Just get Noel, fast." He released the medic and stepped back, glaring after him as he took off.

He actually didn't know if his blood would do anything for Dylan, but Noel would. He knew everything there was to know about wounds contaminated with shadow. Noel had saved Alistair's life after his mother put the Skaath Mark on him, hopefully he could save Dylan too.

***

Dylan screamed through gritted teeth and strained against Blake's hands.

"Lie still, Dylan," Blake said. He glanced over his shoulder at the medic busy behind him but couldn't see more than the top of his head.

"It burns, it burns," Dylan cried.

"Just hang in there, let the medic do his thing." He tried to sound reassuring but couldn't.

Dylan was bleak as snow, the veins under his skin looked darker than they should, and a sheen of sweat covered him. Tears ran freely from his eyes as he looked up at him.

"I think this is it," he panted.

"Don't you dare give up," Blake growled at him.

Dylan smiled. "It's not about giving up. I know you'll look after them for me but I'm asking anyway…" his words broke off into another cry of pain.

Blake didn't know what to say anymore. Gods, was he really watching one of his best friends die?

The door burst open. Blake looked over his shoulder at a silver-haired man carrying a bag of blood. Noel, one of the chief medics, and a younger guy that Blake didn't know.

"I'm starting a transfusion." Noel's blue eyes fixed on Blake as he rounded the bed. "Who are you and what are you doing in here?"

"He's holding the patient down, sir," he heard the medic reply.

"Give the man painkillers, you moron!" Noel yelled.

"I did, it isn't working yet."

The man grumbled and set up the blood on the drip stand. When he finished, he looked down at Dylan and spoke calmly. "I believe Alistair is a friend of yours. His blood has something like an antibody to Skaath, should help you while we patch you up."

"Really?" Dylan's eyes widened as he looked up at the old guy.

"Son, it's the best shot we have." He put a hand on Dylan's arm then turned to look at the medic working on him. "Jared, I want to know exactly what you've done so far. Dominic, get the theatre prepped. You," he stared at Blake, "thanks for your help, now leave."

He looked down at Dylan. "Be strong, man."

"Tell Al there better be whiskey in this blood," he replied.

14

Blake wasn't there when Vinny woke up, an hour later than usual. The house was empty, and she could only assume that whatever happened last night was responsible for this anomaly.

She set off towards the dorms as soon as she was dressed, and jogged all the way through the woods. There was nobody here either. What the hell?

The back of a black SUV was just visible past the far corner of the dorms; parked outside the building across the way. As she got closer, she saw another car, skid marks, and a trail of blood leading to the doors of the building.

White tiles and white walls filled the passage in front of her. Guardians lined the walls, and she heard cries of pain from behind some of the doors she passed. It was easy to find Blake since he was one of only a few not dressed entirely in black. In fact, he was wearing the same clothes he'd run off in last night.

She squeezed into a space next to him and tugged gently at his arm to get his attention.

"Hey." His voice sounded heavy and his features looked strained.

"What happened?" she asked.

"I don't know all the details…Dylan called for backup, but when they got there he and Elise were fighting three wenches. He was already wounded," he sighed heavily. "It looked like he might pull through for a while, but not anymore."

"You guys are close?"

Blake nodded, his jaw clenched tight. She didn't trust herself to say the right thing so she just took his hand and squeezed it gently between both of hers.

A choked wail echoed down the passage. Everyone went silent as a man with a lined face and silver hair appeared through a door. He looked right and left at the men gathered against the walls, and shook his head. He placed his right hand over his heart and everybody else did the same. They lowered their heads and spoke in one voice.

"Seeogayn a gur lees ahr dyurtaar…"

Vinny didn't know the words, barely recognised a few of them, but she mimicked the gesture, placing one hand over her heart.

"…tug shay a sheel le hayavan an sholash."

When they'd finished speaking, Blake walked away from her without saying anything. She followed him out of habit, but paused as he entered the room.

Elise was wiping Dylan's face with a cloth. Her hands were steady, every movement seemed certain and professional, but the atmosphere in the room was as dense as mist. Vinny felt like her throat was swelling shut. When she looked at the dead Guardian's face again, she had to bite her lip to keep from crying.

What a ridiculous reaction, she'd only seen him once, and never spoken to him. Sure, it was sad, but she had no reason to cry for the man.

Blake quietly circled around the foot of the bed and put his arm around Elise. The blonde woman froze then she looked up at him, and her face crumpled. He drew her against his chest and wrapped his arms around her as she wept. Heaven backed away from the Water Wielder's anguish and quietly pulled the door shut.

Many of the Guardians had left now but the evidence of their presence remained in the dirt smudged over the white tiles, and footprints left in Dylan's drying blood. One of them had left a dark smear just outside the door.

A man stood beside a wounded Guardian whose arm was being bandaged. Both looked hollow, and their eyes stared blankly at the floor. They reminded her of photos of war zones; soldiers duty-bound to death and destruction, terrified civilians plunged into a living nightmare.

Violence carved out the most vital parts of humanity and left this emptiness in its wake. She knew this because she'd seen her own eyes in the mirror.

She walked down the hallway and out. Flowers grew in unruly beds around the clinic, and behind the dormitory, and she idly wondered why hospitals always had such beautiful gardens. Was this really supposed to make you feel better? Mortality sucked but at least there were was a rose garden?

There was a wooden bench nearby, half-hidden by a bushy plant taller than she was. Heaven sat down on it and stared at the moss growing through the paving bricks. She should probably leave them to grieve and find something useful to do. She could read the lorebook, practice spells or pyrokinesis, but it didn't seem right.

Her throat was painfully tight and she tilted her head back. Thick clouds hung in the sky, fluffy and white with edges outlined in grey. They were the type of clouds that looked like they'd been painstakingly carved into being, and it was difficult to believe that something that looked so solid, wasn't.

"You feel it too?"

Alistair was looking at her; his normally caramel skin was ashen with dark smudges under his eyes.

"I didn't even know the guy, Alistair." She tried not to stare, but he looked like he wasn't far from death either.

"I know, but when Elise mourns all of us mourn with her. Empaths have that effect on people," he said gruffly.

That explained her meaningless sadness.

He sat down next to her on the bench, leaned forwards and rested his elbows on his knees. It occurred to her that she should probably offer him some form of comfort as well so she tentatively placed one hand on his back, between his shoulder blades.

"Do you understand what happened last night?" His head was turned just enough to see her with one eye.

"That somebody died? Yeah, if it's any consolation he truly is in a better place now."

"No, why he died…why he chose to give his life to save Elise," he said gruffly.

She hadn't even known he'd done that. If she thought about it then she might be able to give him the right answer, but the truth was she didn't know, so she shook her head.

"Part of being a Guardian is understanding that, when it comes to this, our war against the Skaath, we are less valuable than our Wielders," he replied.

"People are equal, it's only our aptitudes that differ." She'd heard that somewhere and always believed it should be true. It had felt true when she was dead.

"That's not what I mean." He sat back and she withdrew her hand, fiddling with a loose thread on the hem of her shirt.

"It's purely strategic," he continued, "sacrificing a knight in order to checkmate your opponent with the queen. We're equal as people but not as weapons."

Weapons…was that what she'd agreed to? Being a weapon, a tool of destruction? How could love and the magnificence of spirit she'd felt in death be a weapon? It didn't sound right.

"I'm not a gun, Alistair, not even a bullet. Far be it for me to take the moral high ground, but I was asked to love in the Between. Killing seems like the opposite of that."

He stared at her until she turned her head to look down at her hands.

"Love may be a long term solution," he said softly. "But hugging Handmaidens in the thick of a fight is just going to get a dagger in your guts. Did you know that Gandhi wrote a letter to Hitler?"

"No…"

"A noble gesture, but it didn't stop the Holocaust. Sometimes people can change because other people care about them, but not everyone wants to change, Vinny, not everyone realises that they're wrong."

She sighed. "Fair enough. Although I really don't see how talking about all of this is useful right now."

"I want you to know how important you are to us."

She stared at him for a long while, but all he really meant was that her abilities would make her more useful than Blake. Her insides turned to cold oatmeal at the thought of him lying dead in Dylan's place. He was by far too good a person to die for her.

"Why didn't they just heal him like they healed me?" she asked.

"Trueborn Handmaidens carry lun skaath, shadow blades. They inflict a wound that Sages can't heal." He glanced away as he spoke.

"Oh...they have some kind of Skaath power, or something?"

He nodded, "The lun skaath is forged with the cold fire of the Never, they're so deadly that a normal person can't even grasp the hilt without getting hurt."

She leaned back against the bench, how could a mere knife be so powerful? Alistair put a hand on her knee. She stopped fiddling with the thread, and turned her head to find him looking at her intently.

"You have to be a weapon, Vinny, it's unavoidable. But it doesn't mean you can't love too."

"I'll keep that in mind," she said, staring back at him.

"Good." He nodded and slowly withdrew his hand. For a moment, he looked lost but then he got up and walked away.

"Alistair," she called after him without thinking.

He stopped and half turned to look at her. She hesitated, not really sure what to do with the urge she felt to try to make things better.

"What is it, Vinny?" he asked.

"Are you okay? You lived with him and I got the idea that you were friends..."

His eyes reminded her of a child, they reflected the type of honest vulnerability that was terrible to destroy, but it was there and gone again in an instant.

"I'm okay...thanks for asking." He walked away and she watched him until he disappeared into the gym.

15

Dylan was cremated the next day. Half his ashes were given to his family, and half kept by the Circle, as was customary. That same evening, Blake got a message from Elise asking him to come with her to scatter his ashes at the ocean. Of course, he agreed.

He left Headrush before dawn to drive to Denysrus to pick her up, and they were on their way shortly after sunrise.

Elise held the small box on her lap; her hands hadn't left it since she got into the car. It broke his heart to see her like this, like a chisel rammed into the crack made by his friend's death. It made everything worse.

He wanted to say…something, anything that would make it better. But his words turned to dust in his throat and the sparing efforts at comfort and conversation that did make it out, hung awkwardly in the air between them.

Dylan was like a brother to him. He'd helped both him and Al get through Bryan's messed up idea of training.

When he first arrived at Headrush, he'd been the awkward kid who'd trained with his uncle instead of going to Hex. Chubby, nerdy, and shy, but thoroughly drilled in martial arts. The others hadn't appreciated his ability to knock them out with a few well-aimed strikes to their pressure points, and Bryan hadn't liked him either. He and Alistair had formed a friendship of sorts, and teamed up to figure out how they could prove themselves and pass training to become Guardians.

Then Dylan caught them climbing the fort. Instead of scolding them, he'd raced them to the top and won. He'd never forget the sight of him leaning over from the top of the water tower, joking that he'd take a piss over his head.

Blake blinked away tears and focused on the road in front of him. There was some comfort in the fact that Dylan's death had been honourable, that he would do the same for Vinny. Saying those things to Elise wouldn't lighten the loss a Wielder felt from the death of her Guardian.

Rochelle had told him that Arnold's death had played as big a role in her decision to retire as her stiffening joints and slowing reactions, that she'd blamed herself, that every Wielder blamed herself.

He'd been thinking so hard about the right things to say that he only realised they were there, that the silence had filled their journey, when he almost drove past the exit turn.

Coastal towns had a strange air to them during the cold months, like dropping in on somebody unannounced and finding them in their pyjamas with their teeth unbrushed. He parked at the beach where Dylan had taught him to surf just last year, and opened the door for Elise. Together they walked down to the pier and stood at the edge with the sound and smell of the sea all around them.

Elise opened the box carefully, as though she might break it, then leaned forward over the railing and tipped Dylan's ashes into the grey ocean. There wasn't enough wind to scatter them; most of it fell straight down into the water while the finer particles disappeared into the air.

It was over so fast.

Elise closed the box without looking, her eyes fixed on the water, and then she leaned back and took a deep breath.

"Are you okay?" Blake asked softly.

She glanced at him, her eyes sparkling with moisture, but didn't reply. She stared out at the waves again and crossed her arms.

Maybe he ought to stop trying to get her to speak. She obviously had no interest in talking to him, maybe she didn't even see him as a friend at all, but just a guy she'd once counselled. Why had she even asked him to come with her?

"I lied to everyone," she said, still watching the waves.

Her voice sounded rough, she must've spent most of the time since Dylan died in tears.

"What do you mean?" Blake asked.

"Dylan and I were already together. He saw the wenches walk past the video store while I was buying popcorn and we both decided to follow them. We hoped they would lead us back to their Coven house."

"Why did you..." he paused, and his heart cracked a little wider. "You and Dylan?"

She nodded then let out a laugh that was all fragile edges. "You know what the irony is? We'd just decided to announce ourselves to Robert, stop hiding and make it official. Now he's gone and I..." she paused and swallowed hard.

"I'm so sorry, Elise, he never even hinted to me that you were a couple."

She nodded, tucked her hair behind her ear, and looked up at him, lost and forlorn. "Blake, part of why we wanted to make it official now is because I'm pregnant, we intended to get married."

He bobbed his head automatically, before his brain fully registered what she'd just said.

"I...I can't raise a child alone, Blake, I can't," she continued. "Dylan was my strength and my stability. He was my lighthouse when my Empathy turned the world into a raging storm. How can I do this without him?" She couldn't wipe the tears away fast enough to keep up with them.

Blake put his arm around her shoulder. "I'll help you," he said with more confidence that he felt. "You just call me anytime you need something, and I'll be there. Dylan was a good friend, it's the least I can do for him, and I owe you one."

"I couldn't possibly expect that of you." Elise shook her head.

"Even if you never take me up on it, the offer stands. Always. You were there for me when Maya died, and I'm here for you now."

"You're such a good person, Blake." She sniffed. "But what you're offering is too much."

"Just accept it, Elise. I don't want you to worry about any of this."

Her bottom lip quivered, and he hugged her as she started sobbing again. When she put her arms around him, all he could feel was the side of the box pressing into his back.

It felt like they stood there like that for a long time, but eventually Elise extricated herself from his embrace and turned back towards the ocean with a determined look.

"I'm selfish," she said, her voice low as she wiped her eyes. "I brought him here so he'd always be a part of me, part of my element. This is selfish too."

"Accepting help isn't selfish, Elise." He reached out to touch her arm.

"Oh, Blake."

"Let's get out of the cold, there's a coffee shop nearby, when last did you eat?"

"Last night." She shrugged and allowed him to lead her away.

"Dylan wouldn't want you to stop taking care of yourself."

"I know that," she snapped. "That's what makes it so difficult. All I want to do is curl into a ball and stay in bed but I can't, it's not just me anymore."

He'd felt the same when Maya died. He'd gone home for the funeral and stayed on; sleeping in her bed to feel close to her, but it hadn't helped. His soul still knew that part of it was gone.

"Nothing is going to make you feel better, not now, and not anytime soon. In time, it gets easier but until then you still have to live. A part of him is still with you, Elise, your child will always be a link to him."

"I know," she sniffed. "He was so happy that he was going to be a father. I only realised recently and he wanted to tell you and Alistair..."

"It's okay, I understand," he said around the lump in his throat.

"No, it isn't. I knew you guys wouldn't betray his trust but I still told him he couldn't do that. I'm such a bitch," she sobbed.

"Don't do this to yourself, things happen and there's nothing that anybody can do to change the past."

"He was so happy…"

"Take that as a good thing." They'd reached the end of the pier and he looked down at her. "We don't have to stay here if it's too difficult; we can get some take-aways and eat in the car."

"Its fine, I don't think I'm ready to go just yet."

"Okay, whatever you want." He placed a hand on the small of her back, and guided her to the coffee shop. It was a small place across from the beach, with an upstairs terrace that looked out over the sea. The last time he'd been here it was full of surfers and stoners, and he'd felt like the stranger he was. Dylan had fit in, of course. His friendly nature had put everyone at ease anywhere he went.

Blake sighed. Life just wouldn't be the same without him.

***

Spot crouched on the piece of bark that filled a quarter of her enclosure. Dylan's father had collected everything else he owned earlier that day, but he wouldn't take the tarantula because his wife was arachnophobic. Judging by the look on his face, she wasn't the only one.

So Alistair had moved the table Spot's terrarium rested on and the small heater beneath it to his room. Now he was sitting here, watching her do absolutely nothing.

"You aren't a very exciting pet, are you, Spot?" He drank some coffee then folded his hands around the mug again.

Spot didn't even twitch.

"Sure, you have the creepy factor going for you, and this book says you like to dig…" He peered at the open book on tarantula care beside him on the bed to check that he remembered correctly. "But that's pretty much it, isn't it?"

Still nothing.

Alistair had never had a pet before. There'd been animals around when he lived with his mother, but they were all Handmaidens' familiars—the furthest from friendly that an animal could get. He still had scars from the one time he'd stroked his mother's German Shepherd, if she hadn't been linked to the dog then it probably would've mauled him.

Logically, he knew that those were twisted creatures in extraordinary circumstances, but it had put him off having animals around. Yet here he was with a pet Tarantula, of all things.

He blew out a sigh and wondered if this was Dylan's last stupid joke.

Alistair drained the rest of his coffee, got up, and placed his empty mug on the desk where he was charging Dylan's phone. He hadn't told his father that he had the phone because he hoped he'd be able to find out who Dylan had been dating. He wanted to meet the girl who'd turned his head, even if it was just to tell her that he was gone.

He switched the phone on and stared at the background picture, a photo of some airborne skateboarder with the ocean behind him. No clues there.

Alistair tapped the icon for the message application and looked at the names on the screen. Mike was there, Blake, himself, Elise, and a few names he didn't recognise—one of them was a girl. He tapped on her name and read the last few messages, a conversation about surfing. No 'chat later, baby' or 'I love you' or cute emoticons.

He looked through the other contacts. Some of the girls had cute couple pictures up but none of them featured Dylan. One girl was pulling a duckface pose, but Dylan had her listed as 'Stalker Ho from Joe's'.

Yeah, he wouldn't have been serious about an easy girl, no man would. Dylan's girlfriend would be a woman with guts and personality, he thought.

The opposite of what he usually looked for.

Alistair sighed, why was he doing this? What would he even say to this girl? 'Hi, I'm a friend of Dylan's and I thought you should know that your boyfriend is dead'.

That was a real winner of a line right there. Line…as if he was planning to chat her up. He shook his head and exited the application. He wasn't the right man for this job. If he really wanted to do Dylan a favour then he'd tell Blake about the mystery girl and give the phone to him, he'd handle it much better than he ever could.

The worst part was that he probably would end up trying to chat her up, that was what he always did. He made a play then threw them away, ever since Erika left him because his mother happened to be a Handmaiden.

It wasn't like he'd chosen her, or the Skaath Mark she gave him. He certainly hadn't chosen to be abandoned by her.

On the other hand, he'd never have become a Guardian if she hadn't left him. He'd read the note she'd tucked into his pocket so often that the words were burnt into his mind,

'I'd hoped the Jackal would overpower his Awakened genes, I didn't know this would happen. He's a kind child, even if he survives, there's no place for him here. Please, take him as one of your own. It's his only chance.'

Kind. He sniffed, maybe by Coven standards but certainly not in general. Dylan had said he was a good guy, but would Gina, Pam, Ella, or any other girl he'd used say the same thing? Alistair doubted it.

And if he couldn't even deliver a message to Dylan's girlfriend, what right did he have to so much as look at Blake's Wielder? Absolutely none.

He thought about what Vinny had said about love, and his reply that she could love and be a weapon. He'd thought he believed it at the time but now…what did he know about love?

***

Blake stopped by his uncle's place to pick up his guitar before returning to Headrush. It was the latter part of the afternoon, and David would be working so he let himself into the townhouse, and padded to the spare room. His guitar case lay on the bed. Blake walked across and grabbed the handle, as he lifted it, he heard a soft click from the passage.

"It's me, Uncle." He turned towards the door.

"Blake? What are you doing here?" David stepped into the doorway. He had a gun in his hand but his arm was relaxed and it was pointing at the ground.

"I missed my guitar," Blake said.

David narrowed his eyes, watching him as he flicked on the safety, and tucked the gun away. His dad had never looked at him so shrewdly, his dad hadn't noticed him much at all, but somehow David reminded him of his father anytime he gave Blake that look.

"Did something happen?" David asked softly.

"Dylan is dead," he replied. "They were able to counter most of the effects of the lun skaath using Al's blood, but she must've given the blade a good twist when she stabbed him. He was all messed up inside."

"I'm sorry, Blake. He was a good man." David came closer and put a hand on his shoulder.

"He was."

"It's never easy when one of us dies," David sighed. His uncle narrowed his eyes at him. "Do they know who it was?"

"No, not yet."

"Ah…but they will be found, and punished for this, no matter how long it may take."

Blake nodded. He knew David was trying to reassure him, but he didn't have the strength for one of his rambles.

"I should get going," he said, moving towards the bedroom door.

"Be strong, lad, and take care of yourself, alright?" David gave him that look again as he moved past him, and Blake wondered how much double meaning was in those few words.

"Always, Uncle." He forced himself to smile weakly.

He wedged the guitar case into the passenger seat so it would be nearby, and glanced at it every now and then as he drove back to Headrush. Every time he looked at it, he felt his heart beat a little bit faster. But he wasn't planning to do anything. He just needed it nearby.

He still couldn't believe everything that had happened in the past few days. Dylan was gone. Gone. And Elise was carrying his child. They'd practically been engaged.

All this time he'd been waiting for the right time to start something with her. Countless hours spent pacing his room at Headrush, wondering if it was fair to ask her out when half an hour's drive separated them. He'd juggled the distance and the dating rule in his head until it drove him crazy. So many nights when he'd gone to bed, sick with longing.

All of it for nothing.

Dylan obviously hadn't felt the same reservations about getting involved with her. How long had they been seeing each other?

Dylan would never see his child, what right did he have to feel jealous over their relationship? Or even to feel sorry for himself because no amount of help he gave Elise would ever make her love him.

The anger he felt was almost tangible, and he hated himself for it. At the end of the day, Dylan had been a far better man than he'd ever be, and Elise had been better off with him. She'd called Dylan her lighthouse, and he knew exactly what she meant by that. It was the same way he felt about her.

He could never give Elise what she needed.

Blake followed the dirt road through the woods to Rochelle's house. It was in awful condition, but he didn't particularly care about his car's suspension today.

He went straight up to his room and shut the door then set the case down on the bed and opened it. The guitar wasn't some expensive make but it played nicely, and the dark, reddish wood produced a good sound.

He sat and drew the guitar across his lap, holding it with one hand as he reached inside the case with the other.

Years ago he'd promised himself that he'd never cut again, but he hadn't been able to throw away his razor blade. Instead, he'd made a slit in the lining of his guitar case and hidden it there. He closed his eyes as he traced his fingers over the outline, his heart beat faster with anticipation, but his breathing slowed. He could almost feel the rush of relief he'd get if he used it.

Blake took a deep breath, removed his hand, and distracted himself from the tactile memory of that shape beneath his fingers by pressing them against the guitar strings.

He began to play a song by Seether, mouthing the words as he poured his pain into the music.

16

"Stop!" Alistair shook his head. "This isn't working."

Heaven straightened up and looked at him. She and Blake had been doing battle training for the past half an hour. She was just starting to think she might be able to do this after all, but now they had to stop?

"You're going too easy on her." Alistair frowned at Blake.

"She's still getting the hang of everything." Blake shook his hair out of his eyes as he stood up straight.

"She's never going to learn that way."

Blake put his hands on his hips and stared at Alistair. "Going full on isn't the best approach here, Al."

"Don't mind me, standing right here," Vinny mumbled to herself as she crossed her arms.

Alistair shook his head and walked right up to Blake, but they spoke too softly to hear what they were saying. Blake had crossed his arms when Alistair approached, but after a minute, he shoved his hands in his pockets and lowered his head, nodding. Alistair slapped him on the arm then walked towards her with his lips curved into a faint smile.

"You're going to play with me for a while, Vinny," he said.

She wasn't sure that she liked this idea, but Blake was already walking away to where Nadia leaned against the tennis court fence.

"Don't worry." Alistair took a step closer. "I'll go easy on you. Ready?"

She gripped the lighter Nadia had given her in her fist and nodded.

He was behind her in a flash, one hand on her shoulder while the other twisted her arm up behind her.

"Focus, Heaven," he said next to her ear. His breath blew warmly against her neck.

"You never even gave me a chance!" Her heart pounded, but it was just training. Nothing to be scared of.

"If you'd been paying attention then you could've dodged me, too late now, but you can still get away before I give you a nice, big hug."

She wrenched and wriggled, elbowed him in the ribs and stomped on his toes. He let her go and she skipped a few paces away to put distance between them.

Those brown eyes watched her with such intensity, like floodlights dragging across every inch of her. She felt a blush rising in her cheeks, but then he was moving towards her again.

She flicked the lighter and sent a short burst of flame at his feet. Any normal person would've paused, but Alistair jumped over the fire before it even hit the ground and made a grab for her. She ducked around and past him, reached for the fire, and manipulated it to arrow across the clay towards him.

It missed by a mile so she called up another fireball, and shot it at him while backing away. She wanted to keep space between them, but he just kept coming.

Trying to focus on both things at once was distracting. She didn't even realise she'd allowed him to get too close until it was too late. She turned to run away and he grabbed her from behind. Alistair's arms tightened around her, trapping hers against her sides as he darn near squeezed all the air from her lungs out against his chest.

"Maybe you just don't mind me hugging you so much after all," he said.

"Is this the real reason you wanted to partner with me?" she gasped. "Get your hands all over me?"

"You have a dirty mind, Vinny."

She'd said it to make him feel uncomfortable, had hoped his arms would relax enough for her to fight free, or he'd feel offended enough to release her entirely. Since it hadn't worked, she lowered her head then whipped it back to hit him on the shoulder. He inhaled sharply then dropped her.

"You're supposed to be practicing with fire," he said.

"While you feel me up, Alistair?" She turned to face him while backing away.

"All right, next time I catch you, I'll take you down hard. Does that work better for you?" He watched her through narrowed eyes.

"And you think my mind is dirty." She had the lighter ready and shot a fireball at him.

"You just proved it is." He had the nerve to laugh as he dodged her attack.

Damn him. She struck a flame and swept her arm through the air, sending a stream of fire blazing towards his face. He ducked sideways but she pulled on the fire and it landed near his feet. As he leapt backwards, the fire followed. Vinny grinned as she chased him around the court with her flames.

It didn't last very long though. After a few minutes, the fire began to sputter and shrink, and then he was after her again. She was concentrating on making another fireball as he tackled her to the ground.

Everything blurred as the back of her head struck the clay. By the time she'd regained her senses, Alistair had her pinned down and was looking at her smugly from a few centimetres away.

Too close, too vulnerable. She squeezed her eyes shut and cried out the first offensive spell that came to mind.

"Arsheel!"

Alistair flew into the air as though he'd caught a hit to his stomach from a massive fist. Vinny rolled away and got up onto her knees.

"Bairt Malla," Alistair cried.

The spell breaker worked and he dropped down, landing on his feet.

He glanced over at her and smiled. "Not bad, sweetheart. You do better under pressure—does it bring out your survival instinct?"

She sneered and turned towards the gate, ignoring his question. She'd panicked, but at least he hadn't noticed.

"Let's try that again," he said behind her.

She swallowed hard and turned to face him. Her body hummed with adrenalin, it screamed at her to flee, but she had to fight instead. Alistair shifted his weight and she prepared herself to fire at him.

He dashed towards her and she dodged, turning to face him as she backed away. She flicked the lighter, held tightly in her gloved hand, but it didn't light and Alistair was already approaching again.

Her stomach knotted and she tried to tell herself that it was just training. It felt real, he was looking at her like she was his prey. She flicked the lighter again.

He was too close, less than two metres between them. Every time she tried to widen that gap, he was fast to close it again.

Trey might be behind her, but it seemed like she'd always be fighting. Always be staring into another person's eyes and trying to read the measure of violence within them. She'd thought her life would be peaceful, hadn't the voices in the Between implied that?

Alistair grabbed her arm. She swung towards him, and thrust her palm up at his face. His eyes widened, and then he twisted and sent her reeling away from him.

"And here I thought you were daydreaming," he called out.

Vinny hit the fence and wrapped her fingers around the chain link.

No. No more victim.

She turned to glare at Alistair. The floating warmth she'd felt on her first morning at Hex spread through her chest. Again, she felt like the flames of the Phoenix were all around her. She wasn't powerless anymore.

This time the lighter shot out an inferno, and she aimed it straight at his chest. Alistair dropped but the edges caught his shirt, and he rolled on the clay, beating at the smoking cloth. She built up a fireball in her hand and threw it at him. It missed, but he rolled right into it.

"Call it back!"

There was pain in his voice, it satisfied her—and that made her feel sick.

The lighter fell through her fingers and she stretched her hand out to the flames, but it was too late. Tongues of orange and red sucked into the air as Nadia rushed towards them, Blake pulling ahead of her.

She felt distant as they helped Alistair up, and watched Nadia fuss over him as though she was seeing it through a telescope.

The warmth still filled her. It didn't feel like she'd done something wrong. Alistair might've been hurt, but he wasn't. His clothes weren't even that badly burnt.

She'd actually beaten him.

She was fire.

All across her upper back, the muscles and skin pulled painfully tight. It was the worst cramp she'd ever experienced, and she clenched her jaw as she turned and leaned against the fence. Her shirt pulled tight over her front for a moment then fell back against her. The weirdest feeling crept across her upper back, like her skin was on fire, but it tickled rather than burnt.

Golden wings spread out on either side of her, and flames rippled along the edge of each feather. They were both brighter and warmer than the bleak winter sun overhead.

"Holy crap! I want to be able to do that!" Nadia called out behind her.

Vinny turned, and almost fell as the wings moved, but they shifted to correct her balance. The Guardians were staring, Alistair on his feet now, and Nadia was bouncing towards her. The Fire Wielder ran her fingers across the long flight feathers, grinning as the flames stuck to her fingers.

"Check it out!" She strode back to Alistair with her hand up. "How awesome would it be if I had wings?"

"Spare me, its hard enough to keep track of you as is," he replied.

He sounded different, and now she did feel a bit bad. She'd gone overboard and could've hurt him. The wings faded away as the warm feeling left her.

"Nicely done." Blake smiled as he approached her.

"What was that?" she asked, even though she thought she already knew.

"It's the Phoenix," he replied. "Heavenly talismans can manifest physically, they serve their wearer's need."

"How does that work?" Heaven looked up at him.

"Generally talismans respond to focused thoughts or intense emotions, thoughts are normally better than emotions to activate them."

"Why?"

"Using emotional triggers takes more out of you, in my opinion. It's like good acting, I suppose, the type where an actor becomes so immersed in their character that they almost literally become them. It might take a little more effort but learning to concentrate is the best method."

"How am I going to do that?"

"Practice." He placed a hand on her shoulder. "I'll teach you."

"Of course you will." She forced a little smile.

"That's enough for one day," Alistair said. He nodded at her. "Good job."

"Thanks," she muttered, avoiding his eyes.

"You're pretty fast, you know." Blake gave her a shrewd look. "Especially on defence."

She narrowed her eyes at him. "So? I'm still not strong."

"Fighting isn't all about strength, Vinny, not everybody is strong, and not everybody is fast. You play to your individual strengths."

***

The fire had shaken Alistair more than he cared to admit. Nadia had had her fair share of accidents over the years, and if anybody was used to being set alight, it was him, but this had been different somehow.

He lined up another golf ball on the green square in front of him then walloped it down the range. It soared skywards like a miniature cannon ball, and he smiled as he lined up the next one.

There were few things as relaxing as hitting something with all your strength, be it a training dummy, a punching bag, a golf ball, or a face. He hadn't gone out looking for a fight since he was fifteen, but faces would always be on the list.

Maybe that was it. There'd been fury behind Vinny's fire, and Nadia had never attacked him like that. And those wings...she'd looked like a vengeful angel sent to burn the world down. It was hot in more ways than one.

He'd come here to clear his mind, not to think about her. Alistair positioned another ball and hit it as hard as he could, then another one. He concentrated on moving as quickly and efficiently as possible: position the ball, grip the club, swing and connect, then place the next ball. It was easy to forget himself this way, and it worked, until he reached into the ball bucket and found it empty.

"Damn," he muttered.

He took the plastic bucket back inside the shop and put it on the counter. The blonde girl at the cash register, Claudia or Carla, something with a 'C', licked her lips and flicked her hair as she straightened up, but he turned around and left before she could say anything.

***

She climbed into bed and sat there. Even now, she was too hyped up to sleep. She spread the shirt she'd worn earlier across her lap, and stared down at it. The material was hard and discoloured around the slits the wings had burnt through it. She pulled the Phoenix free, held it in her palm, and ran her thumb over one of the wings as she remembered what it felt like when they sprouted from her back.

She should've flown, why the heck hadn't she? How often had she dreamed of flying, but when she got the chance, it didn't even occur to her to try it.

She'd lost it with Alistair, how could she face him after that? What the hell was wrong with her? Self-control was a trait she'd nurtured into rigid, infallible strength. It had held under far greater pressure than what she went through today, so why had she snapped like that? She'd been slipping further into chaos ever since she started wearing the Phoenix.

She narrowed her eyes at the talisman. "Are you the reason I'm acting like a crazy person?"

The Phoenix tilted its head to look at her, the ruby chips it had instead of eyes caught the light and reflected it around the room. Vinny was too shocked to do anything except gape at it.

A crest of long feathers unfolded from the bird's neck and it felt warmer for a second, but then it tucked its head in against its chest and went still again.

If it weren't for the fact that its position was entirely different from when she'd received it, she would've thought that she'd dreamed it.

17

"Remember the sensation of the wings coming out. Imagine it strongly and clearly in your mind."

Vinny scrunched her eyes closed and tried to recall the sensation as vividly as possible.

"Have you got it?" Blake asked.

"Uh huh." She nodded.

"Use that memory, picture it happening again now."

She tried; she willed the wings to emerge as hard as she could, but felt nothing.

It was difficult to face, but she replayed the moment with Alistair in her head like a video on repeat. If she could identify what triggered the Phoenix to respond to her then maybe she could repeat it. She'd been angry and scared but all of it had vanished when the warmth filled her body. It had been so good to let it take over.

Her back muscles contracted hard and she tilted forward, but just as she felt like she'd accomplished something, it disappeared.

"Damn it!" she snarled.

Vinny grabbed the talisman through her shirt, the same shirt she'd been wearing when it first happened. At first, it had been a reminder that it really had happened, but now it seemed to be mocking her.

"It'll take time, most things do," he said calmly.

She looked up at Blake with narrowed eyes. He was missing the point without even realising it. It wasn't so much about getting it right as it was about flying, wanting to feel the freedom of open space beneath her and all around her.

"How much time, Blake?" she snapped. "We've been doing this for three days now and nothing happens."

"You can't force it and getting angry won't help either."

"It sure helped the first time."

Blake swept his hair out of his eyes with one hand. "I know it's frustrating, but it will come eventually."

She sighed and slumped down on the grass. They were in a glade at the edge of the woods, roughly halfway between the Guardian complex and Rochelle's house but higher up. The trees spread out here, and she could see the top of the hills and sky between their trunks.

"Let's go punch bags for a while." He gave her a crooked smile. "You need to blow off steam."

"You go…" Her eyes found the top of the water tower. "I think I'll just walk around for a while."

"Sure?"

"Yes." She glanced at him as she got up.

"Don't be too long, it's going to start getting dark soon."

"Not that soon." She tucked her thumbs in her pockets and strolled away up the hill.

She'd had an idea but doubted he would approve of it. Blake had said the talisman responded to the wearer's need, if she could find a high enough spot then maybe the thing would work.

Most of the trees were straight trunks with branches far beyond her reach. There were a couple of huge stones in the area, but they wouldn't be high enough.

Once she was over the top of the hill, she looked at the tower again. It was the tallest thing around, and it would probably have an access ladder, like electric pylons did. She jogged towards it along the bottom of the hill, to reduce the risk of running into anybody. Nobody wandered around here, that's why Blake had picked this area for her to practice.

Soon she saw the dorms and the side of the gym up ahead. Vinny leaned against a tree near the edge of the woods and watched the buildings. A few Guardians came and went, but none of them ventured around the back. She waited until there was nobody around, ran to the edge of the gym, and ducked out of sight behind it.

She made her way along the wall. All the windows were set high up until she reached the back of the clinic, judging by the beds she saw through the first window. Avoiding the windows slowed her down, but eventually she came to the end of the building. The tower was just a few metres away. Fortunately, the gardens provided further cover. It was easy to sneak from one shrub to the next until she reached the rough ground that sloped upwards to the base of the tower.

She circled around the bottom of the structure. There were evenly spaced holes in one section of the tower, they ascended for as high as she could make them out. Intriguing, but useless, since they wouldn't help her get up.

"What are you doing?"

She jumped and spun around. Alistair was standing a short distance away, watching her.

"Looking at the wall," she said, like it was a perfectly normal thing to do. "What are you doing? I thought you left ages ago."

He shook his head. "I've been helping with the investigation into which Coven killed Dylan."

"Coven…makes it sound like they're witches."

"Witches aren't the only people who use that word. Are you having fun?"

"What?"

"Looking at the wall." Alistair smiled as he jerked his head toward the structure.

"Er…" This was awkward.

"What are you really doing here, Vinny?" he walked toward her as he spoke, making surprising little noise as he moved through the dry grass.

"I wanted to climb it. What does it matter anyway? Did I cross some invisible 'no entry past this point' line?"

"Not exactly, climbing the tower is prohibited though. They removed the outer ladder years ago." He gestured towards the holes in the wall. "I presume that's what you were looking for?"

"Yeah…" She narrowed her eyes. "How did you find me if nobody is supposed to be hang around here?"

"I was talking to a guy in the camera room. Going round the back was a smart move, we actually lost you for a while in the gardens."

Vinny looked up at the tower. She would've noticed if there were cameras.

"They're small and well hidden," he said, as though he'd read her mind.

He was grinning like a lottery winner. She groaned and walked away, there had to be a place she could climb around here.

"Why do you want to climb up there anyway?" He fell into step at her side.

"Just because." She shrugged. "How many cameras are there around here?"

"Enough," he laughed. "What are you up to, Vinny?"

"Training, that's what I'm here for, right?"

She picked her way down the hill towards the dorms. It was steeper on this side but she was able to use the stones in the ground almost like stairs. She stepped on a rock and it shifted under her. Before she could fall, Alistair caught her elbow.

"Before you break an ankle, why don't you just tell me what you're doing? Maybe I can help."

He stood so close that she felt the warmth radiating off his body. She bit her lip and eased her arm out of his grip.

"Blake said the talisman responds to need, so I reckoned that if I climbed up high enough…"

"The wings would come out again," he finished her thought. "It might work, but shouldn't Blake be supervising this little experiment?"

"I barely know Blake, but even I realise that he'd never agree to this."

"No Guardian would knowingly put a Wielder in danger, or allow her to endanger herself."

She sighed, his choice of words suggested that he didn't like the idea either.

"You're going to try to stop me?" she asked.

"I'm going to suggest an alternative," he replied, smirking at her with a mischievous look in his eyes.

"Let's hear it then, what's your alternative?" She couldn't help but smile back at him.

"Follow me and I'll show you." He walked off, glancing back at her over his shoulder.

She might as well see what it was, right? She jogged to catch up to him, and walked a little way off to his side as they crossed the lawn in front of the dorms, and headed into the woods.

"I'm guessing you haven't had any luck getting the Phoenix to obey you?" he asked.

"Nope."

Alistair made a thoughtful noise and kept on walking. He was leading her downhill, and soon they were all alone, nothing but chirruping birds and the sounds of their footsteps. It felt awkward. He'd been walking fast before, but now they strolled along.

"So, how's that investigation going?" she asked after a while.

"We have a few leads but nothing concrete yet. A couple of Handmaidens have claimed they did it, but they're obviously lying."

"How can you be so sure?"

"They're posers, a bunch of recruits trying to act like they're important." He turned his head to look at her. "It works in our favour though. Sooner or later, the Trueborns who did it will want to put them in their place for trying to steal the glory."

"Trueborns are more powerful, right?"

"Yes, but it varies. Each Coven serves a particular Skaath Diurga, and whichever Handmaiden their Lord or Lady Diurga favours the most, is the most powerful. Sometimes that's a recruit but usually it's the Matron of the Coven, the leader."

"How many Diurga are there?"

"About twenty, but only six of them are really powerful."

"Only six." She rolled her eyes. "How reassuring."

"Their rivalries make them weak." He was watching her, a slight smile curling his lips. "Competition is fierce, both in the Covens, and amongst the Diurga themselves. They don't do teamwork."

That lorebook the Keeper gave her didn't mention any of this, not that she'd read it from cover to cover, but she had skimmed through it.

"Does that mean Trueborns can summon more Skaath than a recruit?" she asked.

Alistair shook his head. "Recruits can't summon Skaath, but they can use their own shadow to spy on others. High ranked Trueborns, however, can summon more Skaath than those ranked beneath them, more powerful types of Skaath too."

"How many different types are there?" she asked, not much liking the sound of 'more powerful' Skaath.

Alistair slowed even more and frowned at her. "Hasn't Blake told you about this?" he asked.

She shook her head.

"That dumbass and his kid glove treatment." He sniffed. "Listen, being able to summon Skaath beasts doesn't automatically mean that the caller can control them. Munchers, Skaath hounds, are fairly obedient so you'll encounter them the most. Rippers look like cats and are almost as fickle as a feline, and then you get Spitters. They don't look much like anything, but if you picture a big, badass Komodo dragon, you won't be far off."

She almost wished she hadn't asked, but she probably needed to know this, and Alistair either knew more about it, or was simply more willing to discuss it than Blake was.

"Why do you call them Spitters?"

"They spit globs of poison that eat your flesh," he replied matter of factly.

"Why didn't I guess?" she mumbled, mostly to herself.

Alistair sniggered and put a hand on her shoulder. "You can always tell when they're about to spit, makes it relatively easy to dodge it, and you're good at that."

"Very encouraging." She glanced at him through her eyelashes. "What other twisted beasties do I need to look out for?"

"Those are the most common types; the others require a lot of will-power to control. You get big cats, a Skaath that looks like a pterodactyl…"

"What about jackals?" she asked, remembering the creature in her dream.

He stiffened, or maybe she imagined it because when she blinked, he looked just as relaxed as before.

"The Fox Coven used a jackal Skaath given to them by their Diurga, but that Coven was destroyed a long time ago."

"Okay then." She pretended to look straight ahead but stole a glance at him the moment he turned his gaze from her. He still seemed perfectly at ease.

"Almost there," he said a few moments later, walking on ahead of her.

'There' turned out to be the Demon.

She stopped dead and stared at him. "Your idea had better be something more inspired than just me running through an obstacle course."

"It is." He smiled and carried on walking.

Alistair led her to a frame standing nearly three storeys high with a cargo net spanning it from top to bottom.

She leaned back to look up at it then glanced at him. "You're kidding, right?"

He shook his head. "Race to the top?"

Vinny snorted. "Yeah, sure, then we'll have a tea party."

She gripped the net and started up it. It swayed as she moved, more so when he joined her.

"Come on, Vinny, we don't have all day you know?"

She glanced at him, "You've probably climbed this thing thousands of times for fun."

"Your point being?" He arched his eyebrows at her.

"The unfair advantage, obviously."

Alistair laughed and moved past her, headed for the top at double her speed.

What a show off.

Her arms were tired by the time she reached the top and half crawled over. There was a narrow platform beneath her, but she was just too short to reach it, and there was no railing on it for her to catch hold of if she stumbled. She hung from the large top beam and considered her options.

"Want me to help you down?" Alistair placed one hand beside hers, not quite close enough to touch.

"I'm good," she muttered, and reached under the beam to grab the net with one hand before dropping down to her feet.

She let out a deep breath and turned to peer over the edge of the platform.

"Here, give me your hands."

Vinny turned to look at Alistair. There was a spark of joy in his brown eyes as he held his hands, palm upwards, waiting for her.

"Come on, its part of the plan," he said.

She moved towards him and put her hands in his, looking up at him as his fingers closed around her.

"This glove is a bit slippery." He rubbed the back of her hand with his thumb. "Have you got a good enough grip, or do you want to take it off?"

"The glove stays on." She edged backwards, regretting this now. His proximity made her heart beat faster and her mouth dry up.

"Okay then." He shrugged and stepped toward her.

"What exactly is your plan, Alistair?" She stepped back to keep him from getting too close.

He smiled, moved close enough for her to feel his breath against her face, and then swung her out so she dangled over the edge of the platform. One of her feet slipped off the edge and her body swayed.

"I really think you should've taken the glove off." He smiled as he tightened his grip on her left hand.

"Alistair, this isn't funny!" She looked over her shoulder at the earth below her, ruddy brown and packed hard by the passage of feet.

She closed her eyes. He wouldn't drop her; she'd get hurt if she fell—badly fucking hurt. He wouldn't allow that, she really hoped not.

He pulled her up a bit, and let her drop again.

The wings emerged, burning the shirt even more. Near hysterical laughter burst from her mouth as they stretched out on either side of her. Then the wings tilted, lifting her away from the platform. Both her feet were in the air now and she dug her nails into his hands as she bit back a wail.

He tugged on her arms and she crashed into him. She vaguely realised he'd caught her as she reached past him and clenched her hands around the net behind him.

"Easy, you're safe now," he murmured close to her ear.

"You..." her voice sounded shaky, not angry.

"It worked, that was the point," he said softly. "I knew you wouldn't trust me to keep you from falling."

She scowled up at him with angry words on the tip of her tongue, but he looked...sad?

"I don't trust anyone." She was pressed against him, one of his hands was on her hip, holding her, and his other arm was wrapped around her. She didn't know if she liked it or hated it.

The wings had faded without her notice. She'd missed another opportunity to fly.

"You trust Blake," he said, tilting his head to look into her eyes.

"Yeah…" Vinny leaned back and stepped sideways, away from him. "In some ways. Blake's a softie."

"He has frustrated brotherly urges."

That sounded about right. She'd never caught a glimpse of lust in his evident affection for her, and it shed new light on the way he'd had his arm around Paula. She looked at Alistair; maybe he also had frustrated brotherly urges.

"Thanks for your help." She looked around. "Now how do I get down?"

"Vinny, it wouldn't have worked if I'd told you what I was going to do."

She looked at him, it took a moment to realise what he meant.

"I get that," she replied.

"Good." He smiled. "Getting down is the fun part."

He turned and walked to the far edge of the platform and fiddled with something attached to the frame. She followed more cautiously, keeping a hand on the net. A steel cable she hadn't noticed before ran from the frame to the ground at a gentle angle.

"Bonus points for me if your wings make another appearance." He glanced at her as she stopped beside him.

"Could you be any smugger?"

He laughed and gave her a long, steady look. "Maybe."

"Now who has a dirty mind?" She laughed.

"That'll still be you." He turned, holding a simple t-shaped bar attached to the wire. He angled it towards her. "Hold on tight."

"Obviously." She turned and wrapped her hands around the metal. It was rough, like a file, but didn't have the best grip.

He positioned himself behind her and placed one hand on her side. "For the record," his voice was low and warm against her neck, "I like being a feature in your dirty mind."

She turned her head to retort but he pushed her.

Her body jerked as her arms took her weight and she squealed. Everything rushed past her and the wind pressed against her body.

The ground was racing toward her and there weren't any brakes on this thing. Closer, closer, there was a muddy patch near the bottom. If she dropped into that, she might not break her legs.

She let go and time seemed to stop, even her heart stood still, then she splatted into the icy mud. The shock of it snapped her out of her fear and she crawled towards the edge swearing.

***

Alistair laughed as he grabbed a bar for himself, and he was still laughing as he dropped down to the dry ground just past the pit and rolled to his feet.

"Asshole!"

He turned towards her and a lump of mud struck his shoulder.

"Shit, that's cold." He pulled a face as he flicked it off his shirt.

"No need to tell me." She was using her hands to scrape mud off her pants and lower abdomen, giving him a glimpse of skin.

More mud flicked in his direction, some of it landed on his jeans and he took a step back.

"What the hell?"

"You were staring." Vinny gave him a satisfied look. "No wonder you 'like being a feature' in my dirty mind."

Oh crap, did he really say that to her?

"Dirty all over now." He turned away. Couldn't he say something nice instead of crass innuendos? "Come on, best get yourself off to the shower."

"And muddy footsteps all the way there…somehow, I don't think Rochelle will be impressed," she replied, moving closer to him.

"Probably not." He forced a smile and headed back the way they'd come, staring at the ground.

"Suppose I should be glad you didn't make any mud wrestling jokes," she said.

"I think I've skated close enough to making you mad, wouldn't want to be set on fire again."

"I guess I deserve that."

Vinny stared ahead, the humour gone from her face. Now she thought he was picking her out, crap.

"Don't be like that, Vinny. I was trying to make you snap that day, I got what I deserved."

"Still, I got carried away."

He put out his hand and grabbed her arm without thinking, then quickly let it go. "I don't blame you. Honestly, I'd have been disappointed if you hadn't tried to hurt me."

Her grey eyes seemed to look right through him but she didn't say a word.

"Now who's staring?" he asked softly.

She blinked, shook her head and started walking again. Soon they were at the edge of the woods.

"I'm headed that way." He jerked his head in the approximate direction of the fort.

"See you tomorrow then," she almost sighed.

"Probably not."

She turned her head and frowned at him. Was she disappointed?

"I have a few other things to do," he explained. "So you get the day off."

"Lucky me," she replied.

"Cheers, Vinny." He walked away and didn't look back.

Why wasn't she angry with him? Usually, when you hit on a girl like that, the easy ones turned on their charms, and the nice ones tore you to pieces. Vinny had just teased him about it, flirtatiously too. What on earth was that supposed to mean?

He couldn't do this. What good was his resolve to be professional if it fell apart the first time he was alone with her?

By far more troubling though, was her question about the Jackal Skaath. There's no way that was a coincidence. If she'd found out about him then it was only a matter of time before she trampled all over him. Something had to change before any deeper involvement could develop between them.

A plan half formed in his mind, he contemplated it as he drove, and it was near perfect by the time he pulled into the parking lot behind the Sanctuary.

He knocked twice on the door to Robert's office, and the familiar deep voice called for him to enter before he could knock again.

"Afternoon, Keeper." He closed the door behind him.

"Afternoon, Alistair, have a seat." Robert only briefly glanced at him before returning to whatever he was busy with on his laptop.

Alistair sat down and waited, drumming his fingers on his thigh where Robert couldn't see it. His gaze flickered around the room, taking everything in even though he'd been in this room so often. He could tell when one of the books was even slightly out of place, or if one of the chests had been moved.

Details steadied his thoughts and gave him something else to focus on.

"What's on your mind?" Robert's hands were folded on the desk, his green eyes set on him as though he'd been watching him for a while.

Immediately, Alistair pulled himself together,

"I just wanted to tell you that Heaven has been able to summon wings with the Phoenix, it's happened twice now," he said.

"Blake informed me of this." Robert nodded and continued to watch him.

"If we advance her training then I believe she may be ready by the time we find out who was responsible for Dylan's death."

The Keeper's brow furrowed. "Nadia and Janine are capable of delivering justice for that."

"I know, but Earth and Fire aren't naturally compatible, and that could work against us with a powerful Coven. If we mobilised Heaven as well then it would balance the elements and negate the incompatibility," he replied casually. If Robert caught the slightest hint of an ulterior motive from him then he'd pounce on it.

"You have a point, but I could just as easily avoid those aspects by using Paula to complement Nadia's fire. She has more experience than Heaven and her ability is a known factor."

"Known, but no less unpredictable for it. Paula gets insecure when she's separated from Rochelle, that leads her to make mistakes."

Robert lifted his fingers to his beard and twisted a few strands of hair between them. "Heaven, too, is unpredictable. We have no measure of her aptitude yet and she lacks military discipline."

"It's merely a suggestion." Alistair shrugged and leaned back in his seat. "It seemed to me that this would be a good way to see the Spirit element in action."

Robert's eyes narrowed slightly. Alistair knew how curious he was about her abilities; hopefully this would be the key to convincing him.

"I'd planned on having Elise do a psychological evaluation before Heaven began the more intensive training, but she's not taking Dylan's death very well," he paused, still twirling his beard.

Robert was a man of very few 'tells', and it was generally difficult to figure out what was going on in his mind, but this habit of his was a sure sign that he was analysing an idea. He waited quietly until Robert spoke again.

"You have my permission to speed up her training," he continued, eventually. "Provided that you take care in doing so. Once we discover who killed Dylan, I'll see about using her in the raid."

"Understood." Alistair nodded and rose to leave.

"Was that all?"

Robert was giving him an opening, and he was too curious to let it pass.

He cleared his throat. "This Giyarav Shpyorad…do you know who it is?"

Robert smirked through his beard. "I have my suspicions."

"Which you haven't shared with Herman?"

"No. As far as I'm concerned, this person is doing us a favour. Not that I approve of the Skaarav, but the punishment I'd have to hand out to the culprit would be poor thanks for their efforts to lighten our workload."

"I see," he said.

"That being said, I would never allow Herman to use you as a whipping boy for the crimes of another." Robert's eyes seemed to pierce him as he spoke.

"I trust you, Keeper."

"As I trust you, son. Since you're here now, I have an errand for you." Robert opened the top drawer of his desk and removed a cardboard box. "Give this to Heaven tomorrow. It's her legal documents, bankcard, cell phone…everything she requires. There's also a set of keys for the scooter Michael found for her."

"No problem," he said. Crap, now he'd have to see her tomorrow after all.

"Thank you." Robert put the box down near the edge of the desk and began tapping at his laptop.

Alistair tucked the box into his jacket and left.

18

She climbed the frame again, pausing at the top to take a good look at the hard packed earth below. It seemed too high, and not high enough at the same time.

"Come on, Phoenix, I know you can hear me." She placed her hand over the talisman, pressing it against her skin until it almost hurt. "You and I are a team now," she continued. "We work together. I'm high up and I need your wings."

Nothing. Not so much as a pinch in her back.

"God damn it, Phoenix! Do I have to throw myself off here for you to listen to me?"

The amulet twitched against her skin, and she swallowed hard. This was madness, trusting her life to an animated metal bird. What if it didn't work?

She ran both hands through her hair and closed her eyes, focusing like Blake had taught her to. If she thought about it too hard then she'd never go through with it.

She leapt over the edge of the platform.

Too scared to scream, she fell. She didn't even feel it in her back this time, but her body jerked as the wings caught the air. She was gliding now, laughing like an idiot, and tearing up with relief. The obstacles were laid out beneath her, the trees a taller barrier in front of her.

It suddenly occurred to her that she didn't actually know how to fly, and that even birds needed to learn how to do it. She was going to fly into a tree, but she didn't. The wings tilted and took her past the outstretched branches of a pine tree.

So, maybe the wings were more like her catching a ride than telling the Phoenix what to do. She glanced at the sky; she wanted to go higher. The wings flapped down strongly. She felt them cupping and pushing against the air, lifting her up past the treetops, and into the sky.

Amazing, awesome, invigorating, the words passed through her mind but they were poor synonyms for the joy she felt right down to her soul. She soared past birds…birds!

Higher! She could see the entire centre spread out below her, and the endless veld around it. It reminded her of how Africa had looked as the Earth turned.

She folded her wings and fell towards the earth again, diving as fast as a falcon after prey, and only braked when she needed to breathe. She tilted into a glide that carried her toward the house in the trees, and skimmed the treetops before leaning her body to spiral downwards.

Vinny was moving too fast as she approached the roof. She stuck out her feet and hit it hard, turned a somersault, and rolled down the slope. Her fingers caught the edge of the gutter just long enough to give her hope before it came away from the roof, and she fell into the garden below.

A bush crumpled under her weight and the air rushed out of her lungs. The gutter pipe banged down on top of her, and all she could do was laugh wheezily about it.

"Not the best landing, but impressive all the same."

Her laughter died in her throat. She clumsily rolled over onto her knees, and pushed the gutter off her. Alistair was standing behind her. He took a step closer and held out his hand to help her up.

"I thought I had the day off," she said, taking his hand as she got to her feet.

"I'm not here for training." His hand brushed over her arm and she tensed.

"Dirt..." he smiled faintly. "I brought you something from the Keeper."

"What is it?"

He flexed his shoulders as he shrugged off his backpack, and she tried not to look at the material pulling taut across his chest. Instead, she watched his hands as he unzipped the bag, and removed a small cardboard box that he held out to her. She tilted her head then took the box, pulling the flaps loose to open it.

A cell phone lay at the top, beneath it was an identity book, driver's license, and the phone's charger. At the bottom were an envelope and a key ring with three keys on it.

"Congratulations, you officially exist."

Alistair was grinning when she looked at him, but she had no words. Nothing could explain what it was like to find an entire life in a fifteen by twenty centimetre box. Her life.

"Thank you," she murmured.

"Your bank card and the map to your flat are in the envelope and Mike got you a scooter to drive…its ugly, but it runs okay."

She nodded absently and lifted the identity book out of the box. Her fingers fumbled to open it until she pressed it flat against the lid. When had they taken a photo of her? She smiled when she saw her new birthday.

"You made me two years younger…and Capricorn." She glanced at him as she spoke.

"Better than five years older. Is there any coffee left over?" He looked towards the front door.

"Probably, go see for yourself."

"Your manners need attention, you know that?"

"Yes, you wouldn't believe how much effort it takes to override my programming."

He made a thoughtful sound and lightly placed his hand on her shoulder blade, ushering her towards the entrance.

"You're a strange girl, Vinny," he said.

"I'll take that has a compliment."

Blake was in the kitchen, reading a book as he leaned back against the counter. The microwave was working next to him and she caught a vague scent of herbs and bread.

He looked up as they entered and arched his left eyebrow. "Wasn't expecting to see you today, Al."

"I know," Alistair replied.

"Look here." Vinny held the identity book out to Blake and he slowly smiled as he set his own book aside.

"You're legally alive again." He wrapped one arm around her side, and she leaned in to hug him briefly.

"Don't I get a hug? I brought it here, after all." Alistair looked at her with his eyebrows slightly raised and she couldn't tell if he was joking or not. He did want to hug her though.

"Sure." She half smiled as she moved towards him. She could just rest her chin on his shoulder, and she caught a breath of his scent, earthy, like sandalwood. His fingers brushed against her back as they parted and her spine stiffened.

"You missed the show." Alistair smiled at Blake then jerked his thumb at her. "She was flying."

"What?" Blake looked at her with wide eyes. "Really?"

"Yeah." She lowered her head to hide her smile. "Beautiful sight."

She glanced sideways at Alistair, held his gaze for a moment then fiddled with her sleeves.

"How'd you do it?" Blake asked.

"Er...really want to know?"

"Yes..." He quirked a brow at her.

"I jumped off the climbing thingy on the obstacle course." She straightened up, bracing herself for his reaction.

"What?" His expression darkened. "What if it didn't work? You could've been badly injured, killed even! Lain there for hours until somebody found you."

"I had to try," she shrugged.

"No, you didn't. That's what your training is for."

"Relax man." Alistair moved towards Blake and dropped his hand on his shoulder. "Fire is a bold element—it doesn't make what you did any less idiotic." He looked at her. "But maybe that's why it worked."

She rolled her eyes and shoved the I. D book back in the box. It was more about letting go than being bold.

"She's ready for something a little more realistic," Alistair said.

"No."

She looked from one man to the next while they stared at each other.

"It's time, bro. You know it's an important part of training."

"Of course I do, but she isn't ready."

"C'mon, if anybody can prepare her, it's you. She can't punch bags forever."

"I know that…"

Vinny took her box and went to her room. Whatever they were talking about, it didn't matter right now. She existed again.

***

"Just give it another week or so." Blake was on the verge of pleading with him but Alistair wasn't looking at him anymore.

He followed his gaze and saw the kitchen door swing closed. Vinny had left.

"You know I trust your judgement, bro, but I think you're getting mixed up," Alistair said. "You can't protect her by holding her back."

"That's not what I'm doing. It's going to take time to build her confidence, and rushing her could put her right back at square one."

"C'mon, she reacts well to pressure."

"I disagree. I think she's just really good at pretending, like you are."

Alistair narrowed his eyes slightly. "Maybe…it doesn't really matter either way. The Keeper wants her ready for when we find Dylan's killers."

"You've got to be kidding me," he snapped.

"I'm just the messenger, man."

"Being the messenger works both ways in this case, and you need to tell Robert that she isn't ready. Damn it, man, I'm supposed to have six weeks to train her, and I'm not even sure that will be enough. She's barely started coming out of her shell, for pity's sake!"

"You can't always wait for people to be ready. Girl has guts, and she's smart too, you just have to get her to be more aggressive," Alistair said, like it was just that simple.

The microwave beeped and he glared at it. This conversation was going nowhere. Alistair would stand there and listen with that superior look on his face, but it would be a waste of time.

"Can you give me another day?" he asked.

"Sure." Alistair shrugged one shoulder and looked him in the eyes.

This usually meant that he was lying through his teeth. "Al, I know when you're lying…"

Alistair grinned and patted him on the shoulder. "Luckily for me, you're the only one, bro. I'll try to stall but I'm not promising anything."

"Thanks."

"Sure, before I go." Alistair's expression turned sharp. "We have something important to sort out."

"What is it?"

Alistair pulled a phone from his pocket and held it out to him. He arched his eyebrow and took it, turning it over in his hand.

"It's Dylan's," Al said. "A few days ago he told me he was seeing a girl, it sounded serious. She should know…you know."

Blake stared at the phone to avoid his eyes. "He didn't mention a name, did he?"

"No. I glanced through his contacts, but I can't see any likely prospects."

"I'll see what I can do," he said.

"Alright then." Alistair looked down. "I'm off again, see you tomorrow."

"Sure." Blake stared after him as he left the room. Should he tell Al about Elise? Maybe, but not now.

He removed the leftover foccacia from the microwave and took a bite. This business of having Vinny involved in the raid to avenge Dylan didn't sit right with him at all.

Sure, Robert was merciless. He never let a move by the Covens go unanswered, and his reputation was something Guardians whispered about in awe even now, years after he'd taken up the position as Keeper. How many times had uncle David told him about the time they were sent to negotiate with the

Ice Flame? Only ten Guardians were in the group, but they'd killed everybody, except the Matron. Robert had planned it all, including the lie they used to cover up their actions afterwards. All because Robert refused to bargain with Handmaidens, unlike the Keeper before him.

Alistair's motives were less clear. He might simply want to avenge Dylan or he might just want to stick it to the Covens. How he planned to do that with an inexperienced Wielder was beyond him. Al was too smart for such a dumb move; it was almost like he wanted this to fail.

Blake pushed the plate away. He was getting paranoid. Alistair hated the Handmaidens more than anybody else, and for exactly the reason why he doubted him now. The guy couldn't help what he was anymore than people could help the colour of their skin or sexual preferences.

"Damn it all." He shook his hair out of his face and went straight to Vinny's room. The door was ajar but he knocked before entering anyway.

"Come in," she called out.

She was sitting cross-legged on the bed with the contents of the box strewn around her. It almost looked like she was sorting through presents; unsure which one was the best.

"Still looking through it?"

"Yeah…it's a weird feeling." She smiled shyly at him.

"I can only imagine." He sighed. "I hate to interrupt, but we should get some combat practice in."

"Because of what you and Alistair were arguing about?"

"Yeah…" He looked down.

"What's this about anyway? We're going to start playing war games or something, combat simulations?" She climbed off the bed and walked towards him.

"Something like that, Alistair thinks you aren't aggressive enough."

She snorted and edged past him. "Maybe he'd be happy if I set his pants on fire."

"It's worth a try," he chuckled.

When they reached the gym, he got a pair of gloves for Vinny and had her take shots at one of the dummies. It wasn't very life-like but he didn't think he could spar with her. He didn't even like battle training in case he scared her, or hurt her by accident. Maybe Alistair was right and he was holding her back.

"Try to picture the dummy as somebody you knew who you would've loved to punch," he said.

Her head whirled around and she stared at him.

"Er…okay," she said softly then turned to look at the dummy.

Her first punch was hesitant, weaker than the ones she'd been throwing before he spoke. Blake chewed on the inside of his cheek and watched as she hit it again, somewhat harder this time. She kicked at its knee then followed through with a fist to the abdomen.

Then Vinny growled. She launched at the dummy and hit it wildly, the sounds of her gloves meeting the wood echoing around the large room.

Blake took a step back. She'd completely lost her form now, but he didn't dare to stop her.

"Balance, weight, arm straight," he called to her.

She kicked the dummy so hard that it tipped backwards on its stand.

"Good job." He wasn't even sure she was listening anymore.

She was losing her cool and part of him wanted to look away, but he couldn't. Far better that he stay calm, and probably better that she let this out now rather than later. Blake had no doubt that Alistair would come that night, despite what he'd said about stalling. Most of the war games were played at night because most raids were conducted at night. It was often a surprise too. Older Guardians usually waited for the trainees to fall asleep then burst into their rooms announcing that a game would start in a few minutes.

Eventually Vinny began tiring, her movements becoming sluggish and less effective.

"That's enough for one day." He walked closer and gripped the dummy by its shoulder. "Feeling okay?"

"I'm not made out of cotton wool, Blake." Sharp words, but without any malice in her tone.

"I know." He smiled at her. "So we'll jog back to the house, right?"

"Please tell me you're joking."

He looked down at her raised eyebrows and laughed. "Come on, Vinny, let's go."

They walked back to the house in companionable silence, Blake keeping their pace slow.

"You went a bit wild back there," he said calmly.

"You said I should picture somebody I want to punch." She shrugged.

"I know, I just didn't expect it to work so well."

"Want to go back to the plan for setting Alistair's pants on fire?"

He smiled. "Let's keep that as Plan B."

"You guys are pretty close, aren't you?"

"We started hanging out as teenagers. I trained with my uncle instead of going to Hex so I didn't know anybody when I first came here. Al was also an outsider, and my room mate."

"And so began a beautiful bromance?" Vinny grinned.

254

Blake frowned, "Brotherhood is not bromance, Vinny."

"If you say so." She rolled her eyes at him. "Why was Alistair an outsider?"

He looked down at her and swallowed. It wasn't exactly a secret, and she was bound to find out eventually—but he'd seen the way Al looked at her. Blake had no intention of getting in the middle of whatever was brewing between the two of them.

"You should probably ask him about that," he replied.

"Alright." She shrugged.

"Were you close to anybody before you died, Vinny?"

"No," she said.

"And family?"

She looked down and he wondered if he'd struck a nerve.

"I have a sister but we lost touch a long time ago, she could just as well be dead."

"I also had a sister, twin actually."

"She's not around anymore?"

Blake shook his head. "Horse riding accident."

"I'm sorry." Her hand rested gently on his bicep.

"I still miss her, but what can you do except move on?"

"Nothing," she sighed.

They'd reached the house now. Just outside the front door, he stopped her. "I shouldn't tell you this, but I think they'll come tonight so be ready."

19

Blake was right, Alistair returned just before sunset. She, Blake and Darren were just getting ready for their evening game when his bike roared through the front gate. Vinny watched him dismount and remove his helmet. He was dressed all in black, and the smuggest grin she'd seen on him to date.

"Now I understand why she's learning so fast." Alistair ambled to where Blake was standing. "You guys have been practicing without me."

"It's just a game." Blake shrugged.

Vinny quenched the fire she'd been gathering in her hand. Alistair had a point.

"Smart move, bro, but tonight we play a different game."

"Capture the flag?" Darren's angelic features lit up.

"Better, Slayer." Alistair smiled. "Maybe you and Paula can join us next time. Come on, you two, Nadia's waiting."

They walked through the woods at a brisk pace. Vinny thought they were heading towards the Demon, but instead they ended up in a small area covered in gravel. A sign on the far side announced that this parking area was for paintball players only. Nadia's car was parked nearby, music spilled through the open door, and Nadia's long legs.

"Finally!" Nadia abruptly turned the music off and climbed out of the car.

"You weren't waiting that long," Alistair said.

"Was too," Nadia said.

Alistair rolled his eyes and turned to face her. "Right...so, Vinny, the game we're going to play is simple enough. It's a two on two match and the objective is to eliminate your opponent, you do that by forcing them to yield in hand to hand combat, got it so far?"

"I reckon so."

"Good. Once a person has yielded, they're out of the game and return to this area. The game continues until there's a winner. Now, since you don't know the field I'll show you the basic layout. So there's no unfair advantage." He arched his eyebrows at her.

Vinny sniggered. "Once was bad enough," she replied in a low voice.

Alistair smirked, knelt down, and lifted one of the larger pieces of gravel. Vinny crouched beside him and watched as he quickly scratched out a rough map.

"Those are the bunkers." He pointed to squares on opposite sides of the field. "There's a platform built between the trees in the middle, and everything else is basically just there to provide cover. Along this side are sections of wall that separate this field from the next one—don't pass them. Leaving the field is an automatic disqualification."

"Got it."

"Now then, rules." He stood up and brushed his hands off on his pants. "No weapons, no fighting dirty, no fighting after an opponent has yielded…" He looked at Blake. "Anything else?"

"One on one combat only and a two metre limit on ranged attacks, unless you hold the platform."

"Like there's so much we can do with fire around trees." Nadia crossed her arms and pulled a face. "Can we just start already?"

"As milady wishes." Alistair gave her a mocking bow.

"Awesome, in that case, I declare this match as girls versus guys." She sidled up to Vinny and hooked her arm through hers.

Vinny stared at her. Blake quirked an eyebrow.

Alistair shrugged. "Fine by me. Blake and I will take the far side, we'll shout when we get there, and the game starts exactly five minutes after that."

"Roger that." Nadia gave him a casual salute then started walking, dragging Vinny along with her. The men took off at a run.

"They're bound to split up when they leave the bunker," Nadia said. "Our best bet is to head for the platform and try to pick them off, but they know that too…they'll try to cut us off."

"Maybe we should split up too, one of us moves in front and the other hangs back to provide cover or something."

Nadia glanced at her. "That's actually not a bad idea."

They came to a short wooden wall about a metre high and one and a half metres long. A copse of trees grew directly in front of it, and everything beyond that was grey and indefinite, camouflaged by the encroaching night.

"We'll strike off to the right. I'll take the lead so I'll be the first to run into either one of them."

"Suits me." Vinny was vaguely impressed, Nadia came across as such an airhead yet here she was, talking strategy like an army general.

"We might be able to simply pick them off one at a time…well, assuming they're going to try to flank us. They might just decide to guard the platform instead."

A shout carried across the field and Nadia lifted her arm to check her watch.

"What do we do if they are guarding the platform?" Vinny asked.

"Try to draw them off then ambush them."

"Right." Somehow, she doubted it would be as easy as Nadia made it sound.

A few moments of silence passed then Nadia looked up. "Let's move"

Nadia stalked away and Vinny followed, staying back while still keeping her in sight. Insects sang in the woods and all around them but their footsteps still sounded so loud. Nadia paused at the last tree then sprinted to a row of empty drums, and crouched down in their shadow. Vinny waited, listened carefully as she looked around, then ran across to join Nadia.

As soon as they were crouched together, Nadia leaned in to whisper next to her ear. "Right again, I'll approach the platform at an angle to try to get behind them, you keep to the outside on a parallel path."

Vinny nodded, and then Nadia was off again. She counted to five then moved out. The grass grew long here but other wise it was open. Nadia was a dark silhouette prowling off to her left, and ahead of her was the dark outline of another hiding place. She moved towards it slowly.

There was a sound to her left and a yell. Where Nadia had been there were now two shapes scuffling in the dark. The shorter one had to be

Nadia, but she couldn't tell if the other was Blake or Alistair.

A flash of fire lit up the dark and she ducked behind the concrete drainage pipes in front of her so she wouldn't be seen.

A thump and a cry, a sharp crack that she knew was a hard slap connecting with bare skin. Vinny scurried to the far end of the pipes and peered around them in time to see the larger shape fall.

"Yield," he called loudly.

Nadia ran for the trees to her right, and Vinny caught sight of a second shadow moving to intercept her. The way to the platform was clear but she hesitated, wondering if she ought to go after Nadia instead.

Nah, she left the cover of the pipes and stalked across to the trees in the centre of the field. Whichever one of the guys Nadia had defeated was already gone and soon she ducked down at the base of the nearest tree.

The structure built among the trees was a dark outline over her head, but how did she get up there? She moved to the next tree then stopped as a high-pitched squeal carried to her.

"Yield."

Nadia, which meant that it was just her and one of the guys now. She looked around but couldn't see a ladder or anything else to help her reach the platform. Nadia had been right about them knowing that they'd try to get here. Since she couldn't get up, the next best thing seemed to be abandoning the obvious.

She moved through the trees and stared in the direction where she'd last heard Nadia. No signs of movement. She ran to a bush and crouched behind it.

The dark shapes of structures were visible to her left, one off to the front, and another behind her. Retreat was probably her best option for now.

She headed for the structure behind her, and was almost halfway there when she caught a flash of movement in her peripheral vision. As she turned her head, the figure ducked, skidded, and knocked her legs out from under her.

Vinny fell. A large hand gripped her side and jerked her, but as she rolled onto her back, she struck out and kicked him. A hissed breath, close by, she pulled her left leg in to her chest then thrust it forwards.

"Fuck, Vinny, that was almost my face."

Alistair's voice. His hand closed around her thigh, just above her knee, and she reached for her lighter. He pulled on her leg and she struck a flame.

Alistair grabbed her wrist and then they were rolling around in the grass, squabbling like children. The fire was out and she couldn't light another one like this. She kicked and hit at him but he didn't seem to feel it. She was good at being slippery, but he had more stamina. Eventually he managed to pin her on her back.

"Say the magic word, Vinny," he said in a low voice.

"Abracadabra." She headbutted him.

"Bloody hell." He reared back and she threw him off then ran back to the trees in the centre.

She ducked behind the closest one and pressed her back up against the rough bark. Fire was her greatest advantage, but with all this dry grass around her...bad idea.

She was supposed to be more aggressive, right? He was coming. She could hear his footsteps, and the rustle of the long grass as it brushed against him. She waited until he was close enough then rushed out and drove her fist at his stomach.

It glanced off him as he twisted away, and he lashed out, her side stung as he slapped her. His other arm darted towards her, but she angled her arm down in time to block him.

Alistair chuckled and she looked up at his face.

"You aren't going to make this easy, are you?" he asked.

"Why should I?"

She couldn't see it but she just knew that he was smiling. He took a quick step forwards. She thrust her palm up towards his nose but he shifted. The blow landed on his jaw instead, and he smacked her arm away.

She aimed another punch at his stomach but he blocked her, so she stomped on his foot.

Alistair laughed. "Steel toe caps, sweetheart."

He slapped her on her side again then shoved her backwards. She slammed into the tree and lost her balance for a moment, long enough for Alistair to kick her on the thigh, and send her sprawling in the grass again.

"It doesn't really matter," he said. "I'll get you to give in sooner or later." The side of his boot roughly bumped her hip.

Vinny stared up at him looming over her, a dark figure silhouetted against the night.

Like hell.

She'd imagined that the dummy was Trey earlier on. It was easy to do the same with Alistair when she couldn't see his face.

She punched the side of his knee with as much fury as she could muster then twisted her body to use a clumsy sweep kick on him. It worked, and she hit at his stomach as he fell but missed. He was trying to get up, but she launched at him, straddled his hips as she beat at his upper body with her fists. He blocked most of her blows, but enough of them made contact for her to feel powerful.

Alistair grabbed her left wrist, next his palm cracked loudly against her thigh. The area was numb for a moment before the sting rushed in.

Vinny froze for an instant where fear saturated her, but she'd been hit much harder before. Rage swept away the fear, and night retreated as wings unfurled from her back. She pulled back her arm to punch him in the face but stopped.

Alistair stared at her with the same look as when he'd first seen her, and his eyes reflected her fire as though it burned inside of him. He wasn't handsome; he was beautiful like a sunset over the ocean or a falling star. She lowered her fist uncertainly and laid her hand on his chest, felt his ribs rise and fall with his breath.

"Yield," he said roughly.

Her eyes snapped back to his face, and the guarded look in his eyes. She nodded and stumbled to her feet then stepped away from him. Her wings stretched out then folded back and faded away, like the Phoenix knew it had been a false alarm.

Alistair cleared his throat. "Not bad at all, Vinny."

"Thanks." Her voice sounded high, like a little girl's.

He stood close to her, and she felt nervous and excited at the same time. She glanced up at him then looked away.

"We should get back to Nadia and Blake," he said.

"Yeah." She looked at anything but him, then pointed off to her left. "That way?"

"This way." His hand folded loosely over her shoulder.

For a moment, his arm was around her as he turned her in the right direction, but then it was gone.

"Just follow me." He stepped past her, walking a little way in front until she saw light up ahead.

With her next few steps, Nadia's car came into view, the door open, as it had been earlier. Blake was leaning against the rear fender and Nadia was sitting on the boot, but she slid down the moment she saw them.

"Who won?" she asked.

"Vinny," Alistair muttered.

"High five," Nadia exclaimed, presenting her hand to Vinny. She couldn't help but smile as she slapped her palm.

"And," Nadia continued. "Since I took Blake out, I'd say that makes us girls the overall winners. I so wish we'd made a bet on this now."

"Maybe next time." Blake smiled at Nadia.

"Next time, they won't be so lucky," Alistair said. "Give us a lift to Rochelle's house, princess?"

"Sure, winner's treat." Nadia winked as she turned and climbed into her car, and they all got in after her.

**

Alistair followed the others into the house, and froze when he saw Rochelle sitting in front of the TV.

"How did the game go?" Rochelle asked, smiling as she sat up and turned to look at them.

"Blake tore my shirt." Nadia pouted, forever seeking the spotlight.

His Wielder strode to the couch and sat down beside Rochelle, pulling up the hem to display a small rip.

"Easily mended, dear." Rochelle stroked her hair.

"Sounds like the two of you had a real good time." He turned to look at Blake as he teased him.

"Alistair, manners." Rochelle gave him a hard look and he stared back at her. He couldn't even make a joke without her getting on his case. It was really starting to piss him off.

"What you think of as a joke, is rude and insensitive."

He heard her voice in his mind, as clearly as if she'd spoken aloud.

"If Nadia and Blake don't take offense, why should you?" he replied in his head.

"It's not them I'm concerned about." An image of Vinny's face accompanied her words.

"You and Blake are two peas in a pod," he thought angrily. *"Just because she's had it rough,*

doesn't mean she should be treated like a child, give her some credit."

"Oh, I do." The older woman's lips curled into a subtle smile. *"But you lack objectivity, dear. She's not as unfamiliar with kindness as you were, and I think she could benefit from remembering what its like to feel cared about. Everyone needs that, even you."*

Anger flared white-hot inside of him, he didn't bother trying to hide it from Rochelle, but he didn't want the others to see it. From the corner of his eye, he saw them watching him and Rochelle. He stuffed his hands in his pockets and forced his shoulders and jaw to relax.

"I'm not saying you should stop being yourself around her," Rochelle continued. *"Just try to be more considerate, you also care about her, don't you?"*

"Alright, alright," he said aloud, hoping that would make it clear to her that he had no interest in continuing their telepathic conversation.

"Thank you." Rochelle smiled, then turned and patted Nadia's knee. "Its late, why don't you two stay over? There's plenty of room."

Alistair stifled a groan. The last thing he wanted was to stay here overnight.

Nadia beamed. "That'd be great!"

"Just let your father know," Rochelle said.

"I shouldn't leave Stillwater empty," Alistair said, the quickest excuse he think of.

"Nonsense, Stillwater is well protected and it's not good for you to be alone in that old house all the time. Dylan must've left a big shadow."

She just wouldn't quit. He nodded and turned away, anything to keep her from bugging him any more. Vinny was watching him, her head tilted slightly and a calm expression on her face.

"It's decided then," Rochelle said.

A moment later, the woman was dragging Nadia and himself towards the staircase. He tried to keep his mind blank as he followed her upstairs. She chatted to Nadia while digging linen out of a cupboard in the hallway. Alistair leaned against the wall, focusing on the weave of the carpet.

"Good night, you guys," Blake said as he passed them.

"Night, bro," he muttered.

"Night," Vinny said.

She sounded amused and he looked up sharply to find her smirking at him. He was tempted to grab her and tickle her, its what he would do to Nadia if she looked at him like that, but he rolled his eyes instead. Having her in his arms could only lead to trouble, or third degree burns.

"Here you go." Rochelle held out a pile of blankets to him. "Take the room just over there, the bathroom is two doors down, on the right."

"Sure, thanks," he muttered, clutching the blankets and getting away from her as fast as he could.

The room was tiny, not that he cared much. For most of his childhood, he'd slept on a floor in a cellar with nine other boys around his age, all of them huddling together for warmth in the winter.

Enough moonlight came in through the window for him to see what he was doing without turning on the light. He pulled back the bedspread and tossed the blankets onto the bed, removed his belt and dropped it on the floor before sitting down to untie his bootlaces.

People like Rochelle would never truly understand hardship. No doubt, she could intellectualise it, but however much she saw of it in other people's minds, it would never be the same as experiencing it for herself.

He climbed into bed then shook the blankets out over his body and lay down. The woman had some nerve, looking into everyone's heads like that, messing around with things that were better left alone.

The sooner this assignment was over, the better. He could go back to comfortably avoiding all the people who annoyed him…and Vinny. It probably wouldn't be that hard to make sure they didn't see much of each other.

He sighed and put his hand on his chest, remembering what her hand had felt like on him. The look on her face...gods above and devils below.

But it didn't matter. She hadn't been raised to loathe anything remotely connected to the Skaath, but when she found out about his Mark, and his mother, everything would change.

He'd already watched one girl's expression change from affection to disgust. Not again. No matter how different Vinny seemed.

Yeah, the tactics of avoiding her would be easy, but changing his desire to see her, not so much.

20

Nadia joined them for the morning exercise in a tracksuit borrowed from Paula. Her tawny hair was tied back in a ponytail, she wore hardly any make-up, and she somehow managed to jog and flirt with the Guardians at the same time.

Vinny couldn't understand it. The girl who flounced around like an idiot was so different compared to the side of Nadia she'd seen last night.

When they got back to the house, Alistair was glaring at a plate of scrambled eggs while Rochelle sipped coffee at the head of the dining room table.

"…been in the same position, you could provide a lot of guidance," Rochelle was saying.

"I told you, I don't want to talk about it," Alistair replied. His voice was gruff and edgy.

Vinny cleared her throat and edged into the room.

"Morning, Heaven." Rochelle smiled.

"Morning." She glanced at Alistair and he quickly looked away.

"Well, I should be off." Rochelle rose, gave Alistair's shoulder a brief squeeze, then left.

"Odd woman," Vinny muttered.

"Nosy woman," Alistair growled, he pushed away his plate of food and took a swig of coffee.

"That why you're so grouchy?"

He glared sideways at her, half turned in his seat and smiled. "No, my side is bruised to hell thanks to you."

Vinny sniffed. "Sure it is."

"See for yourself," he said, rising from his seat.

Vinny had assumed that Alistair was just tanned, but even under his clothes, his skin was a light caramel. The edges of his abs were defined by shadows and light rather than bulging mass, and there was a splotch of purple over the outer edge of his stomach.

"Oh yes, take it off."

She snapped her head around. Nadia was winking at Alistair from the doorway.

"Princess, I'm seriously thinking of putting you on hormone therapy." Alistair said.

"Dude, you're such a wet blanket." Nadia pouted at him.

"And you're a pervert!" He laughed. "I'm surprised you haven't put spy cams in the Gym showers."

"Oh my God, Alistair!" Nadia grinned mischievously. "You're a genius."

Vinny poured herself some coffee and kept her head down as she slowly stirred in sugar and milk.

"Not even the slightest show of remorse, Vinny? You're breaking my heart," Alistair sighed.

She almost spat her first mouthful of coffee over the table.

"I have your hand imprinted on my thigh from last night." She glared at him.

"Damn, Al, you should know that spankings stop being fun when they leave marks," Nadia chipped in.

"That generally depends on who's getting spanked."

"Nobody is going to be spanking me," Vinny muttered.

"You sound like a bunch of horny teenagers," Blake said from the door.

"Come on, Blake, we're all adults." Nadia smiled.

"Nadia was way worse as a horny teenager…back then I was considering holy water," Alistair said.

"Screw you!" Nadia laughed.

As she watched Nadia attempt to slap Alistair across the table, Vinny wondered if the two of them hadn't already slept together. She gritted her teeth and leaned back in her chair.

Alistair's phone rang, interrupting his foreplay with Nadia. He left the room as he answered it and Vinny went back to sipping her coffee.

"You really need to loosen up Blakey...next time I hit the town, you're coming with me." Nadia smiled.

"What?" Blake stared at her as he spooned eggs onto his plate. "No, I couldn't, it's really not my scene, Nadia."

Nadia giggled. "I was telling you, not asking. It'll be fun, you'll see."

Vinny wondered if the look on Blake's face was anything like the way she'd looked every time he told her that something was fun.

Alistair reappeared in the doorway with a grave expression on his face. "The Keeper is on his way."

"What?" Blake spun in his chair and a lump of scrambled eggs dropped off his fork, landing on his plate with a plop.

"He wants to see her in action," he said.

"What happened to stalling, Al?" Blake snapped, standing up so fast that his chair toppled to the floor. He circled round the table toward Alistair.

"They found Dylan's killers."

Blake stopped dead and stared at him, his facial muscles had been scrunched into a thunderous expression, but now they went slack.

"Couple of the Ice Flame Handmaidens put down some recruits last night for bragging about their accomplishment," Alistair continued. "Arthur followed the Trueborns back to their Coven house."

"When do we hit them?" Nadia's expression was all business now.

"Not so fast…Keeper thinks we're going to need everything we've got." Alistair's eyes turned to Vinny. "That means you, sweetheart."

"She isn't ready." Blake's voice sounded like a century without sleep, and his eyes flickered with emotion.

"Have a little faith, Blake, she's tough as nails," Alistair said.

Blake shook his head and pinched the bridge of his nose lightly between his fingers.

"Look, we don't have a whole variety of options here," Alistair continued. "Elise is still without a Guardian, and Paula is too young, her abilities too unpredictable. Rochelle is retired, and the nearest Circle we could send to for back up Wielders is Joburg. Even if they catch a plane, the procedural bullshit could take a week or more. We're left with Janine and Nadia. Fire and Earth aren't naturally compatible, but Vinny's the Spirit Wielder. Her essence can combine any two elements regardless of whether they're well-matched or not."

"Her essence hasn't even Awakened," Blake yelled.

"Awakened or not, its still there. Passive facilitation is better than nothing."

"I'm sitting right here, you know," Vinny spoke loudly.

Nadia looked at her but the men were oblivious. She picked up a teaspoon and hurled it between them to clatter against the door. Both turned to look at her then.

"For one thing." She glared at both Guardians. "I can make my own decisions. Stop talking about me like I'm a child."

Blake sighed.

Alistair continued to stare. "And the other things?" he asked.

"You're discussing me doing something when I don't have a clue what you're on about."

"Your essence...Spirit Wielders can merge any of the elements together, even Water and Fire. Spirit is the one thing that is a component of everything, remember?" Blake said.

"Yeah, but I don't understand..."

Blake opened his mouth to continue, but Alistair spoke first. "The breath of the Mother gives life to all things, fish, animals, plants, birds. It's all around us all the time. No matter the differences between us all, the Mother binds us together through the Spirit element. It brought life to the Geead Lyana, therefore its part of the material elements."

"It's like the internet," Nadia added. "And you're the super computer that can control everything. It'd be like smashing Google and Yahoo together and turning it into Goohoo."

"Goohoo…" Alistair groaned and shook his head. "Just kill me now."

"It's better than Yagle." Nadia shrugged.

"Please, don't." He dragged his hand over his face. "You're blaspheming all that's good in tech."

"I think I get it." Vinny looked at Nadia. "That's why a Spirit Wielder can use any of the Spirit talismans?"

"Because Spirit is in everything, so it can be anything." She nodded.

"So, what do you actually expect me to do?" Vinny turned to look at the Guardians again.

"You can't really do anything yet but…"

"You're basically going to be something like a multi purpose battery," Blake interrupted. "They're going to risk your life so that they can use you."

"For fuck sakes, Blake!" Alistair rounded on him. "This is for Dylan, our brother. You and I both owe him this."

"Like I don't know how much he did for us?"

"You seem to need a reminder."

"Fuck you, Al!"

"Both of you, stop this!" Nadia shouted. "Do you really think Dylan would want you fighting like this? He'd slap both of you, and you know it."

They glared at each other like two bull elephants about to clash. Vinny could almost smell the tension and it made her shiver. Blake had been close to Dylan too, he must also want revenge, and who could blame him?

"I'll do it," she said.

She was looking at Blake when she spoke, his shock was evident but there was something more than that in his eyes.

"Not so fast..." Alistair was cut short by the sound of the doorbell.

"I'll get it, it's probably the Keeper so you all should wrap this up." Nadia strode from the room like she meant business.

Vinny stood up, but made no move towards the door. The men were still staring at each other, and the vibe between them was just as intense as before she spoke.

"Blake, trust me." Alistair put a hand on his shoulder.

There was something bordering on desperation in his voice and it occurred to her that she'd never seen Alistair quite so exposed before.

"I do, that's not the problem," Blake replied.

"Brotherhood, man. Nothing's changed there."

"Good morning." Robert appeared in the doorway. His eyes flickered over her before settling on the Guardians. Both had turned to face him.

"Morning, Keeper," Alistair and Blake said at much the same time.

Vinny just nodded.

"I trust Alistair has filled you in on the details, Blake?" Robert asked.

"Yes, Keeper." Blake nodded stiffly.

"Very good." Robert turned to look at her. "Are you ready for your assessment?"

"I guess so," she replied.

"You've found your voice." He smiled thinly, then turned. "If you all would follow me…"

He strode off without waiting for a reply. Alistair filed after him, but Blake lingered at the door, watching her.

"You don't have to do this, Vinny," he said in a low voice.

"It's okay, I'll just give it a shot and whatever happens…" She shrugged.

21

Vinny felt strangely calm. She hadn't known Blake for very long but she'd come to care about him, something that surprised her. If Dylan had mattered so much to him then the least she could do was give him the chance to kick the asses of some of the Handmaidens who'd killed his friend.

The Earth Wielder was leaning against the tennis court fence, twirling a knife in her hand. Her hair was braided in cornrows and she wore tight black pants, knee-high boots, and a loose jersey.

"Janine is going to assist us." The Keeper glanced back over his shoulder in her general direction.

The tall woman looked up at the sound of her name and straightened up.

"Howzit people." She nodded at them as she tucked the knife away.

Alistair grabbed the gate, pulled it open for the Keeper, and followed him through. Soon they were all gathered around the man on the court.

"The first test will focus on precision, Janine will control the targets." He pointed to a pile of disks the size of dinner plates. "Hit the red ones only, not the blue."

"Right." Vinny nodded.

"Take position on that side and we'll begin."

She walked away to the side he'd indicated and turned around, removing the lighter from her pocket and gripping it in her left hand. Janine sauntered to the pile of disks with the grace of a cat and held one hand over them as she looked at her. Vinny had just enough time to wonder what she was waiting for before disks began whizzing towards her.

The lighter flared and she shot down the first two disks easily. The third was blue and she nearly hit it, but diverted the fireball at the last second.

Time seemed to stand still as she aimed and fired repeatedly, focusing intently on the colour of the missiles shooting towards her. Once or twice, she missed. Sometimes there were too many coming at her to get all of them, and she had to dodge, but she felt good—powerful and capable.

Her body was gears in relentless motion, and the warmth of the Phoenix was a drug charging through her bloodstream. Another volley of disks zoomed towards her, and she hit three of them. The last one was seconds away from knocking her off her feet when she struck it with her elbow. Pain sang through her arm but, for a change, it didn't bother her.

A few more disks flew at her, and then they stopped. She took notice of her surroundings again and saw that Janine had used up the whole pile.

"Simulated combat," Robert's voice boomed off the clay. "If you're down for longer than a count of five, you're metaphorically dead."

Vinny sniffed then shifted her balance to the balls of her feet as Janine stalked towards her. All the advice Blake had given her ran through her head.

Janine ran the last few metres. Vinny jumped back just as her boot swept past her face, then a fist headed for her gut and she pivoted to one side. She needed a strategy. She kicked at Janine's side, where her side had been a moment ago anyway, then stumbled sideways with her ear ringing from a hard blow. A kick swept her legs out from under her, and she landed on her back.

She had five seconds. Vinny rolled away, came up on her knees, and shot a burst of flame at the Earth Wielder. Janine held out her hand and it stopped in mid air. With a flick of her fingers, she brushed the fire aside then thrust her other arm forwards. Vinny left the ground, and flew backwards until she slammed into the fence.

She fell and landed on her knees. This bitch was worse than Alistair, but she still had a trick left.

"Come on, Phoenix, let's do this," she muttered.

Heat rushed through her spine and the muscles twinged. Her wings spread out at her sides. Janine's eyebrows arched just before she smacked at her with her right wing. Janine blocked it with one arm and Vinny moved in. She aimed the edge of her left wing at Janine's head, but it was the kick she'd directed at the woman's stomach that found its mark. Janine folded forward but still managed to dodge the blow Vinny aimed at the back of her shoulder.

For the first time, she felt like she could win, and it made her smile. She jumped and the fire on her wings roared as they flapped downwards. She kicked at the woman's head, but hit some kind of barrier instead.

"Damn it." She flew higher, the jolt from the impact juddered through her leg bones.

Janine held both hands up with the fingers splayed. She must be using some trick tied to her abilities rather than her element.

She'd have more to work with if she could use her wings to shoot fireballs.

With the next downwards flap of her pinions, she pushed her arms forwards. Tongues of flame fell from her wings like rain. They spread across whatever force field the Earth Wielder was using until she could barely see the woman anymore. Heat shimmered through the air and she focused on increasing the intensity.

"Enough! Put it out," Robert shouted.

She dropped her arms and frowned. Did he really expect her to give up her advantage?

"Now!"

She drew the flames away from the invisible bubble, and quenched them as she lowered herself to the ground.

Janine was panting, her dark skin covered in sweat.

"Ma se dinges," she exclaimed. "Any longer and I would've been medium rare"

"Sorry," Vinny muttered, uncertain if the pang in her guts was from guilt or disappointment.

"It's cool." Janine got up and slung her arm around Vinny's shoulders. "But I'll never shield myself against fire again."

Vinny stiffened, but Janine didn't seem to notice, and they walked back to the Keeper like that.

"That last manoeuvre was quite impressive," Robert said.

He didn't look very impressed to Vinny.

"Cheaper than a sauna," Janine added.

Robert just looked at her. "I'm sure..." he replied. "Thank you for your time, Janine, now you'd best return to the fort."

"My pleasure, Keeper." Janine grinned, and waved her good-byes as she left.

"Alistair, over here." Robert jerked his head as he walked away.

Was her assessment over? It seemed way too easy.

"Is that it?" she called after him. "You're going to judge me based on a few minutes?"

Alistair arched his eyebrows at her. Robert stopped dead and glanced at her over his shoulder.

"Hardly," he replied. "Nadia was kind enough to record some of your training sessions for me so I have a fair idea of your capabilities, Heaven."

She blinked, and turned to look at Nadia.

"Sorry, but it was part of the job." The Fire Wielder smiled sheepishly.

The deceit didn't disturb her nearly as much as the fact that she'd never expected it. She moved over to stand beside Blake, and stared at Alistair and Robert while they spoke. Both men had perfect posture and exactly the same deadpan expression on their faces. Neither of them used any body language as they discussed her; no head movements or gestures, their facial muscles barely moved. It was freaky.

"Are Alistair and Robert related?" She leaned a bit closer to Blake and kept her voice soft.

"No," he answered very fast.

When she looked up at him, he was frowning deeply.

She couldn't hear what they were saying. She couldn't read lips either, but she stared at their mouths all the same, and tried to make out a word or two.

Eventually the Keeper gave Alistair a curt nod and they both walked back towards them.

"You have done well during a rather short period of time, Heaven," the Keeper said evenly. "I believe we can consider your basic training completed, your final test will take place this evening."

"I thought this was my final test." She frowned.

"Technically, it is, but tonight you will have your first experience with fighting Handmaidens, and that is a test in itself."

22

They all wore black. At least forty Guardians plus Nadia, herself, Janine, Mike, and Blake looked on as Robert outlined the plan. A satellite image of a house was projected on the curved wall behind him, covered with arrows and different coloured rectangles to represent their different groups.

Alistair leaned against the wall just next to the image with a tablet in his hand. Two swords were strapped in an X on his back, and he wore a black knitted cap that she suspected was a balaclava. His gaze focused on the tablet, and hers kept finding its way back to him.

"Alpha Team will clear these outbuildings before moving round to put gas canisters through the side windows. You'll work in sync with Bravo." Robert pointed at the image as he turned to look at a different part of the group. "Lee-Roy and Richard, you'll disable any cars in this garage area while the rest of Bravo circles around to the

289

back and puts gas canisters through those windows. You'll then draw back to these trees to cover the rear. Our main objective is to flush them out the front." He pointed to the image. "Earth Team will intercept them on this open area in front of the house. They're predictable—they'll send out the recruits, familiars, low-ranked Handmaidens, and Thralls in a direct charge. Once they're out, Janine will open a trench at the front of the house. Around three metres deep should do it."

"Are we going to drive them into it?" Janine asked.

"If possible, yes. The Trueborns will probably close themselves off in the upper level with their personal Thralls. In general, it takes a minimum of ten minutes to summon Skaath. Fire Team, your objective is to get through these trees undetected, and set fire to the house as soon as possible after Janine sinks that trench. The less Skaath we have to deal with, the better. Members of both Alpha and Bravo will put Firestarters through the upper windows to help it spread. Afterwards, Alpha will move through this gap to flank the Handmaidens in the front. Any questions?"

Vinny had quite a few, but she hadn't even been mentioned yet so none of this seemed to apply to her.

Blake stood at her side, restlessly flipping a four point throwing star of black steel over his knuckles then back again. It was a skilful act in itself, but what really impressed her was that he hadn't cut any of his fingers on the sharp edges. He didn't seem too concerned about this plan so she took that as a sign that it was a good one. That, and the fact that nobody seemed inclined to ask a question.

"Very well then. Heaven and Blake will hold this position." Robert pointed to a copse of trees between and slightly to the rear of Nadia and Janine's positions. "Your objective is mainly to back up Fire Team. If they run into trouble then it falls to you to start that fire, understood?"

"Yes, Keeper," Blake replied.

Vinny simply nodded.

"Alistair will take the Field Command, may the Mother watch over all of you." Robert nodded curtly.

"Let's hope that half-wench doesn't lead us to our deaths."

The words were said in little more than a whisper behind her. She tilted her head slightly to her right to hear if they said anything more.

"He won't," a hesitant reply. "Keeper trusts him."

"He's filth, and the Keeper is blind to it."

Blake's shoulders had tensed and he'd stopped playing with the throwing star. He must have heard them too. She watched as he turned his head and fixed his gaze on somebody outside her field of vision.

"Don't give me that look, Cake," the first voice spoke again.

Blake smiled viciously. "Sleep with one eye open, Gary."

She heard a mutter behind her and turned to look at Alistair. He had to be 'half-wench', but what did that mean? She'd heard Blake call Handmaidens wenches...could one of Alistair's parents be a Handmaiden, or Thrall?

No, for all the righteous good attitudes of the Circle, they wouldn't take pity on their enemy to the extreme of embracing him as one of their own. The Keeper certainly wouldn't be so buddy, buddy with him either if that was the case. But then why call him that name?

"Let's go kick ass!" Alistair yelled.

The Guardians roared back and it echoed through the room, a circular space at the base of the water tower.

This was yet another deceit she was kicking herself for not anticipating. Of course the water tower was a secret headquarters, of course a bunch of men would call it 'the fort', and of course this was known as the war room. Her hands weren't large enough for the sort of facepalm such lameness deserved.

She followed Blake out of the room and through the underground maze of passages to the door which led outside, an entrance hidden in the back of the gym.

Four Black SUVs were parked on the paving and she glanced across at the medical building to her left, remembering skid marks and blood, the reason she was doing this.

"Heaven!"

Janine was jogging towards her. As she made her way through the Guardians closest to her, Vinny noticed she was holding something.

"Here." Janine pressed the object into her hand. "You can sommer keep this, like a graduation present. Strap it to your thigh, and may you not have to use it this time."

Vinny looked down, gripped the hilt amidst the straps, and pulled out a sharp looking dagger. When she looked back up to thank Janine, she was already gone.

***

Something had gone wrong. They'd barely reached their position when Vinny heard a woman shrieking. It had pierced the night just long enough to chill her before coming to an abrupt end. She thought it came from the direction of the outbuildings Alpha Team was supposed to be clearing.

Blake had pressed her into a tangled bush then crouched down in front of her. He put his finger to his earpiece and frowned. She didn't have to ask what was happening because soon afterwards the earth rumbled beneath her, followed by a crash. A choir of roaring voices followed, gunshots, and screams of fury and pain.

It had been going on for at least fifteen minutes now. Her legs had pins and needles. Branches scratched at her cheeks, and leaves brushed against her neck, making her itch. She tapped Blake on the arm and leaned in closer to him.

"Shouldn't we do something?" she asked.

"No." He turned his head to look at her. "The original plan has fallen apart, Vinny, Al is improvising. He'll let me know if we're needed and until then, we stay put."

"I'm not sure we can do that," she replied, staring past him.

At least two dark creatures were moving towards them through the unkempt grass beneath the trees. Low slung shadows with long necks and eyes that burnt like hot coals.

"Spitters," he whispered.

Blake moved fast. In the next instant, he was standing a short distance away with his arm extended. He must've thrown something because one of the Skaath vanished. The other one rushed toward him.

He put his hand to his hip then suddenly threw himself to one side, rolling onto his feet. The Skaath whirled and she heard a sound like a whip then Blake went down. Vinny pulled out her lighter and fired a burst of flame at the Spitter.

It caught on the grass in front of it and the Skaath recoiled, hissing. A broad reptilian head swung towards her, and a fringe of skin unfolded around its head. The long neck arched as it opened its jaws wide, and she threw the flames into its face. It shrieked before breaking apart into thousands of little black motes.

"Come on." Blake grabbed her hand and ran, forcing her to run too.

A shadow moved in front of them but before she could react, Blake's arm pulled back and he threw something at it, never slowing. As they ran through the black mist it left behind, she smelled cold ash.

Blake pulled her behind a shed that appeared before them, hidden by a tangle of young trees.

"Spitters forced Heaven from position," Blake was talking into his earpiece. "We're at a derelict shed somewhere behind Fire."

She stared at what she could see of his face as he nodded curtly.

"Roger." He turned to Vinny. "We're joining up with Al, follow me and stay close."

"Got it," she replied.

They moved from one tree to the next. Vinny was wary of every shadow. She watched them for the slightest indication that any one of them might be more than what they seemed.

Blake stopped and crouched down beside a fallen tree, the bottom part of the trunk was partially attached to the stump. The upper floor of the house reared over the trees, a shape against the sky with horizontal bars of light escaping from the windows.

There was a soft thud behind her. She pulled the knife from the sheath on her thigh and whirled around. Metal sang against metal as a sword blocked her blade.

"Not bad, Vinny."

She looked up into a face hidden by a balaclava and lowered her knife. All she could see was his dark eyes, but it had to be Alistair.

"What now?" Blake joined them.

Alistair turned to look at him as he put his sword away but before he could answer, Nadia appeared very literally out of nowhere, bumping against Blake as she materialised.

"They've got Earth and Alpha surrounded. If you order Alpha to get those Firestarters over the wenches then we can burn them from behind," Nadia said.

"And start a veld fire? It's too risky." Alistair shook his head.

"Let Janine drop another trench then." Nadia stared up at Alistair as she spoke. "I seriously doubt we'll get them into the first one at this rate so we might as well make another."

"Yes, with the Firestarters at the bottom." Alistair straightened up. "It ought to buy us a chance to fire up the house."

While Alistair spoke into his earpiece, Vinny looked up at the house again.

"They've boarded up the windows." Nadia leaned toward her as she spoke. "Bravo tried firing through them but it didn't work."

"Isn't there some way we could smash the windows in first?" she asked.

"No." Alistair looked at her. "We have to go in."

"Al…" Blake looked at him but Alistair held up his hand.

"Not her," he said. "Vinny, I want you to take up Bravo's position. Once we pull out of the house, you feed power to the fire, got it?"

"That's it?"

"Yes, it's a quick in and out job but you'll be alone so it's best you don't draw attention to yourself."

"No way in hell." Blake spoke harshly.

"We have to, brother. Best compromise I have is giving you rear guard."

Blake let out a strangled growl, and then the ground beneath them shook. Vinny lost her balance and stumbled sideways against him.

"That's your cue, princess." Alistair turned to Nadia. "Fall back as soon as the trenches are lit, and be careful."

"Always." She smiled at her Guardian then vanished.

"Come on." Alistair took off through the trees. Blake followed him so she did too.

They soon emerged in a paved area. The far side had undercover parking for five cars in a basic structure with an open front. Two more cars were parked on this side. Alistair slipped between them, but Vinny hesitated to leave the cover of the trees.

Alistair ran low across the paving to the far end of the structure. The last parking bay was closed off by a gate and looked empty. Blake moved to the space between the cars so Vinny joined him. She might not like being exposed but it beat being alone.

Unearthly screaming came from the direction of the fight. It sent a shiver down her spine and she pressed closer to Blake. Just a few short weeks ago, she'd never have believed she could take comfort from physical contact.

"Count to two then follow me," Blake spoke close to her ear.

"Okay."

"I'm proud of you, Vinny." He squeezed her arm and then took off after Alistair.

She completely forgot about counting and stared after him, stunned by his words. He was halfway there when she remembered what she was supposed to be doing and ran after him.

She ducked around the corner of the building and flattened herself against the wall. Figures moved in the dark off to her left, two of them stood very close together and spoke in low, harsh voices.

"...take orders from you, half-wench, this is insane."

"You take orders from the Keeper, and he put me in charge. Feel free to raise a complaint after we get the job done." Alistair said.

"Assuming we survive..."

"It's either this, or insubordination, Gary. I'm not going to waste time arguing with you."

The slimmer shadow moved off and everyone else followed. As Heaven passed Gary, she heard him curse then fall in behind her.

They moved silently around the back of the garage then crouched down. Voices whispered and then the Guardians started running across to the corner of the house one by one.

Blake turned towards her. "Be safe, Vinny, and if anything goes wrong, get out of here."

She nodded, but she wasn't sure she meant it. Blake ran across the open stretch to the house then Alistair ordered Gary to go.

"Okay, this is where we split up," Alistair said. "As soon as I'm gone, you count to ten then run across to those trees there and climb the closest one. When we come out, you take over the fire."

"Got it," she muttered.

"Don't move unless you absolutely have to, just sit tight and be safe."

"You be safe too." She found his wrist and moved her hand down to his. "You and Blake."

"No promises, sweetheart." He squeezed her hand. "But I'll do my best."

He let go of her and ran off. As she watched him, she slowly started counting.

23

It took two tries to break the back door down. Blake wasn't surprised to find Skaath hounds waiting for them in the kitchen on the other side. Alistair moved before anyone else could, slashing the munchers to dust with his swords.

Lee-Roy and Chris ran across to the kitchen door and burst through it. A dark shape reared up in front of them but Chris stabbed it. The rest of them followed, and moved down the passage while Chris and Lee-Roy cleared the way.

The passage opened into a large room. Portions of the walls had been crudely knocked down to make it even larger, and stained linoleum covered the floors. Near the centre, six Handmaidens stood over kneeling Thralls. Blood ran down the men's bodies and formed pools around them, which were surrounded by the inky shadows of Skaath.

As Blake watched, a broad head with red eyes rose from the floor with its ears flattened against its skull. Massive paws appeared, a wide chest, and broad shoulders. The Skaath hound growled as it heaved itself from the darkness.

He pulled out two shuriken, but one of the others was faster. A gunshot cracked loudly, and he briefly glimpsed the dog's yellowed fangs before it broke apart.

Blake's ears were still ringing from the first shot when the next one was fired. Two Thralls had appeared through one of the broken walls, but one fell back through with a bullet in his head.

"Give him the fire, quick."

Dane moved forwards and hurled a Firestarter at the dead man. Shadows had already claimed his corpse, it jerked as their formless mounds heaved upwards. Pairs of crimson eyes appeared as the Skaath crowded each other in their eagerness to enter this realm.

The specialised grenade burst at the body's twitching feet and flames leapt up in a radius around it. Shrill yowls echoed off the walls as the fire consumed the shadows.

One of the Handmaidens shrieked and grabbed a handful of hair on the Thrall kneeling before her. She pulled his head back then plunged her dagger through his throat. The Thrall's body lurched as he choked on the blade. Blood spurted over her hand as she twisted the dagger then jerked it free. His body fell sideways and the Handmaiden held her other hand over him as he died.

"Adoor, gowin Skaath," she commanded.

Blake hurled shuriken as several pairs of burning eyes rose from the darkness covering the man. Another Firestarter hit the floor near the Handmaiden, and she screamed again as her jeans caught fire.

Another Firestarter hit a broken wall, spewing fire over the group of Thralls charging through it. Blake heard them yell, but then shadows crawled around the wall in front of him.

He pulled his knife free as a muncher reared out of the wall. Jaws snapped in his face, bathing him with its cold, stale breath. His blade slashed through it and it burst apart. Motes of darkness stung his eyes and he coughed.

A more solid figure appeared through the mist-like remains of Skaath, and hit him in the face. He reeled back against the wall and kicked out at the Thrall. Blake blocked his next punch, and jabbed at the pressure point on the upper curve of his chest. His eyes bugged and he doubled over. Blake struck the back of his head with the hilt of his knife and the Thrall crumpled to the floor.

Crushing knives pierced his calf, then his knife arm. He shouted with pain as he grabbed for the Skaath attached to his arm, but its shoulders bent into its body like liquid and his fingers closed over air.

Silver flashed past him and the hound biting his arm burst apart as a sword sliced through it. He almost dropped his knife, but forced his fingers to close around the hilt as he stabbed the Skaath biting his calf.

He coughed again, not just because of the Skaath. A couch and curtains were burning on one side of the open space. The cloth that covered a small table, and whatever had been the centrepiece on top of it, blazed brightly near the centre of the room and the entire area was filling with smoke.

A Handmaiden yelled from somewhere close by and the wall in front of Blake heaved. He ducked aside as it crumpled, falling as a lump of bricks struck his hip.

A hand closed around his arm. "On your feet, Blake."

He looked up and recognised Dane then grimaced as he got up and looked back. The entrance to the kitchen was blocked by rubble.

"Now we all die, Guardians!" One of the Handmaidens shouted.

***

Vinny was worried even before she heard the crash from inside the house and saw a puff of dust, or maybe smoke, blow the back door wide open. She stared and waited for Blake, Alistair, and the others to appear, but they didn't.

There was nobody about so she climbed down the tree and cautiously approached the open door. Her left hand clenched around her lighter as she moved to a position where she could look into the house.

Light sparkled off a metal sink and she slunk closer. She couldn't see or hear anything moving inside. Vinny stopped to one side of the door, took a deep breath, then flicked the lighter and stepped into the doorway.

Empty. She was relieved until she noticed the misshapen doorframe and pile of broken bricks blocking it. Her head turned as though the Guardians would spring from the kitchen cupboards, but she already knew…if they weren't in here then they had to be trapped behind that.

She stepped out the back door and ran her fingers through her hair. They'd told her to take off if something went wrong, but how could she? Blake was in there—she couldn't just save herself after everything he'd done for her—and Alistair, he was in there too.

Blast their orders. She looked back at the house, there had to be another way in. The front door?

The Phoenix wings unfolded and she flew up to the roof and over it, but hesitated when she saw the battle at the far end of the front lawn.

She couldn't tell friend from foe, they were all just dark figures eerily lit by the glow of flames she couldn't see. Screams, shouting, and cries of pain carried up to her along with the crashing song of metal against metal. A section of the group flew backwards, briefly silhouetted against the orange glow of fire. Tongues of flame rose to meet them, and then they were gone.

Vinny stared. Killing in the abstract sense was a very different thing from witnessing it in reality. Such violence and suffering. Could this really be justified? Wasn't there any other way to fight them?

Fighting begat violence simply by definition so no, there probably wasn't any other way to 'fight' them. But did it really have to be this brutal?

Wasting time on philosophy, what kind of an idiot was she? She flew down the front of the house, hovering over Janine's trench as she grabbed the front door handle and turned it.

Inside was a small, but tastefully decorated foyer. A Persian style rug covered the wooden floorboards, and a narrow table stood against the wall with a vase of flowers on it. Not at all what she'd been expecting. There was even a replica of a Monet painting hanging on the wall.

There was an archway just past the edge of the table; light flickered from the other side of it. Vinny tiptoed closer and peeked into a large, open space.

Smoke, and what looked like fine ash, drifted on the air. Some of the furniture was ablaze, and a few of the people too. A woman lay prone on the floor not too far from her and a man was running around, screaming as he burned.

Nobody seemed to have noticed her so she moved right into the doorway to get a better look. None of the Guardians were visible, but the far side of the room was shrouded in twisting shadows and black mist. Skaath...there was only one logical reason why they'd be gathered in one place.

A table was burning a few metres away. She spread her fingers, focused on the flames, and willed them to obey her as she fed her essence into the fire.

The entire conflagration roared into the air, setting another Handmaiden alight. The flames hit the ceiling and spread over it, eagerly seeking something to devour.

A man shouted, and Vinny turned as a tall figure appeared through the smoke in front of her. She quickly directed the fiery mass at the Skaath on the other side of the space then turned to face the Thrall.

His fist slammed into her abdomen and she folded, choking for air. His next blow landed on her shoulder blade and then she was on the floor, rolling away from him.

"Pathetic little Wielder," he snarled as he kicked her.

For a moment, she was airborne, then the floor smacked into her and she skidded against the wall. She pushed up on her arms and he kicked her again, the hard toe of his boot connected with her hipbone so hard that she screamed.

The Thrall's large hand closed around the side of her neck and he lifted her as though she weighed nothing. Her hip was in agony, shooting pains radiated up her side and down her thigh. She clutched at the man's wrist and stared into his night-dark eyes as he pulled his arm back to punch her face.

"Ar…" she croaked, "Arsheel!"

He staggered backwards and she fell. The force vibrated up her injured leg and she bit her lip, tears springing to her eyes.

The Thrall stomped back to her and she instinctively threw up her arms to protect herself. She heard crackling and felt heat on her face. When she opened her eyes, her forearms were enfolded by flames.

Without thinking at all, she shot the flames at the man and hit him on his chest. He yelled and beat at the fire with his hands, and she hit him again. He backed away from her and she watched him fall out the front door and into the trench.

A short burst of hysterical laughter escaped her. Vinny lifted her hands in front of her face and stared at the fire flickering around her arms. She just made fire, and kicked a man's ass.

A wave of darkness crashed against the archway and streamed past it, towards the door. A cacophony of baying, hissing, and snarling echoed around the small room as the mass divided into bestial forms with gleaming eyes and large fangs. Claws scratched on the floor as they turned toward her.

She raised her arms and shot a jet of fire at the Skaath. A large rift appeared in the mass and fine, black particles exploded into the air. Another burst of flame consumed most of the beasts near the door.

A smaller shape pulled free from the darkness and galloped toward her across the ceiling. It yodelled like a cat as it leapt at Vinny. She glimpsed claws and a wedge shaped mouth opened unnaturally wide.

She flung her arms up in front of her face. Nails raked down her arm, and then there was just a cloud of black mist. It caught in her throat and obscured her vision. She shot fireballs through it at random, and the air grew thicker as more of the creatures burnt away.

Sweat beaded her forehead, but turned icy in the cold mist that surrounded her now. Nobody

309

had warned her that the remains of Skaath held danger too. She coughed again and crawled towards the murky shape of the archway.

A figure appeared in front of her. Vinny shot a fireball at it and threw herself to the side. She pressed her back against the wall. The air was clearer on this side of the room, a quick glance towards the front door showed that the black mist was clearing rapidly.

A hand and some of a woman's face appeared in the archway. She said something, and the wall shuddered behind Vinny. Several long cracks traced jagged paths through the plaster, and dust puffed out of them. Vinny shot another fireball at the Handmaiden then dragged herself away from the wall.

"The Guardians that came in here are all dead, Wielder, their blood fed the Skaath you just burnt," the Handmaiden called out to her.

No, they couldn't be dead. This bitch was just trying to psych her out.

"Here's the proof."

Something long and dark landed on the carpet with a soft thud. It took her a moment to realise that it was an arm clothed in a black sleeve.

Vinny couldn't breathe. She stared at the arm. The hand was too pale to be Alistair's, but what about Blake? They were all so muscular, she couldn't tell if it was his or not.

There was a loud cracking sound and splinters burst from the floor near her knee. Her ears were ringing and there was a hole in the floor.

The next shot hit her in the calf. Vinny didn't know if she cried out, everything seemed distant, except for the warmth of the Phoenix inside her.

She could let go, die and return to the Between, but all of them would burn first.

Her wings filled the foyer with light and she floated, more than flew off the floor. As she hovered, she became aware of all the fire in the house. It was all part of her, a wild dance of destruction. The carpet burst into flames, then the painting. She heard shouting and closed her eyes, revelling in her sense of the fire. She felt it spread through the house, consuming anything that could fuel it.

Another crack, pain blossomed in her belly, and Vinny fell. She rolled over on her back and stared into the barrel of a gun.

"I hate these things; they're a coward's weapon." A dark haired woman was staring down at her. Dimples appeared in her cheeks as she smiled at Vinny. "But sometimes you just have to use what fate presents you with."

"I couldn't agree more." A thin blade of dark metal slid beneath the Handmaidens jaw, pressing lightly against her throat.

Vinny recognised the balaclava immediately.

"Do you really think you can kill me faster than I can pull this trigger?" the Handmaiden asked.

"No, I intend to make sure you bleed out slowly enough for me to complete the Skaarav," Alistair said.

The woman's eyes widened and rolled in their sockets to stare at him. "You're bluffing."

"Are you really willing to risk that?" Alistair sounded like he was smiling. "This isn't just your body at stake here. Your soul will never join with the Void and your Lord Diurga will not know you. Skaath will hunt you through the Never, you'll feel the pain every time they catch you and tear at you, but you'll never die. You'll wander for all of eternity as a lost soul with no chance of reincarnation…well, you know how it works," he said.

"Are you him, Mashkduv, the one who's been hunting us?" the Handmaiden asked softly.

"I wish I was. I've actually never performed Skaarav before so this could turn out very badly for you, but it'll be good practice for me either way."

The Handmaiden muttered something under her breath.

Alistair chuckled. "Actually, I'm not that bad. I'll even let you live if you give me the gun."

"And I should take your word for it?"

"This house is going to burn down. You have ten seconds before I cut your throat anyway."

He spoke so casually that Vinny thought maybe he really meant it. Not that it mattered, at this rate she was probably going to bleed to death, again. She started to laugh but ended up coughing and choking.

She turned her head to the side and closed her eyes to slits. Oh well, it had been good while it lasted.

The gun went off but she was still in pain, still leaking blood on the floor and watching fire flicker around the leg of the table.

"You reckless, stupid, thoughtless girl." Arms slid under her shoulders and thighs, and he lifted her. "You were supposed to stay safe."

"So were you," she muttered. "Is Blake okay?"

"Way more okay than you are." He looked into her eyes.

"Whose arm did she toss at me then?"

"Who gives a crap? You need to get to a Sage, fast."

"She said you were all dead."

"It was a lie. Hold on tight and no more talking." He adjusted his grip and started walking. Vinny curled her arm around his neck and put her head on his shoulder. He smelt like fire, and the cold, ashy scent of Skaath.

24

Vinny woke up in a white room, lying on a hospital gurney. She jerked upright and looked at herself, but she felt no pain, nor was she bleeding anywhere.

"Easy, you're okay." Blake sat up in the chair beside the bed to her left.

She was happier to see him than she'd expected.

"Are you okay?" she asked.

"The Sages healed both of us. I'm just relieved that you're alright, you scared the crap out of me, Vinny."

"I could say the same to you...where are we?"

"Headrush. We got back about an hour ago but you didn't come round after being healed. Sage Helana said something about your essence being depleted, but I wasn't really paying attention."

There was a rapping knock at the door and Blake rose from the chair beside the bed.

"That's probably Al," he said, glancing sideways at her.

"It's okay, he can come in." She swung her legs over the side of the bed but Blake reached the door before her feet touched the floor.

Just as he'd predicted, Alistair stood in the doorway with one arm crossed over his chest and his jaw clenched. He glanced at Blake before turning his gaze to her.

"How long has she been awake?" Alistair asked as his eyes practically drilled holes into her.

"Just a few minutes," Blake replied.

"Give us a moment, bro."

Blake gave her a look, unwilling and a little doubtful, but then he nodded. "Sure, I'll go get some coffee or something," he said.

"Take your time," Alistair replied, still glaring at her.

Vinny sighed and slid off the bed as Alistair closed the door. She was obviously in trouble.

"You disobeyed a direct order, and in doing so, placed all of us in danger. I can't discipline you because you're a Wielder, but I..."

"Excuse me? How exactly did I place everyone in danger?" she asked.

"You went into that house alone. They could've taken you as a hostage."

"Can't say I got the impression that they're keen on hostages."

"Damn it all, Vinny! Do you honestly not realise how much danger you put yourself in, or are you

315

being glib on purpose? She nearly killed you, I had your blood all over me…" He broke off, hands held before him. He wasn't wearing his hoodie anymore, and his shirt had a tear across his chest that showed red beneath.

"You're hurt." She frowned and moved closer to get a better look, but he leaned back, away from her.

"I'm fine, don't change the subject." He narrowed his eyes at her. "You might not care for your own safety but Blake nearly went in after you, did he tell you that? He was already hurt and I can promise you he wouldn't have handled that situation as well as I did. He would've died, both of you would've died. Does that register with you, or do you just not give a crap about anything?"

"Fuck you." She slapped him without even thinking.

Alistair's eyes widened and his mouth opened, but she didn't give him a chance to speak.

"The only reason I went in there was because I was worried. When I realised that you guys were trapped…how could I just leave you in there?"

"You're a Wielder, we're supposed to protect you. I told you this already, you matter more than any Guardian."

"Shut up, Alistair, just shut up!" Her hands formed fists at her sides and she stared into his eyes. "I can't think that way. I can't just leave people I care about to die because that's what I'm supposed to do. Maybe it's because I wasn't born with Awakened genes and trained to think that I'm so important, I don't know, and I don't care. I won't be that way."

He uncrossed his arms and stared at her, his lips moving as though he were biting them from inside his mouth. "People, you said...plural."

"Yes, you big dumbass, you and Blake."

He smiled a shy sort of smile that seemed so contrary on him that she smiled too. Then he looked away.

"Look, Vinny, I get that its not easy being the outsider," he sighed. "You have to work harder than everyone else and they all seem so strange on top of it, but you need to start thinking like you're part of a whole. Sometimes, that means following orders."

She tilted her head and looked up at him,

"How could you know what it's like? All Guardians are born into the Circle," she said.

"Not all." He shook his head.

So, maybe one of his parents was a Coven member after all. How on earth had he ended up not just a Guardian, but entrusted with protecting Nadia?

"Why does all of this even matter to you?" she asked.

"The Circle is my family." He shrugged.

"So, what does that make me, your screw up sister?"

Alistair smirked. "Not exactly, sweetheart."

"Good." She couldn't believe her own brazen attitude, but if he wasn't going to do something, she would.

She moved closer and leaned in to brush her lips against his. For a moment, she was terrified he wouldn't respond—his eyes were impossible to read.

As she was about to pull away, one of his hands pressed against her. Fingertips curled around her side and his lips pushed against hers.

Sweet, soft, intense in the slow way their tongues entwined around each other. Vinny circled her arms around Alistair's neck and leaned into him, raising her heels off the ground for a little added height. His other arm folded around her and pulled her tight against him as he kissed her harder.

The last time she'd kissed a guy was Nick in Grade 10, and it had been nothing like this. She understood what people meant about chemistry and butterflies now, what it might be like to have sex with a man because you were attracted to him, and not because you had to.

She traced her fingers down the side of his neck to his chest and pressed her palm over his heart. She hadn't known if any guy would want her now that she didn't look like Anna anymore. Heck, she hadn't thought she'd even want a guy to want her.

But she did. She fisted her fingers in his shirt, tugging it as she navigated her way to the bed backwards. Soon her behind bumped against the side of the bed. His last step pressed their bodies together, and she had to cling to him to keep her balance.

Alistair lifted his head, looked over her shoulder and frowned.

"What?" she asked. Had she done something wrong?

It was unnerving, being this close to the look in his eyes as he stared at her. She might've expected the lustful glint, but not the affection that softened it.

"I don't know what to make of you sometimes," he told her in a low voice.

"It's simple." She smiled. "I'm messed up."

"Aren't we all?" he muttered, moving his hand to lightly trace down the side of her face with his fingers. "You don't have to drag me to bed, sweetheart. Not that I'm not sorely tempted to ravish you, but it's too soon. I need you to be sure that you want what you want."

"What's that supposed to mean?"

"I have a theory." He kissed her lower lip softly. "I think some guy was violent with you, and I don't want you to be scared of me."

She stared down at his chest as she frowned. Was she that obvious or was he that good?

"Some men are bastards, it's not your fault."

"Shut up, Alistair." She pressed a finger to his lips but that didn't stop him,

"Vinny, look at me."

She braced herself for pity, but it wasn't there. His eyes were soft but dark, and she couldn't interpret the emotion in them but it made her stomach turn somersaults.

"You're staring at me..." she muttered.

He smiled but said nothing.

She moved her hand to trace his jaw line before stroking her fingers through his hair. Alistair sighed deeply and leaned his forehead against hers.

"What you did tonight, please, don't ever do it again," he whispered.

"You don't want me to kiss you again?" she teased.

Alistair groaned. "You know what I mean."

"Yeah."

"Although, kissing isn't really something we can openly do. Robert wouldn't be happy at all."

"I remember, weird rules and stuff."

"It's not really that weird, can't have everybody dating everybody else or people would lose focus, feelings would be hurt, and over-protective Guardians would rampage. At the end of the day, we still have a job to do."

320

"This topic is such a turn on." She rolled her eyes at him. "Quit being so serious already."

"Who knew there was so much spark behind those grey eyes?" He smiled as he stepped back. "I should go, wouldn't want Blake thinking that I'm being too harsh on you."

"I guess not," she sighed.

He pulled her towards him and kissed her, grazing her lower lip with his teeth as he pulled away. "Another time, Vinny."

She bit her lip as she watched him leave. He left the door open and she heard voices, then Blake entered with two Styrofoam cups of coffee.

"I hope he wasn't too hard on you." He held out one of the cups to her and she shook her head, biting her lip to stop herself from smiling.

"He was pissed off but it went okay." She stared into her coffee to avoid his eyes.

"Al is very strict about people following his orders, tends to take it personally when you don't," Blake said.

"Like that Gary dude?"

"Gary is…well, he's just an asshole. He's had an issue with Al since we were teenagers."

"Like some kind of grudge?"

"Yeah." Blake pulled a face. "I don't want to rush you, but we should probably clear out of here now. A couple of guys were wounded and they might need this room."

"Sure." She glanced around the room but everything was still on her, even the knife was still strapped to her thigh. Blake retrieved his jacket from the chair and they walked down the white corridor with their coffee.

"Blake, would you give me an honest answer to something?" she asked as they walked.

"Sure, what is it?"

"Did it help at all? When I went into that house tonight."

He went quiet and she looked at him, waiting.

Eventually, he spoke. "We were in a pretty tight spot back there, I won't deny it. They had us pinned down when this wall of fire came towards us. It cleared the Skaath, and gave us a chance to retreat through one of the rear windows, but came pretty close to burning us too."

"Oh…I'm sorry, I would've done more to control it but I was attacked."

"My heart stopped when we got outside and realised that you must've gone in. Al ordered the others to take me away and then he went back in…" Blake shook his head. "What a night."

"I second that. But we got them, right? We won or whatever, Dylan's death was avenged?"

"After the house went up many of the Coven members outside took off, and we managed to finish off the rest. It counts as a victory but it was a close call, we're lucky things worked out in our favour."

They walked in silence, sipping their coffee. There were plenty of Guardians about but none of the wounded seemed to be in particularly bad shape. One man was bandaging the hand of another, and there was a Guardian draped in a chair who had several long scratches across the side of his face. His eyes were closed and he appeared to be sleeping.

She supposed that anybody with a serious injury was treated first, leaving these guys to wait until a medic was available.

It was cold outside, a dark night with no sign of the moon. She was surprised to see the constellations of Pleiades and Orion. It must be almost morning, and almost spring too if the stars of summer were appearing in the sky.

"What happens now?" she asked. "Is my training over or did I fail?"

"You didn't fail, but I'm going to continue to train you. There's still quite a way to go, Vinny, and you weren't ready for a raid in the first place. But you are a full member of the Circle now and there's already a flat waiting for you to move in," Blake said.

"Really?" She smiled.

He nodded. "It's off to Denysrus for you and I, first thing in the morning, in fact."

Vinny snorted. "It's already morning."

"First light then." He smiled at her.

"And the Coven house? Won't the cops notice something strange happened there?"

Blake chuckled. "This is South Africa, Vinny...they might notice, but they'd never find us. Besides, nearly an eighth of the police force are Guardians who didn't pass combat training, Inactives, their loyalty lies with us."

"Don't leave anything to chance, do you people?"

"Of course not." Blake started walking towards the woods and she followed.

25

They didn't leave at first light after all; Rochelle wouldn't let them. The woman had arranged a party for Vinny, and out of all the things that had happened to her recently, she found that the strangest by far.

There was a vase of fresh flowers on the dining room table, nestled between plates of snacks and two bottles of champagne. Rochelle had also ordered enough cupcakes for all the Guardians and partial Wielders at Headrush. Vinny overheard her joke about the three hundred cupcakes to Blake and nearly choked on the one she was eating at the time. She'd known there were a lot of them running around but she was certain that she hadn't seen more than a hundred so where was everyone else?

They probably spent their days in the fort. She imagined a bunch of deathly pale Guardians emerging into the sunlight blinking, and smiled to herself.

"Why wasn't I invited to the party?" Alistair stood in the doorway with a man just behind him.

"I thought you drove back last night," Blake said.

Alistair shook his head. "Change of plans, that's why I'm here actually. James is coming back with us to replace Dylan and I don't have a spare helmet with me, I thought he could catch a lift with you."

All eyes turned to James, a man with an angular face, pale green eyes and coppery brown hair, who smiled shyly at them. Darren walked forward, gave him a man-hug and his congratulations then led him to the table.

"Sure," Blake replied, his tone suddenly wooden. "We aren't leaving yet though."

"Plenty of time for cake then." Alistair smiled and helped himself to one of the cupcakes on the table.

Vinny watched him a moment then turned and slipped into the kitchen to throw the wrapper from her cupcake away in the scullery.

She looked at the door to the basement and thought of how anxious she'd been when she first arrived here. That person had been different from the one who woke up in a morgue drawer, and this person, Vinny, was also different.

Like a caterpillar in its chrysalis, she was slowly changing; shedding what she had been in order to become something new. But who would she be when the metamorphosis was over? There was too much damage in her soul, under her skin, for her to be beautiful. The stains would show through, they always did.

"I'm certain there's some kind of rule that the person a party has been thrown for is not supposed to spend it hiding in a pantry."

"I'm not hiding, Alistair."

"Sure, sweetheart?"

"I was just thinking." She turned and stepped in front of him.

His lips curved into a smile as he cupped her cheek with one hand. "How're you feeling? You used up a lot of your essence last night."

"I'm fine." She touched one finger to his chest. "How's your scratch?"

"It will heal a bit faster if you stop poking it."

Vinny rolled her eyes, and resisted the impulse to kiss him by moving past him.

"What happened with that Handmaiden last night? I heard you tell her you'd cut her throat anyway then the gun went off." She turned in the centre of the kitchen to face him.

"She tried to shoot me instead."

"And…?"

He sighed. "And I shoved that lun skaath through her throat."

"You didn't do that Skaarav thing?"

He shook his head. "Even if I knew the entire process, it's complicated and time-consuming to separate a soul from the body in such a way that it loses its identity. It was a very rare ritual until some vigilante started hunting down Handmaidens."

"Like a serial killer?"

"Exactly. They call him Giyarav Shpyorad, which basically means the one who severs souls."

"Charming," she said sarcastically. "That reminds me, why'd she call you..." she wrinkled her nose as she tried to remember the word, "mashed dove?"

He blinked, arched his eyebrows and smiled. "Say that again."

"Mashed dove."

He chuckled. "Mashkduv, it means black mask."

"Mashed dove sounds way more badass...dove for short."

"Don't you dare, Vinny."

She smiled. "What, call you dove? I wouldn't dream of it...dove."

"You shouldn't tease me when you know how easily I can catch you." He smirked as he took a step closer to her.

"Is that a threat?"

"Definitely. I've been wondering if you're ticklish."

"I'm not," she lied quickly.

"I'll see about that." He brushed his fingers lightly over her side.

"Vinny?"

Alistair quickly withdrew his hand and they both turned as Blake appeared in the kitchen doorway.

"Time for the toast," he said, jerking his head slightly to indicate she should follow him.

"Sure," she replied, her voice a little higher than normal.

She trailed behind him to the dining room and took the elegant glass that Darren offered to her, looking at the bubbles rising in the yellow-gold liquid. It felt uncomfortable in her hand, but she kept her features composed and forced herself to smile. They'd done this as a nice thing for her. None of them could possibly understand that, for her, alcohol was a painkiller, stolen from bottles in gulps or slipped into cool drink and coffee to disguise it.

"To Heaven." Rochelle lifted her glass, smiling at her as she spoke. "Welcome to the Circle, to our family."

She forced her smile wider and clinked her glass with the others then sipped her champagne.

***

For most of the way to Denysrus, Alistair drove ahead on his bike, kicking up dust on the dirt road and weaving through traffic on the highway. She hadn't thought an off-road bike could go that fast. It looked almost as good as flying.

When they pulled into the parking lot behind the Sanctuary, he was leaning against the wall, waiting for them.

"You drive like an old lady, Blake."

"Because I have a car full of people, if you want to race then you'll have to wait until I'm driving alone."

"Deal." Alistair grinned and the two bumped fists.

Blake walked inside, with James just behind him and Vinny trailing behind. As she passed Alistair, he caught her arm and pointed to a mound covered by a tarpaulin, just in front of where his bike was parked,

"That's yours," he said.

"Great, I always wanted a tarp."

"Underneath it." He rolled his eyes. "The scooter Mike dug up for you."

"Oh…"

He nodded then turned abruptly and entered the building. "Come on, the Keeper isn't very patient," he said over his shoulder.

She followed him down the passage to the office where she'd first met him. As they reached the door, the Keeper came out.

"Alistair, wait for me inside." He turned to look at her. "Sage Helana wants to speak to you, Heaven."

She glanced towards Alistair, uncertain if this was a good thing, but his face was smooth and inexpressive. He barely met her eyes before walking into the Keeper's office.

Vinny frowned as she followed Robert back down the passage toward another door. This one opened into a small room with a table on the far side. The air in here felt charged, as though every atom was vibrating or setting off sparks.

"Helana?" Robert called softly.

Even his voice sounded different in here, lighter somehow.

A person seemed to step out of the air, Helana, she assumed. She looked almost transparent at first, nothing more than a fuzz of mauve and dark. Vinny blinked, and she'd already become more solid. Helana was freaking tall, even taller than Robert. The same violet and bright white eyes as Adnes seemed even more striking in contrast to her chocolate coloured skin.

Vinny recognised her instantly.

"Thank you, Robert." Helana smiled peacefully at him. "Would you excuse us? I know you have much to do."

"Certainly." Robert nodded.

Vinny heard the door close but she wasn't paying much attention to the Keeper anymore.

"You were there," she said.

"Indeed." The Sage nodded. "You have grown since we last met, Chantelle."

Vinny shook her head. "I'm not using that name anymore. They call me Vinny, or Heaven."

"I see…does it help?"

Such an astute question, it stunned her for a moment so she just nodded.

"That is good."

"What do you mean, that I've grown?"

"Not physically, internally." Helana smiled as she reached out to lightly press warm fingertips against Vinny's chest, over her heart. "Being a Spirit Wielder is a unique experience. Even before we die, we endure so much more than others realise. We inevitably come to think of our compassion as weakness and build barriers around it, but in truth, it's our sensitivity that makes us strong."

Vinny frowned and the Sage smiled, as though she understood the fact that Vinny didn't.

"It takes great courage to open your heart to the world when it seems to do such little good, but you cannot let pain and fear dictate to you. People will always hurt each other, but it doesn't mean they do it intentionally, or that they cannot redeem themselves afterward."

"Okay…" she replied uncertainly.

"You will know what I mean when you are ready for it. Until then, trust your heart and your intuition, they will not lead you astray. Your essence has already recovered from your ordeal with the Skaath. We will speak again, Child of Heaven."

With those words, Helana faded back into the air and left Vinny standing alone in the room. She felt like she'd just been told the sacred meaning of life, but in a language she couldn't understand.

She walked out the door and glanced down the passage. The door to the office was closed, and she didn't think Robert wanted to see her anyway. He hadn't said that she should come to see him after Helana, so she turned right and went outside to check out her new wheels.

The scooter was a squat, blue thing, the type you rode with your feet pressed together, that had little capability for leaning around curves. It was practical, safe in that it probably only reached the speed limit on long, downhill straights, and doubtless economical when it came to petrol consumption. A thing that took one from point A to point B in an efficient manner.

In other words, it was one of the most un-cool things she'd ever seen.

The seat was unlocked. She flapped it open, removed the helmet stored there, and put it down on the footrest as she opened her backpack. The box Alistair had brought her was right on top, and it only took a moment to remove the key chain and map. She had to squash the bag down into the storage compartment, but eventually it fit.

Vinny studied the map, then turned it around in case she had it upside down. She knew where she was supposed to go, it was marked with a red dot, but she had no idea where she was now. Couldn't they just have drawn a route on a piece of paper like normal people? Even GPS co-ordinates would've helped. She hadn't spent too much time looking through her new phone but it probably had an application that could've mapped out a route for her.

She sighed, seeing as she couldn't check out her new place yet, she walked back inside to wait for Blake. She leaned against the wall outside the door to the Keeper's office and hoped they weren't going to take much longer in there.

"...I'm saying is it's not unreasonable to think she has a death wish, she committed suicide after all."

What? She inched closer, that had sounded like Alistair.

"No, she just needs more training."

"She charged into a house full of Trueborns and Thralls, no logical person would've done that. She's not just a sad girl who killed herself, Keeper, she's completely unstable. Whatever she went through before she died has damaged her in ways that might never come right. I doubt she'll ever be reliable."

Definitely Alistair's voice. Vinny clenched her jaw and stared at the floor, she couldn't tell if it hurt to hear because it was true, or because it was his opinion.

"Every Spirit Wielder has their problems, but in time her emotional wounds will heal, and training will become instinctive reactions. That is the way it always is."

"I'm not so certain of that."

"I am." Blake's voice. "She's already made so much progress since I found her, it can only get better."

"You may think her attitude is an improvement but I don't, definitely not in terms of being a good Wielder. Anybody who plays hero is a liability."

She'd heard enough. She moved quickly down the passage to the back door, gulping in a deep breath of air as she closed the door behind her.

Why had he been so nice to her if he thought she was so awful? It didn't make sense. The emotions of last night, his affection, it had seemed so real. It still felt so real. She'd truly believed that he liked her, how did a person fake something like that and why?

Was that why he hadn't wanted to sleep with her, because he thought she was crazy? Vinny clenched her hands in her hair and squeezed her eyes shut. What kind of dumbass believes a jerk like Alistair is suddenly going to be so kind?

"Fuck him," she snarled to herself as she climbed on to the scooter. Blake had stood up for her, even Robert. One asshole wasn't going to ruin her new life.

And she'd find her own way to the flat.

She shoved her helmet on and started the engine, turning a little too sharply at the entrance to the parking area.

She went right on a whim then continued to follow her impulses until a splash of colour caught her eye ahead.

It was a bar with a large sign in Rastafarian colours declaring the place was called 'Marley's'. Better yet, it was open.

She turned into a print shop's driveway, backtracked over the sidewalk, and parked right outside the entrance. Stoners were generally friendly, and maybe somebody tell her where she lived now.

It was dim inside, and empty.

"Hello?" she called out as she stomped towards the bar.

"We aren't open yet," a male voice replied.

"Your doors are…look, I just need directions."

A lanky figure rose behind the bar, a blonde guy with glasses. He looked at her and smiled.

"Directions, I can do."

"Good." She pulled out the map and spread it on the counter. "How the hell do I get to that red dot?"

"It's close by, the bar is just here." He pointed to a spot just one street away.

"Any bottle stores on the way there? Since you aren't open." She smiled sarcastically at him.

"Nope." He frowned. "But since you're obviously new in town, I'll pour you a drink to welcome you here."

"Thanks," she muttered.

"No worries. I'm Justin, by the way."

"Vinny. And I'd like a vodka and lime."

"Denysrus tends to do that to a person." He grinned as he set a glass on the bar.

"Sure," she sighed, watching as he poured her drink.

***

"This was Mike's room," Alistair said. "Should be fine for you."

"It is," James replied. He looked around as he entered the room, not that there was much to see. A bed, a desk, curtains, and a built in cupboard with a picture of a hot girl stuck on it.

"Don't take Cindy down." Alistair pointed at the picture. "She's covering a hole, and don't call me if

337

you need anything, look around and help yourself, this is home now."

James flashed him a smile. "Sure," he replied.

"We'll figure out your chores tomorrow."

Alistair walked back down the hallway to the room Blake was in, right next to James. The door was ajar, and he leaned in.

"You still pissed off, or can we have a beer to celebrate?" he asked.

"I'm still pissed," Blake grumbled, appearing at the door. "You had no right to say those things about Vinny."

"It's not like I lied…"

"You didn't tell the truth either!" he glared at Alistair. "You purposefully put things out of context when you know as well as I do that Vinny isn't half as bad as you made her out to be."

"I'll just leave you to finish unpacking." Alistair turned away and walked to the kitchen.

There was a full six-pack in the fridge. He'd bought it a few days ago, thinking they could have a drink when Blake had finished unpacking. So much for that idea.

"Oh well," he muttered to himself as he reached in, tore the container open, and removed a bottle of beer.

He looked around the kitchen as he twisted the cap off. The house still felt empty. It was supposed to be better now, but it wasn't. Just a few weeks ago, Dylan had teased him about Vinny right here...

Vinny lived pretty close by. He pulled his phone from his pocket and dialled her number. He'd have a beer with her in her new place if nobody wanted to celebrate with him here.

Her number went straight to voicemail, so he hung up.

Maybe it was for the best, if Blake found out he'd been chilling with Vinny, it would just piss him off more. The dude had never quite gotten the concept of subterfuge. He didn't blame him for being pissed; everything Blake had said was true, but what else could he have done? Robert could never suspect he liked Vinny, and the man knew him too well to believe he'd take a forgiving stance on her actions.

He took the bottle of beer to his room and lay on the bed. Past his feet, he could see Spot moving through the walls of her terrarium.

"This is what comes from following your heart, Spot," he said. "You wind up tangled in a situation where somebody's bound to get hurt. You're lucky, all you have to worry about is whether to eat your mate now, or later." He drank a mouthful of beer. "Then again, at least I don't have to give my life for sex."

There had to be a simpler way to do this. He pulled his phone out again and dialled Janine's number.

"Aweh, my bru," she greeted him.

"Hey, Jay, hope I'm not interrupting anything saucy."

"Like I would've answered if you were." She laughed happily. "What's up?"

"Oh, nothing much. I'm just bored, and I got to thinking…" he cleared his throat.

"Yeah?"

"How did you know you and Mike were the real thing?"

"Ooh…is there something going on with you and Nadia?"

"No, don't be silly. I was just thinking…it couldn't have been easy, what with the Keeper's rules and all."

Janine gave an amused snort. "Robert is too uptight. It wasn't easy to tell him we were together, but it was easier than trying to pretend we didn't have feelings for each other. Mike got the worst of it; Robert asked to speak to him alone and laid on the heavy guilt trip. He told me later."

"I see," he muttered. Mike didn't owe Robert nearly as much as he did, how much heavier would his guilt trip be?

"Al."

"Yeah?"

"People are either worth it, or they aren't. When they are worth it, letting them go is the worst mistake you can make. There isn't much space for emotions in the Keeper's well-oiled machine, but that doesn't mean you have to just be a good little gear for the rest of your life, you know?"

"Jay, you're going to make a really good mother one day," he said.

"Just make sure you're a good uncle, if you teach my kids too many naughty tricks, I'll beat you."

Alistair laughed. "That's unfair, you know I won't fight back."

"You're welcome to try, bru, I'll still kick your ass. I have to go, Mike's burning something in the kitchen. Cheers, man."

"Bye, Jay," he said.

He put the phone down on the nightstand and had a swallow from his beer. He had a lot to think about.

About The Author

Caitlin O'Connor searches for truth in fiction, and drags her characters through hell to find it.

A proud eccentric who aspires to be omniscient, she enjoys listening to music, trying to understand physics, and admiring unusual works of art.

She lives in South Africa with her son.

You can keep in touch with Caitlin O'Connor on her website, InspiredChaos.weebly.com

She also loves to connect with readers on these social networks:

Facebook:
www.facebook.com/caitlinoconnorauthor
Twitter: @caity_connor
Instagram: @caity_connor855

GLOSSARY OF SOUTH AFRICAN VERNACULAR

Askies: An Afrikaans word which means 'excuse me'

Masekind: Similar in meaning to 'brother from another mother', often used in the same context as followers of rap and hip hop culture call each other 'nigga'.

Mealie meal: Ground maize porridge, similar to Polenta, but finer. It can be eaten for breakfast, flavoured with sugar and milk, or as a side dish with a meal (in place of rice, for example)

Veld: Open grassland, fields.

Joburg: Shortened version of Johannesburg.

Howzit: A greeting.

Ma se dinges: An Afrikaans phrase that translates to 'Mother's thing'. A polite version of a far cruder phrase usually used to insult others.

Sommer: Similar in meaning to the phrases 'just because' or 'might as well'.

Aweh: A greeting.

BONUS FEATURES

PLAYLIST

These songs all inspired me in some way while writing this book. It's a mixed bag of genres, but I hope you enjoy them.

Falling Awake by Tarja Turunen, featuring Joe Satriani. (This song just fits with Vinny's understanding of the Between.)

Leave the Light On by Beth Hart.

Heart Attack by Demi Lovato. (It might be from a woman's perspective, but this song reminds me of Alistair.)

Roar by Katy Perry.

KleinTambotieboom by Die Heuwels Fantasties. (An Afrikaans song. Dylan isn't a main character, but this one is for him.)

A Truth for Me by Dark Moor.

Sympathetic by Seether.

Take Me to Church by Hozier.

Those Who Slay Together by Chiodos. (My fight scene inspiration song.)

351

Maak of Braak by Fokofpolisiekar. (Another Afrikaans song, links to translations of both songs are available on my website, InspiredChaos.weebly.com)

For legal purposes, please note that none of these songs are officially associated with Finding the Phoenix, I simply listened to them a lot while revising this book.

SCAR

BOOK TWO OF THE CELESTIAL TALISMAN

Available July 2016

Secrets surface when a traitor returns

The scar on Vinny's wrist is nothing compared to the scars on her psyche. She isn't a hero, she isn't even a good person, and when a skirmish with one of the Handmaidens of the Skaath Diurga ends badly, she knows it's partly her fault.

Nobody in the Circle could've guessed at the truths that attack would uncover.

One woman has sacrificed everything to end the war between Handmaidens and Awakened. Now, she's prepared to damn everyone for her freedom. One final betrayal is all it will take to change our world forever.

As soon as the door closed behind him, Samantha began the calling.

"Ghlishaayl dorm, Toornu Braard, ashmu agisish kowaghtayr daegogh…"

Nothing seemed to be happening, but Amanda knew the blood was running along the grooves, mixing with the cremated remains of previous sacrifices, and singing to the Skaath Lord trapped in the Never.

Sometimes she wondered how it had come to this, that she, a Wielder, should have to plead with Diurga for mercy and aid.

The ash rose from the altar as it absorbed the life essence from the blood. Ever thickening grey-black drifts filled the air above the granite table, and the shadows in the room drew closer. They stretched across the floor like lovers reaching for each other's hands, and ran up the sides of the altar until all was dark. She couldn't see Samantha anymore, and her chanting became distant as the mass grew denser.

Shadows and ash shaped into broad shoulders and a thick neck. A head crowned with two pairs of gracefully curved horns took shape. Small, human ears tilted forwards, and the nostrils on the end of the Diurga's muzzle flared as he took in his surrounds.

It never failed to unnerve Amanda, how much of the human scaffolding remained in the Diurga. He even had eyebrows.

"Lord Braard, your presence honours and humbles your loyal Handmaidens." Amanda's voice was weak, but she tried to sound suitably awed.

The Diurga's head swivelled toward her, and his eyes glowed a muddy shade of vermillion as they fastened on her.

"I have been anticipating this summons, Betrayer. The Phoenix has awoken." His voice was a sing-song, a growling rumble, and a nails on chalkboard screech all at once.

Amanda gritted her teeth and resisted the temptation to cover her ears.

"Yes, Lord, the Child of Heaven has been born again."

"And been found by the Circle—that was not the plan."

She gulped. Maybe this was a mistake. "Her watcher betrayed me and when I found out, it was too late to rectify his actions, but I will make this work, this may even be advantageous to us."

The mass shifted as the Diurga leaned closer to her. A clawed hand formed in the floating ash and pressed against her cheek. Thick fingers wrapped around her skull, so cold that her skin burned beneath the touch.

"How?" Braard growled, claws pricking her scalp as his grip tightened.

Amanda coughed. Thank the Mother this was just a manifestation and not the fully summoned being in its corporeal form. The ash may have choked her, but it was better than the nauseating stench of hot metal and decay.

"I can still capture her." She coughed again. "And when I do we'll imprison the Phoenix as well. The Black Rose will then hold two of the Heavenly talismans, to your glory, Braard."

The Diurga continued to stare at her as his lips pulled back in a sharp-toothed grin. Black fangs the length of her fingers hovered in front of her face, dark bands through which the cold fire of the Skaath glowed with ruddy light. Even a manifestation could tear the soul from her flesh with those fangs. She'd seen it happen with countless sacrifices.

Terror wormed in her guts as the great jaws parted.

Braard tilted her head and snuffled the burnt half of her face. "As if the stench of the Stone Giant wasn't bad enough," he rumbled. "You stink of them both, Phoenix and Heaven Child. If those wounds are the result of your first attempt then it doesn't bode well for this venture."

"She got lucky, next time I will be better prepared."

"If you get another chance, Betrayer." His nostrils flared as he pulled back. "You may not survive this night, but that is why you called me, correct?"

"I'd be most thankful if my Lord would heal his servant," she stuttered.

"Aye…but you are a traitor to your own kind, and have failed in every endeavour to capture the Heaven Child. Why should I favour you?"

She couldn't die now, like this. Her thighs felt damp, had she pissed herself? If only he wouldn't speak so close to her, it was like needles stabbing her ears and she couldn't think.

"My treachery aided the Skaath Diurga, and I have been faithful ever since I made Pact with you, Lord Braard. The Black Rose serves you devotedly…"

"You dare to lie before me?" Braard's screeching roar echoed off the walls and the mass reared back. The tips of his horns broke apart as they scraped against the ceiling. "As though I do not keep close watch over this venture?"

A slender tail of ash and shadow slapped down alongside her, bursting into thick mist as it struck the floor.

Amanda made herself as small as possible. If he knew what she was up to, it was all over. "But my Lord…"

"Silence, Betrayer." He grabbed the back of her head and pulled on her skull until she was forced to look into his eyes. "You are a mistake. A weakling, unfit to rule a Coven in my honour. Too stupid to see that the daughters I sent with you to found this Coven have grown lax under your leadership, too complacent to care for my Vessels."

Her heart almost beat normally again. It wasn't as bad as she'd thought.

"I will rectify this immediately, Lord Braard. I will honour our agreement."

"You have much to atone for, Betrayer, and I will have what I am owed. Fortunately for you, you are still in the best position to capture the Heaven Child. What have you to offer in return for your health?"

"I will bring you a holy man or woman, a human who devoutly serves the light."

"A feeble offering, I want a morsel that tastes of power, an Awakened mortal."

Amanda swallowed hard. Even with Samantha's help, she was too weak to hunt down a member of the Circle now. She had to save her strength for Chantelle.

"It will take time to capture a member of the Circle, my Lord."

"The Circle are not the only Awakened." The Diurga grinned again and his eyes flared. "You are one, and there are others amongst the Trueborn— filthy runts. A traitor such as yourself will have no trouble finding one of your own to satiate me."

Her mouth opened as she realised the potential repercussions of what he was asking her. To sacrifice one of her followers would weaken the Coven, and if anybody found out…Handmaidens may well believe there was glory in dying for their Diurga, but not for their Matron. They'd denounce her. All her hard work would be for nothing.

"My Lord Diurga shall have whatever pleases him." Samantha knelt down beside her. "Forgive my intrusion, Lord Braard, but I could no longer contain my awe for your power. It would be a great honour if my Lord would permit me to aid the Matron in satisfying your hunger."

"Is this your whelp, Betrayer?" The dark cloud of ash and shadow heaved as he turned towards Samantha.

"Yes, my Lord. She's Trueborn, sired during the Honouring of the Faithful, and born with the Mark," Amanda said, hoping this information would temper his anger.

The hand dropped from her head and moved toward her daughter. He reached for her with a single finger, scraping a dark, curved nail against Sam's cheek. Amanda glimpsed a line of blood then her view was obscured as the Diurga moved closer. She leaned back in time to avoid his horns, and see him lick the blood on Samantha's cheek.

"Yes," he rumbled. "I taste myself in you, despite the foul Awakened blood of your dam."

"I am humbled to receive such compliments from my Lord." Samantha replied.

The Diurga pulled back, his eyes glowing as a gruff sound came from him. It was difficult to tell whether Braard was laughing or roaring until he smiled again.

"I will allow this. Bring me an Awakened and this holy person, and I will heal you in return. But be aware, Betrayer, it is your daughter who pleases me, not you."

"I will not cease until I have regained your approval, Lord Braard."

Braard snorted, sending plumes of ash over their heads. "If it weren't for the fact that you've come closer to completing the Vessel spell than any other, I'd devour you now. Keep that in mind, Betrayer. I only take your kind into my service because you are more useful than a mortal." His eyes turned towards Samantha. "If she fails again then I will entrust you with fulfilling the terms of your dam's agreement. Her burden will fall to you, as well as my good graces, should you succeed."

"I understand, Lord Braard." Samantha looked up at the Diurga with a broad smile.

"Excellent." Braard turned back to Amanda. His eyes narrowed, and then his body collapsed. The mass engulfed her.

Ash clung to her skin while shadows spread across it, sticking to her like oil. Her nerve endings screamed. It felt like she was burning all over again, but then the pain was gone.

The ash fell to the floor as the last of the shadows crept across her skin and disappeared under her shirt. Her wounds were still weeping and raw, but no longer painful, and she felt her strength returning as Samantha helped her to her feet.

"You stupid girl," she muttered. "Do you have any idea what you've done?"

"I was trying to save you, and it worked."

"To the detriment of the Coven! We can't afford to lose powerful members, or risk a mass defection when the others discover what we've done."

"We won't let them find out."

"A child would think it's that simple. What about the risk to yourself? You're just as responsible for capturing Chantelle as I am now. You have no idea how powerful a Spirit Wielder can be!"

The girl's cheeks flushed, but Amanda remembered that smile when she accepted Braard's terms. You would've thought the Diurga had granted her dearest wish from the way she beamed at him.

She pulled herself up to her full height and walked away, striding down the passage toward her rooms. Anyone who passed her would know their Matron was strong once again. Hopefully they'd assume she paid the Diurga in full.